THE
BROKER

TARA CRESCENT

THE
BROKER

To everyone who enjoys a little bit of stabbing with their spice

Trigger Warning

The Broker contains explicit sex, violence, attempted murder, murder, intimate partner violence (historical, off-page, and not between the protagonists) and child abduction (the child is unharmed.)

VALENTINA

CHAPTER ONE

When you're a hacker working for the Venetian mafia, there aren't many opportunities for field missions. It's mostly desk work—shoring up our defenses against incursions, accessing people's information, that kind of thing. Most of the time, I work out of my home office. I've been here for almost ten years, and I've never been out in the field, not even once.

Today's the exception.

It's a bright November day. The sun shines

down on us, summer seemingly reluctant to relinquish its grip on northern Italy. I'm sitting in a car on the outskirts of Bergamo, palms sweating and nerves on edge, waiting to get the all-clear from our security chief before I embark on my first field mission.

I'm here to steal Salvatore Verratti's computer.

Verratti is the head of the Bergamo Mafia. He seems to have formed an alliance with a Russia Mafia outfit to smuggle guns through Northern Italy into France and the UK. This makes no sense. A partnership with the Russians is the first step on a road that will end with the *bratva* taking over Verratti's territory, and he knows it.

But something's made him desperate. Either the Russians have something on him, or he's broke.

After weeks of searching, I've tracked down the location of the Verratti server to a ramshackle farmhouse just outside Bergamo. The answers I seek are in there.

Now, I just have to go in and get them.

Andreas, an up-and-coming soldier in the Venice mafia, drums his fingers impatiently on the steering wheel and gives me a sideways glance. "You look nervous," he says. "There's nothing to worry about. Verratti isn't there. The only person in the farmhouse is an old caretaker. My baby sister could take him, and she's the same size as you." He grins. "Maybe I should call Cecelia. She lives close by and can be here in less than ten minutes."

"I'm not nervous," I lie, tamping down my irritation. Andreas is concerned. His voice isn't condescending, and he's not hinting that I'm not strong enough for this. Not like Dante would. I tap my earpiece. "Leo, what's the holdup? It's almost twelve. Are we good to go?"

Leonardo Cesari, our security chief, answers immediately. "Not yet."

Every noon, the caretaker leaves to eat lunch at the local pub, and he's gone for an hour. That's our window, and it's tightening every minute we sit here. "Why not? We're ten minutes away from the farmhouse, and I'm going to need all the time I can get."

"I have orders to wait," Leo replies calmly.

"Orders from who? The padrino?"

Leo hesitates for an instant too long before answering my question. I immediately have a bad feeling about this. If Leo doesn't want to tell me why we're stalled, it means that the order to wait didn't come from the padrino.

It came from Dante Colonna.

The Broker.

Second-in-command of the Venetian Mafia, my daughter's uncle (it's complicated, okay?) and *my personal nemesis.*

Ugh.

I'm about to open my mouth and say something cutting and unwise when I glance in the rearview mirror. A vintage cherry-red Ferrari roars toward us and screeches to a stop in front of our Fiat. The driver's door swings open, and Dante gets out.

He's wearing a white linen shirt and expensive jeans that hug his muscular thighs. His dark hair is styled perfectly, and his smoky gray eyes are hidden behind sunglasses. He looks like he stepped out of a fashion magazine.

The devil has no business looking this good.

He strides toward us and opens Andreas's door. "I'm taking over," he says to the foot soldier, his voice a low rumble. "Head back to Venice."

Andreas was hurt this summer, and he told me on the drive here that he's been looking forward to getting back in the field. But when Dante gives him his marching orders, he doesn't say a word in protest. Traitor. Instead, his eyes dart to the Ferrari. "Should I drive your car back?" he asks, a little too eagerly.

Dante gives him a long glance. "No. Find a different way back." He finally deigns to look at me. "Hello, Valentina."

I wait until he puts the car in motion to reply. "Dante," I reply shortly. "How's Andreas going to get back? Walk? Would it kill you to let somebody drive your precious car?"

"No, but if he damages it, I might have to kill him."

What? My eyes fly to his expressionless face. I have no idea if he's joking, and I don't want to find out. "What are you doing here, anyway?"

"Isn't it obvious? I'm your security."

I give him a derisive glance, irritation bubbling up inside me. "Don't you have anything better to do? You should get a hobby. I hear knitting is good for the nerves." I rest my gaze on his strong hands and neatly manicured nails. "Are you even capable of getting your hands dirty anymore?"

Ignoring my taunting, he calmly changes gear. "Let's hope we don't have to find out."

Fifteen minutes later, we park the car out of sight and arrive at the farmhouse on foot. The place looks deserted. It rained last night, and only one set of car tracks is in the mud—the caretaker's, leaving for lunch.

There is nobody here, but my heart still races. I am all too aware that I have a nine-year-old daughter, Angelica, and her only two blood relatives are about to walk into enemy territory. If something were to happen to us. . .

If you don't want Dante to see you as a victim, don't act like one.

I take a deep breath and then another. Dante pretends he doesn't see my fear, a kindness I wasn't expecting. "Shall we?" he asks, putting on his earpiece and opening his door.

"Yes." I get out of the car, and the two of us walk to the entrance, Dante a half-step in front of me. The sturdy wooden door is locked, but he picks it in under a minute. I must look reluctantly impressed because he holds out his hands, his lips curling into a smug smile. "Looks like they're good for some things."

So self-satisfied. I ignore him and launch a drone in the air. It's programed to fly in concentric circles around its launch spot and transmit live camera footage back to headquarters. "Leo, can you see the drone feed?"

It takes him a moment to respond. "Yes, I have eyes now."

"Good." I let myself relax a little. We still don't have cameras inside the farmhouse, but at least we'll know if anyone approaches the perimeter.

Dante turns the handle and pushes the door open. "Let's go."

We walk quickly through the farmhouse. The interior looks exactly like I'd expect from the outside. The curtains are faded; the couch is threadbare. The floor is bare, covered with a thin layer of dust. The kitchen sink houses dirty dishes, and the refrigerator looks like it's even older than Dante's precious Ferrari.

Everything looks exactly like it should until we come to the cellar door. The cellar door that's shut and locked with a Yale lock that needs a ten-digit code to open.

Crap.

Dante looks at the lock and then at me. "Can you get in?"

"In seven hours," I mutter. Brute-force hacking a ten-digit numeric code. . . We don't have enough time for that. I plug my codebreaker into the port and pull my laptop out of my backpack.

Dante folds his arms across his chest, his bulging biceps straining his sleeves. "Valentina, I hate to point out the obvious, but we don't have seven hours."

With heroic effort, I resist the urge to strangle him. "Shockingly, I know that." Salvatore Verratti is not computer savvy; he's unlikely to pick ten random digits. I look up his birthday—January 12, 1979—and type 01121979 into the codebreaker. That's eight of the ten digits. Most people pick easy-to-remember passwords. With any luck, the Bergamo head is one of them.

The birthday doesn't work, but the next date I try, the date Verratti got married, is a hit. Who'd have thought he was a romantic? Three minutes after I started, the lock clicks open. I resist giving Dante a smug grin and get to my feet. "Shall we?"

A gun appears in Dante's hand. "I'll go first," he says. "Wait here until I give the all-clear. If you hear me shout out, don't follow me." He holds my gaze in his. "Do you understand, Valentina? If I'm in trouble, get the hell out. That's an order."

I snap to attention. "Yes, sir," I say, giving him a mocking salute. "Whatever you say, sir. Or," I pull a small drone out, no bigger than the palm of my hand. "I could just send a camera in."

He gives me a speaking look. "So that's where the budget goes," he murmurs, cracking the cellar door open.

I send the drone swooping in, my eyes on my phone screen. "Nobody in sight," I say after a moment.

He steps in front of me, his solid body shielding me from imaginary harm. "Stay behind me."

"As you wish," I mutter with another roll of my eyes. Dante is technically my boss, but the master-of-the-universe act gets pretty old. I lift my chin in the air, step around him, and take the stairs down into the cellar.

The cellar is empty except for a desk in the middle of the room. On it is the server. I take one look at it and swear out loud.

"Problem?"

"It's ancient."

That's not the only problem. Leo's voice isn't in my ear either—the cellar is a dead zone. I try not to feel spooked as I boot up the computer. It takes forever before I can navigate the settings, and I swear again. "There's no built-in Wi-Fi." I look at the back. "No USB port either."

Dante, to his credit, immediately identifies the problem. "You won't be able to save data off it." He nods decisively. "We'll just take the computer."

"No need." I rummage through my backpack

and triumphantly pull out a compact disk. "I came prepared." I slide the disk into the CD-ROM drive. "Give me a few minutes."

He taps his earpiece, a frown on his face. "Hurry up."

I start copying data files. The process is glacially slow. It takes seventeen minutes to transfer everything I need, and my nerves are on edge the entire time. Finally, I hit eject and grab my disk. "Done."

Dante lifts his hand, a tense look on his face. Then I hear it. Footsteps above us.

Shit, shit, shit.

His grip tightens on the hilt of a gleaming knife, his eyes focused and determined. He holds up three fingers. Three men, then. "I need to use you as a diversion, Valentina," he whispers into my ear. "Can you scream? The shriller, the better."

I nod, my heart hammering in my chest. We're in enemy territory, and I have no illusions about my nonexistent combat skills. It's three against one, and if something were to happen to Dante, I'd be defenseless.

Angelica is *nine*.

The room plunges into darkness. I instinctively turn to Dante, but he's gone, melted into the shadows. For a moment, panic fills me, and then my brain starts to work again. He's not going to leave me here. The Broker is like superglue, sticky, and impossible to get rid of.

I open my mouth and emit a scream, loud and shrill.

The men upstairs respond immediately, throwing open the cellar door and running down the stairs. I have only a brief glimpse of bulging muscles and guns, and then. . .

And then Dante attacks.

He moves with lightning speed, his movements fluid and precise. My eyes are still adjusting to the dimness, but I see enough. Dante steps between the two guys in the rear, smashes his fist into the jaw of the man on the right, shifts to the left and drives his knife into the other man's shoulder. The guy in front barely has time to pivot before the Broker throat punches him and, for good measure, stabs him in the thigh.

When he's done, all three men are unconscious. Dante pats them down, taking their guns and knives. Then he holds his hand out to me, his knuckles covered in blood. "It's good that they didn't see our faces," he says. "And to answer your earlier question, Valentina, I *am* capable of getting my hands dirty. Shall we go?"

My mouth has fallen open. Three against one, and the fight was over in seconds. Reluctant admiration stirs in me. That was. . .

Impressive.

Terrifying.

Hot as hell.

Remembering to close my mouth, ignoring Dante's outstretched hand, I step over the bodies on the floor. "Sure."

DANTE

Chapter Two

I was *forced* to use Valentina as *bait*.

She could have been hurt.

Shot.

Killed.

As we sprint back to our getaway vehicle, I'm so angry I'm shaking. "Drive," I growl. If I take the wheel right now, I might wreck the car.

What the hell is Valentina doing, barreling headfirst into enemy territory? She should have told me if she had a lead, and I would have sent somebody into that farmhouse to get the damn computer she needed.

No. She didn't do that. Instead, she put herself in danger.

I seethe in silence as we drive back to where I parked my Ferrari. "Will those men live?" Valentina asks as she drives.

"Probably," I say tersely. "Pity."

She gives me a sidelong glance, taking in the rage in my eyes and my tightly clenched fists. "I'm not fragile, you know."

She's looking for a fight, and I'm in no condition to give her one. I'm too on edge. I take a deep breath and make myself calm down. "You've never shot anyone. You've never *killed* anyone."

"That's your problem? Give me a gun, then."

I count to ten in my head. "Guns require training, Valentina. And it needs a certain ruthlessness to hold a weapon up and shoot a man between the eyes. That's not who you are."

"You're saying I'm weak."

I remember the first time I saw Valentina ten years ago. My brother Roberto was using her as a punching bag, hitting her hard enough that she ended up in the hospital. She was lying on the bed, her face and body covered with bruises, two broken ribs, and her arm in a cast, waiting stoically to find out if she'd lost her baby. Valentina Linari is the strongest person I know. "You're not weak. You're human."

"And what are you?"

"I'm a killer," I say bluntly. "The difference between you and me, Valentina, is that you'll wait until somebody threatens you to open fire. And I will shoot first."

Thankfully, Verratti's goons didn't see either of us in the darkness. If they'd caught sight of my face, they would have definitely recognized me, and it would have started a war. And if they managed to identify Valentina, figure out who she is. . .

It didn't happen, I remind myself. Crisis averted. Valentina is safe. I take another calming breath and change the topic for good measure. "Does Angelica like her new school?"

At the mention of her daughter, Valentina's face softens. "Yes," she says. "She's already made a friend."

"Mabel."

"If you already knew that, why did you ask me?"

"Angelica knows I worry about her. She tells me what I want to hear. *As does her mother.*" My face hardens as I remember how close to danger we were today. "I never would've okayed this excursion, and you know it. You took advantage of the fact that I was away from Venice to convince Leo to go along with this ridiculous scheme."

"I did no such thing," she snaps. "We're getting nowhere with Verratti. We needed the information on that computer, so I did what was necessary to get it."

"You didn't need to go in yourself," I retort. "Any one of the guys could have retrieved that computer for you."

"Really? And could any of the guys have cracked the cellar door code?" She gives me a smug glance. "Yeah, I didn't think so."

"Don't tell me you can't train someone to use your precious hacker gadget, Valentina, because I know that's not true." Stubborn woman. She drives me crazy. "I didn't think I had to explicitly forbid you from doing stupid things, but here we are. No more field missions. No more farmhouse visits in hostile territory. No more idiotic, unnecessary risks. Do I make myself clear?"

Her smug look vanishes. "Why not?" she demands. "Why can't I go into the field?"

"You have a child."

"So?" She gives me a truly murderous glare. "That's sexist. I don't see you worry about the men with families under your command."

I open my mouth to respond and think better of it. For fuck's sake. I'm not being sexist; I'm being protective. Ten years ago, my brother beat Valentina so hard she almost died. It wasn't the first time he hit her, either. He'd been beating her for a year and a half.

Nobody in Venice intervened. Nobody stepped up to defend her.

I didn't know he was abusing her, *but I should have.* I knew Roberto was a bully, quick to anger. When we were children, I was his favorite target. And there were whispers. *Roberto is out of control. He's drinking too much, flying into rages at the slightest provocation. He's a favorite of the padrino, and it's gone to his head. His poor girlfriend. . .*

I should have paid attention to the rumors, but I

didn't. My brother wasn't my problem, and I was in Rome, busy with my own career. There was a power vacuum in the capital, and I was determined to take advantage. I worked for various organizations, increasing my skills and making my reputation.

And the entire time I was ruthlessly maneuvering for power, Roberto was beating Valentina.

When I saw her in that hospital bed, bruised and battered, I looked in the mirror and didn't like what I saw. Sure, I didn't hit her myself, but I put my career ahead of her safety. I was *culpable*.

That day, I made a promise. I could never atone for my past failures. But I could make sure it never happened again.

And I intend to keep my vow.

"None of my men barge into danger with such a reckless disregard for their own safety," I snap. "And all of my men are trained. They know how to defend themselves."

"Perfect," she bites out, screeching to a halt inches away from my Ferrari. "I'll sign up for shooting lessons. I'm sure Leo will train me in no time."

Leo chooses that moment to speak up. "Leave

me out of it," he says in our earpieces. "I want no part of your lover's quarrel."

Valentina snorts out loud. "Not even if he was the last man on Earth, Leo."

I roll my eyes. "Because men are lining up to date stubborn women who refuse to see good sense. Trust me, sparrow. I feel the same way."

VALENTINA

CHAPTER THREE

I meet my friend Rosa for dinner that evening. Rosa Tran is twenty-five and an insanely talented fashion designer with a boutique in my neighborhood. She's already at the restaurant when I arrive. "Your best friend is in town," she says once we're done with greetings. "I'm surprised you still have time for me."

Lucia Petrucci, my best friend since high school, is back in Venice after ten years, working at the Palazzo Ducale on a three-month contract. The week after she arrived, she decided to steal a priceless masterpiece from Antonio Moretti, the head of the Venetian Mafia. I thought she had gotten herself into serious trouble and was prepared to rush into the padrino's office and advocate for her, but shockingly, I didn't need to. The painting is a distraction. The two of them are attracted to each other and dancing around it.

Lucia *is* one of my best friends. But then, so is Rosa.

I give her an exasperated look. "Are we still in high school?" Rosa has reasons for her insecurity, but she has nothing to worry about with me. "Don't you start with me. It's not a competition between you and Lucia, and you know it."

My friend makes a face. "Sorry. Bad habit. So, the farmhouse, how did it go?"

Rosa knows I work for the Mafia. About six months ago, her landlord started to jerk her around after she sank all her savings into opening her new boutique. I got Daniel, the lawyer we have on retainer, involved. I don't share many details with her about what I'm working on—it's best if she doesn't know the particulars—but I did tell her I would be in Bergamo today.

"Dante showed up."

"He did?" She leans forward, her eyes gleaming with interest. "Wasn't he supposed to be in Milan?"

"That's what I thought," I say grouchily. Okay, fine. Dante might have been right about me waiting for him to leave Venice before suggesting the trip to the farmhouse. "Unfortunately, I was wrong. He roared up in his Ferrari at the last minute, ordered Andreas out of the car, and informed me that he was going to be my bodyguard."

Rosa's mouth falls open. "No, really? And then what happened?"

"Three guards showed up out of nowhere, and Dante took care of it." I barely had time to be afraid before they were rendered helpless. Even more annoying, I found his competence incredibly hot.

She pretends to swoon. "I think he likes you."

"I think he likes to tell me what to do." I fall silent as Franca walks over to take our order. I get my usual lasagna, Rosa orders a salad, and I continue once the waitress is out of earshot.

"Do you know what he said to me on the way back

to Venice? That I was taking an unnecessary risk and should have known better. And then, he *forbade* me from going on any more field missions without his express permission." Thinking about the encounter sets my blood pressure skyrocketing. "Have I mentioned I hate him? Because I do."

My friend tilts her head to the side. "I'm not defending Dante here, but isn't he right?"

My conscience prickles. "Okay, maybe I was a little too eager to go to the farmhouse, but can you blame me? Dante treats me like I'm made of glass, and I'm tired of it. I just want to be one of the guys."

"But you're not one of them, Valentina," she points out. "None of the men can hack into computer systems the way you can. You don't need to bash in people's faces to be valuable to the organization. Why are you comparing yourself with them?"

"If the fashion designer thing doesn't work out, you could always become a therapist," I grumble. "I don't know why, okay?"

Except I'm lying. I do know why; I just don't want to say it out loud. Roberto is dead; Antonio Moretti killed him before Angelica was born. But when Dante sees me, he still sees the girl in the hospital.

And it *stings*. I'm not a victim. I refuse to let myself be defined by an abusive relationship that happened ten years ago. I've left that version of me in the past.

But Dante can't see it. *He refuses to see me.*

"Enough about me. What's going on with you?"

"Let's see. I emailed a hundred influencers last week, asking if they'd be interested in collaborating," she says wearily. "So far, none of them have bothered to reply. Oh, and I have a date this week."

"You do? With whom?"

"Some guy I met online." She doesn't sound too enthusiastic. "This is our second date."

"Second? How come I didn't hear about the first?"

"Because I never talk about first dates. The only purpose of a first date is to figure out if you want to see that person again. I have a rule—I only start swooning about a man if he makes it past the third date."

I fight to keep from grinning. "How very practical of you."

Rosa ignores my mirth. "Anyway, Franco has a single friend. Do you want to double-date?"

And there it is. The question that rips away the illusion that Roberto didn't affect me. My palms go clammy, and my throat closes up. "When were you thinking?" I make myself ask.

"Thursday."

I let out a relieved breath. "I can't. I'm meeting Enzo at Casanova."

"Enzo," Rosa says, disapproval vibrating through her voice. "Your friend-with-benefits that you only meet once a month at a sex club."

"Yep." I busy myself with my lasagna to avoid meeting her gaze. I'm not a good liar, and Rosa isn't a fool. If she sees my face, she'll immediately know I'm hiding something. "I have a job and a kid. Once a month at a sex club is all I have time and energy for."

"Hmm." She sounds unconvinced. "And at this sex club, you let him tie you up?"

The thought of being bound, restrained and unable to get free makes me panic. "Yes," I lie again.

"Maybe I'll come to Casanova on Thursday and

see what the fuss is about."

I freeze. "Really?"

Rosa bursts out laughing. "Valentina, you should see your face. You look like you're about to have an aneurysm. Relax, I'm not going to show up at your sex club. It's not my thing. I just think you could do better than someone who only wants to see you once a month."

I hide my trembling fingers in my lap. Rosa can't come to Casanova—not this Thursday, not ever. Because if she does, she'll know at once that Enzo and I aren't involved.

And then my carefully constructed web of lies will start to unravel.

I can never let that happen.

The next morning, once I make Angelica breakfast and set her up with her Sunday morning cartoons, I get to work on the Verratti files and immediately hit a wall.

The files are encrypted.

Nothing I throw at the encryption works. None of the tools in my arsenal can break through. And as I work through one failure after another, I wonder if I'm missing something.

Salvatore Verratti is not tech-savvy. Family Verratti earns their money through extortion, smuggling, and drugs. They're old-school to a fault. Federico, Salvatore's father, doesn't use computers at all, and his son isn't much better.

And yet, I can't make any headway decrypting the data.

Where are all these sophisticated tools coming from? The ten-digit electronic lock on the cellar door, the encrypted data files stored on a computer that isn't routinely connected to the Internet—these precautions betray an understanding of data security that nobody in Verratti's organization should have.

There's only one possible explanation. Salvatore Verratti has hired his own hacker. And not just any hacker—this is someone with formidable skills.

I have a rival.

Breaking this encryption and defeating my

adversary is a challenge, and I normally love those. But something about this one makes me uneasy.

Four days later, the only thing I've figured out is that my mystery hacker is Revenant.

Revenant isn't the man's real name, of course. It's his hacker handle, the same way mine is Sparrow. He isn't a stranger to me. On the hacker forums, he's most likely to leave a scathing reply when a newbie asks a question. He posts long screeds about random topics, implies he's leaps and bounds ahead of the rest of us, and generally acts like an obnoxious asshole.

Unfortunately, it's not all bluster. Revenant really does know his job.

But he made a mistake branding his work. Now that I know it's him, I can comb through every one of his posts. If he's ever expressed a preference for an algorithm or endorsed a product, I have a way in.

I'm deep in source code on Thursday when my phone beeps with a message from Antonio Moretti. He wants to meet me in his office in an hour.

This is. . . *unusual.*

Did Dante snitch on me? Is Antonio going to yell at me about the farmhouse expedition? Damn it all to hell.

The padrino is something of an enigma. He's very private and rarely volunteers information about himself. But he's a good boss, fair and reasonable, and even if he weren't, I'd still work for him. Antonio killed Roberto so my daughter wouldn't have to grow up with a violent and terrifying father, and that's a debt I can never repay.

I board the ferry and take the short ride to our headquarters in Giudecca. From the outside, the building looks like every other palazzo in Venice— slightly rundown and crumbling under the weight of its own history. Inside is a different story. The walls are made of steel-reinforced concrete; the windows are covered with bulletproof glass, and it's equipped with a panic room that cannot be breached.

Stefano and Goran are guarding the front. Stefano waves me inside. "He's expecting you."

That's not ominous at all.

I open the door and almost collide with a broad chest.

Dante.

He's dressed in his customary tailored suit. Today's outfit is charcoal gray, with a narrow pinstripe running through it. I don't know fabric as well as Rosa, but I'm pretty sure his suit cost more than a year's tuition at Angelica's frighteningly expensive private school.

"What are you doing here?" I snap, and then my brain catches up with my mouth. I'm not being smart. First, Leo heard us squabble yesterday, and now there's a chance the padrino will overhear us. Bad idea. Men can rage and carry on, and somehow that's macho, but if I let someone glimpse how irritating I find Dante's hovering overprotectiveness, I'll be considered shrill and emotional.

I get my expression under control and smile at Dante, a smile so sweet it sets my teeth on edge. "I didn't think I'd see you here. What an unexpected pleasure."

Dante's eyes laugh at me. "Likewise, Valentina," he says. "Antonio's waiting for us." He gestures to Antonio's office with a wide sweep of his hand. "After you."

DANTE

CHAPTER FOUR

Antonio is already in his office. He glances up as we enter, studies Valentina, and then me. "Everything all right with the two of you?"

Valentina opens her mouth, but I interject before she can say something. "Everything's fine, Padrino. You wanted to see us?"

"Yes." He waves us to our seats. "The more I think about this Bergamo situation, the more uneasy I get."

He's not the only one. Something about this

feels *off*. Verratti inherited the organization from his father seven years ago when Federico retired. Since then, he's made no attempt to expand his territory, no attempt to reach new markets. He's also not the sharpest thinker in the world, nor is he possessed by burning ambition. So why ally with the Russians?

"He might be hard up for money. It's rumored that he's putting up his 1973 Jaguar in an auction next month."

I can tell from the surprise that flashes across Valentina's face that she didn't know that particular tidbit of information. She recovers quickly, though. "Of course, you'd keep track of auto auctions," she says sweetly, tucking a strand of her hair behind her ear, her sarcasm buried under a thick layer of sugar. Today, blue streaks twine through the blonde tresses. Last month, it was purple, matching the frame of her glasses. "I'm assuming you have an alert whenever a classic car comes up for sale. Six cars in a city where you can't drive should be enough, but—"

"Seven," I interrupt, my lips twitching. Bantering with Valentina is always fun. "It's seven cars, not six. Although I don't buy Jaguars. Too English for me."

She pushes her glasses up her nose with her middle finger—a subtle fuck-you—and I almost laugh out loud. "Isn't your suit from Savile Row? Ted Baker, if I'm not wrong."

Her observation takes me by surprise. Dressed as she is in her customary gray sweatshirt and olive-green cargo pants, I had no idea Valentina paid attention to fine suiting. Her friend Rosa's influence, no doubt.

That'll teach me to underestimate her.

Antonio clears his throat. "If the two of you are done squabbling," he says acerbically, "perhaps we can get back to the problem at hand. The Russians cannot gain a foothold into Bergamo. I will not allow that."

I snap into alertness. "You want to take over Verratti's territory."

He nods. "Salvatore hasn't left me any other choice. I'm putting you in charge, Dante. Figure out how to take Bergamo with a minimum of bloodshed."

We haven't expanded our territory in many

years. I'm not going to lie—a part of me is looking forward to the challenge. "I'll take care of it," I promise.

"Good." He turns to Valentina and says something that makes my smile vanish. "Dante told me you went to Bergamo and retrieved some of Verratti's data files."

She lifts her chin in the air. "I did, Padrino, but I haven't yet succeeded in decoding them."

"But you will. I'm impressed by your initiative, Valentina. I want you to work with Dante on Bergamo. Do what you can to destabilize Family Verratti. Hack into their data, disrupt their organizations from afar, siphon off their money so they can't make payroll, that kind of thing. Yes?"

Valentina shoots me a triumphant glance. "Yes, Padrino."

So much for keeping her safe and out of the line of fire.

VALENTINA

I'm in a great mood as I leave the padrino's office. Antonio Moretti thought I showed initiative going to Bergamo. He's confident that I can hack into the Verratti files. He's got faith in me. After the last few frustrating days, it's nice to feel appreciated.

Even the fact that I'll be working closely with Dante on my next assignment can't derail my good mood.

Outside the office, I turn to Dante. "Listen, about Bergamo. Salvatore Verratti has hired a hacker. Anyway, we have to go on the offense—"

"No," Dante interjects harshly. He looks *pissed*. "Absolutely not. If you think the padrino just gave you the green light to do as many stupidly dangerous things as you want, I have bad news for you, Valentina. You work *for me,* and I haven't changed my mind about your involvement. I can take over Bergamo on my own."

I see red. One hot, angry thing after the other explodes through my mind. I try one more attempt. "It won't be as easy as you think, but we can set an electronic trap for Revenant. I think—"

He holds up his hand, his expression closed off. "You're not listening to me, Valentina."

I grit my teeth. I'm not listening to Dante? It's him who's not listening to me. I'm not sure if Dante thinks all his problems can be solved with his fists or if he underestimates how much damage a motivated hacker can cause.

Either way, it's time for an object lesson.

I look around. Leo and Joao are having an animated conversation about pasta in the break room, and Tomas is trying not to laugh at the two of them. I walk up to the trio. "Hey, can you guys come to the conference room for a second? Bring your laptops, please. You too, Dante."

There's one problem with good data security. It's invisible. Nobody pays attention when their data is safe, so they tend to overestimate how protected they are. But part of my job is penetration testing our own network, and every week, I get in at least half a dozen times.

When everyone's seated around the table, I look at Dante. "If I show you that I was able to hack into all of your accounts, will you listen to me?"

He raises an eyebrow. "I follow your guidelines," he says confidently. "Maybe you can hack into their accounts, but not mine."

It's going to be glorious when I get into his account. I'm *really* going to enjoy the next five minutes. "Want to bet?"

He leans back in his seat. "Sure," he says. "Do your worst."

Arrogant asshole.

I survey my targets. "Tomas, you got an email from Antonio on Wednesday night asking you for your opinion on an investment opportunity. Antonio sends emails at all times of the day, so you didn't think anything of it, and you clicked on the link. Only one problem: that email wasn't from Antonio, it was from me. I installed a keylogger on your computer."

I press a key, and Tomas's screen goes dark. Then, a cartoon monkey dressed in a yellow raincoat dances across the screen, carrying a banner that says, 'You've been hacked.'

"Ouch." Tomas makes a face. "That was stupid of me."

Tomas is a nice guy, so I don't rub his nose in it. "Onto Joao. Sorry, Joao, you were even easier. You wanted to watch a Brazilian soap opera last Saturday, so you installed a free VPN on your home computer." Joao winces, knowing where this is going. "Unfortunately, the program you chose has a security flaw big enough to drive Dante's Ferrari through. You didn't install it on your work computer, but since you log into work from home..."

The hacker monkey waltzes across Joao's screen.

I turn to Leo. "Joao wanted some help with a presentation. He put it on a USB key and gave it to you. You trusted him, so you plugged it into your computer. Only problem? Joao was already infected." I press a key, and the monkey dances on Leo's screen. "You've been hacked."

Dante's watching me with an unreadable expression on his face. Is he impressed? Annoyed? I have no idea. "And me?"

"You were the hardest," I admit grudgingly. "All your devices are secured. You even wipe your phone every week, the way I outline in my best practices manual. I didn't think anyone even read that thing."

"I read it."

Huh. Who knew? "I had to work at it. I sent a drone outside your house to record your keystrokes. Did you know each key makes a different noise when you type? I could detect your keystrokes and get your password that way."

The hacker monkey appears on Dante's screen. I give him a long, pointed look. "Will you listen to me now?"

I leave a chastened trio in the break room with copies of my best practices manual. Now I'm sitting in Dante's office, across the table from him.

"You think Verratti has a hacker."

"He definitely does. It's Revenant. He was vain enough to put his handle in the source code." I tell him what I know about the man. "Revenant's cocky, but he's good. If you're going to go after Verratti, we have to be prepared for Revenant to come after us."

Dante's lips twist. "What do you recommend we do?"

"First things first, we shore up our defenses." He inclines his head in agreement. "I need to decrypt Verratti's files. That'll give me something to work with, maybe even a clue into Revenant's real identity."

"Okay."

What a shocker. Dante Colonna is actually being agreeable. My demo must have rattled him more than he let on. Flushed with triumph, I continue enthusiastically. "Also, once I access their data files, we can attack. Set a trap for Revenant and take him out before he can cause too much damage."

Dante's expression shutters. "That could be dangerous."

"He's a *hacker*. We sit in front of computers all day. We're basically indistinguishable from mushrooms. Take our gadgets away, and we're powerless."

He considers me for a long instant. I'm beginning to think he sees the situation my way when he shakes his head. "No. I'm not going to take the chance."

"You aren't letting me do my job," I seethe.

"And you aren't letting me do mine," he replies calmly. "This discussion is over."

Dante's got his master-of-the-universe, I-know-best expression again, and I *cannot* with him. The Broker can go fuck himself. "Fine," I snap, jumping to my feet. "Whatever you say. I don't have time to argue with you. Call me when you decide that you need my help."

He steps in front of me, blocking my way. "Why don't you have time to argue with me?"

"Because I have a date tonight," I throw at him.

If I'm expecting a reaction, I don't get one. He simply raises an eyebrow, as calm and collected as ever. "What about Angelica?"

"Are you suggesting I shouldn't date because I'm a single mother?" I snarl.

He gives me an exaggeratedly patient look. "I meant, who is watching Angelica while you're out?"

"Oh." I feel exceedingly foolish. Of course, he doesn't care that I have a date. He's just concerned about his niece. "She's having a sleepover at Mabel's house. Bye, Dante."

VALENTINA

CHAPTER SIX

I'm still fuming as I text Mabel's mom, Zadie, to confirm that Angelica's sleepover is still on. She responds immediately in the affirmative. Dante brings out the *worst* in me. Around everyone else, I am calm and controlled, and I think before I speak. Not with Dante. He goads me, and in response, I blurt out the first thing on my mind and then regret the hell out of it. Like telling him I'm going on a date. Why did I do that? *Not a clue.*

Dumb move, Valentina. *Really dumb.*

I can't believe he wouldn't listen to me about

the Verratti hacker. Impossible, infuriating, *stubborn* man. I wasn't proposing another field trip, dangerous or otherwise, but did he listen to me long enough to find that out? *No.* I'm a skilled hacker and keep a detailed dossier on every mafia organization in Italy. Did he give me a chance to tell him what I knew? *Of course not.*

I picture Dante roaring into Bergamo in one of his idiotic sports cars and falling flat on his face. It's a glorious vision. I imagine a movie car chase, with Family Verratti shooting at Dante's precious automobile, smashing out the tires. Giant Humvees colliding into the red vehicle from either side, squashing it like a bug. . .

My phone alarm beeps. I take a deep breath and straighten my shoulders. No matter how annoying I find him, I can't dwell on Dante right now. It's time to pick up my daughter from school.

"Mama. . ." Angelica's voice is a little too casual. "Can I ask you something?"

I glance down at her, something I won't be able to do much longer. Angelica had a growth spurt this summer, and she comes up to my shoulder now. Next year, my baby will be taller than me. "Sure."

"Can you tell me something about my dad?"

Damn it. As if my day couldn't get worse.

Angelica is nine. In her last school, she'd been bullied by a group of girls who taunted her for not having a father. She asked me about Roberto then, but I wasn't prepared for the question, and I shut her down so badly that she hasn't brought up the topic for a year.

But now that she's gathered the courage to ask again, I just have to put on my big girl panties and deal. When I wanted out of my relationship with Roberto, I couldn't go to my parents for help. I don't want that for my kid. I don't want her to think there are topics that are off-limits to talk about. She needs to know that whatever the problem is, I have her back. I *will* protect her, whatever the cost.

Not just me. I've tried really hard to gather a family around Angelica, not bound by blood but by the bonds of love. Lucia, Rosa, even Dante. These are Angelica's family, her people.

"Your father's name was Roberto."

She rolls her eyes at me in a way only a nine-year-old can. "I knew that already, Mama," she says. "What was he like?"

I don't know how to respond. I don't want to shield her from the truth, but I don't want to give her nightmares. "He was very charming," I say finally. "He laughed often. But he wasn't always nice. He used to drink a lot, and when he drank, he got mean."

"Oh." Angelica digests my words in silence. We cross a bridge and are almost home before she asks, "Is Uncle Dante a nice person?"

I stop walking. "What?"

"They're brothers," Angelica says, as if that explains everything. "Victoria and Diana are sisters, and they're both mean."

As infuriating as I find Dante, he is nothing like his brother. The contrast between the two of them could not be starker. "Your Uncle Dante is not mean," I say firmly. "If he was, I wouldn't let you see him. I would not let you spend time with anyone I didn't trust completely. Okay?"

"Okay." Angelica switches topics with dizzying speed. "Can I have a puppy?"

Nine-year-olds. "No, you cannot have a puppy. Dogs are a lot of work, and besides, there's no room in our apartment for one." Yet. Fingers crossed, we'll soon be able to move to a bigger place. Of course, I'll have to keep from strangling Dante long enough to collect my paycheck, and right now, homicide is looking much likelier than a pet.

"Uncle Dante said if you were okay with it, I could get a puppy, and he would keep it at his house."

I narrow my eyes. "Did he now?" I can't think of anyone less likely to tolerate a puppy than Dante. Maybe the dog will chew his precious Ted Baker suit and his handmade Italian loafers. I savor that mental image. "Let's discuss this later. You have a sleepover to get ready for."

Angelica has been excited about this sleepover for the last two weeks. Besides being her new best friend, Mabel has a kitten *and* a puppy. But today, her thoughts run elsewhere. "If you got married to someone, I could get a new father."

What the hell? Should have kept talking about the puppy. "I'm not interested in getting married to someone, kiddo," I say lightly. "You're stuck with me."

"Patricia says her mother goes on dates. Why don't you go on dates?"

I'm going to a sex club tonight, does that count? I close my eyes and count to ten. What has gotten into Angelica this afternoon? "I'm happy being single. Can we change the subject, please?"

"Is Aunt Lucia going to marry Signor Moretti?"

I give her a sharp glance. What has she overheard now? This is probably a good time to remind her not to eavesdrop on conversations that aren't meant for her, but I don't have the energy. "Maybe."

"If she does, can I be a flower girl?"

I laugh. "I'm pretty sure you're the first person she'll ask."

"Would Uncle Dante ask me to be a flower girl?"

My footsteps stutter to a halt before I realize what's happening and force myself to keep walking. "Is Dante getting married?"

"You could marry Uncle Dante. He's nice. You said so yourself."

I should have guessed Dante wasn't seeing someone seriously. He spends most of his hours making my life miserable—where would he have the time to date?

I harden my heart against the hope in Angelica's voice. The saints preserve me from matchmaking children. "I'm not interested in Uncle Dante that way. Now, about the sleepover. If you don't want to be there for any reason at all, you can call me, and I'll come get you. Okay?"

Angelica gives me an exasperated look. "Mama, it's Mabel. I'll be fine. Stop worrying."

DANTE

CHAPTER SEVEN

The moment Valentina says she's going on a date, I freeze.

Of course. I'd almost forgotten. It's the second Thursday of the month, the night she meets Enzo Peron at Casanova. All thoughts of Bergamo instantly flee from my brain, replaced by Valentina having an intimate dinner with Peron. Laughing with him. *Touching him.*

She asked me if she shouldn't date because she's a single mother. She has it so wrong—this has nothing to do with Angelica. Valentina shouldn't date because the world is filled with assholes who don't deserve her.

I head downstairs to grab some coffee. Silvio and Omar are in the break room. They take one look at my face and make themselves scarce. I make myself an espresso and head back to my office. It's going to be busy for a while. The situation in Bergamo is a priority, but unfortunately, it doesn't mean that the day-to-day job of running the Mafia goes away.

I turn on my computer and look at everything requiring my attention. Tomas wants my opinion on an investment opportunity before he takes it to Antonio. Joao needs more warehouse space. Leo's informant in the Venice police is getting restless, and our security chief thinks we should remind him it's a very bad idea to cross the mafia. In theory, Tomas, Joao, and Leo report to Antonio, not me. In practice, they run ideas by me before presenting them to the padrino.

I work my way through the list, but my mind is on the Verratti problem. It's dark outside, and I'm deep in spreadsheets when Leo shows up. He lifts his hand to knock at the door, looking like he's a lamb heading to slaughter. "Sorry to bother you," he says. "I normally wouldn't bother you today, but—"

I fix him with a glare. The security chief is a good friend, but he's skating on very thin ice. "What is that supposed to mean, you normally wouldn't bother me today?"

"Everyone knows to avoid you on the second Thursday of the month," he replies. "You're as grouchy as a bear. Anyway, Andreas just called me. He's keeping an eye on Valentina tonight, but he's run into a problem and wants your advice on what to do."

It's nothing urgent or life-threatening; otherwise, Leo and I wouldn't be having this leisurely chat. "If he wanted my advice, why didn't he call me?"

"Because he thinks you're still mad at him about the Bergamo field op. He didn't realize how irrational you are about Valentina."

Andreas is right; I am still mad. "Irrational. Was that his choice of words or yours?" I ask, my voice frosty. "The entire op was a mistake, Leo. Someone with no combat experience has no business being in the field. Call it irrational if you want, but I don't want my niece to grow up without her mother."

"That's all it is, huh?" Leo's expression is a little too knowing. "Back to Andreas's problem. You know Valentina is at Casanova tonight? Well, she just walked into the club, but she wasn't alone."

She's never entered Casanova with Peron, not once in the last two years. She's never left with him, either. What's changed now? Something akin to panic fills me. Before I can open my mouth and demand that Leo stop beating around the bush, he adds, "Lucia Petrucci is with her."

"Fuck." Antonio is obsessed with Lucia. He's not going to take this well. Not at all. I get to my feet. "The padrino will want to know. I'll tell him."

The moment I tell Antonio that his girlfriend is at a sex club, he tears out of there. I return to my office, shaking my head. It's so easy for my friend. So uncomplicated. He likes this girl, and she likes him back. There's no painful past gaping like a chasm between them. No searing guilt. No deep-seated trauma.

I pull up Tomas's spreadsheet again, but my thoughts aren't on his calculations. They're on Valentina. Not on whatever she's doing at Casanova—I'm not picturing Peron's lips on her mouth, on her neck, kissing her fluttering pulse. I'm not imagining his hands roaming all over her curves, his fingers trailing through the turquoise strands of her hair.

No, that's definitely not what I'm thinking about.

I'm thinking about the Bergamo hacker. Revenant.

Valentina might act with reckless disregard for her own safety, but she's very, very good at what she does. Today's demo chastened everyone, me included. She warned us before that threats are everywhere, but her dancing monkey brought it home.

On a hunch, I call my informant in Verratti's organization. Giorgio Acerbi is one of Salvatore's enforcers. His father worked for Salvatore's father, and his grandfather worked for Massimo. He was loyal and dedicated.

Then Giorgio's kid was born with a heart defect, and Salvatore decided to cheap out on medical care.

There's nothing as desperate as a father with a child who needs to fly to the United States for expensive surgery. I saw my opening and paid for everything.

Giorgio picks up on the first ring. "It's you," he says. "What do you want?"

Interesting. The enforcer isn't usually this terse. "A list of everyone working for Salvatore Verratti. Especially anyone hired within the last two years."

"You think that's easy?" Giorgio demands. "It's not like there's an HR department I can go to for this, you know. The list of employees is carefully guarded."

"I don't pay you for easy things, Giorgio," I reply coolly. "How is little Liliana doing? She's coming up on the fifth anniversary of her transplant, isn't she?"

The other man heaves a resigned sigh. "I'll see what I can do," he says. "But I have a bad feeling about this. Everything's too quiet. There's a storm building, Colonna, and it's going to be a big one."

Giorgio is spooked. *His daughter is six*, my conscience prods me with a red-hot poker. Just three years younger than Angelica. "Be careful," I tell him. "Don't take any unnecessary chances. I'll be in touch."

I hang up and stare into the distance. Then there's another knock on the door. I look up, and Leo is in the doorway, out of breath as if he's been running. "Valentina just left the club," he says, his chest heaving. "But there's a big problem."

VALENTINA

CHAPTER EIGHT

"What are we doing here?"

Enzo and I are at the bar at Casanova. There's no one around us. I came here with my friend Lucia, but then Antonio Moretti showed up, and they disappeared into a private room, leaving me and Enzo to stare at each other in awkward silence.

"What do you mean?" I hedge, though I have a very good idea of what he's talking about.

He looks around to make sure we're not being overheard. "You and me. This elaborate charade.

When are you going to stop pretending, Valentina?"

I take a sip of my wine to give myself time to think. It tastes bitter on my tongue. Two years ago, Rosa set me up on a blind date with Enzo. I thought I was okay with dating again, but I ended up having a panic attack outside the restaurant.

If I told Rosa, she would have just worried. That's when I'd come up with what I thought was a perfect plan. Enzo and I would meet at Casanova once a month, supposedly to have hot sex in a private room, and I'd tell my friends that I didn't have energy for anything more involved than that. For reasons of his own, Enzo agreed to my proposal and went along with the subterfuge.

Until now.

Enzo's expression softens. "I thought this was temporary," he says quietly. "You needed people to get off your back about dating again, and I agreed to help because I've been there. I understood what you were going through. But Valentina, we've been pretending for *two years*. I don't think I'm helping you any longer. You're using this as a crutch when you should be walking on your own."

"I—" My voice trails off. I don't know what to say to Enzo. If I tell him I'm fine, I'll be lying. The panic that swept through me when Rosa invited me to double-date is proof. "Did you meet someone?"

"This isn't about me. I'm concerned about you, Valentina. You're still traumatized by your relationship with Angelica's father. You should be in therapy."

"I tried that once. It didn't work."

"Try again," he says bluntly. He sips his whiskey, a troubled look on his face. "What you're doing isn't healthy."

"Why? Is it a rule that everyone has to be in a relationship?" I take another sip of my wine and abandon it on the counter. "Why can't I just be single?"

"You can absolutely be single if that's your choice. But that's not what's happening here, is it? You're afraid of dating."

It's not dating I'm afraid of. It's sex. It's intimacy. It's being naked and vulnerable. That last time with Roberto. . . I feel a headache coming on and squeeze my eyes shut. "You're right. I know you are. I'll work on it."

"I want to believe you," he says. He hasn't raised his voice, but it's too loud. The music, the crack of the riding crop on the stage, are all too much. "I won't be here next month."

"Okay." There were warning signs of my migraine earlier, but I wasn't paying attention, and now I'm fighting off waves of pain and nausea. "I'm going to leave now."

"Are you okay?"

"Fine," I say, trying not to hurl on the expensive carpet. "I'm perfectly fine."

I barely make it a block when another wave of nausea hits, and I lose the contents of my stomach against the side of a building. Offering the store owner a mental apology for the mess, I stumble toward home, but my headache is crippling, and my vision is blurry. I sink onto a bench, cradling my head in my hands. I'll get up, I promise myself. I'll make it home, make myself a cup of tea, and then curl up on my bed and fall asleep. Soon. As soon as this wave of pain passes.

Some minutes later, someone sits next to me. "How bad is the pain?" Dante asks, handing me a bottle of water. "Can you see?"

"It's blurry." I hurt too much to ask him what he's doing here, so I rinse my mouth with the blissfully cool water, grope in my purse for my medication, and swallow two pills. "If you're planning on lecturing me about my irresponsible behavior, I will burst into tears and hate you forever."

"How about we call a truce on the hatred until I get you home?" He holds a travel mug out to me. "Drink the coffee. The caffeine will help."

Water *and* coffee? I take a sip of the steaming hot beverage and then another. "How did you know coffee helps?"

"I'm very clever," he says dryly. He waits patiently until I empty the mug and then says, "Lean on me. You don't have to open your eyes; I won't let you fall."

Why are you being nice to me? I almost ask. Instead, I lurch to my feet. Dante is immediately at my side, lending me support. "You want me to carry you?"

"No." He feels like a rock, solid and steady. "Just don't let me hit a lamppost."

Ten minutes later, we arrive at my house. "Thank you," I murmur. "I'm good now."

"No, you're not," he responds. "I'm coming in and making you soup. I'll leave once you eat it."

"Do you eat soup or drink it?" I wonder out loud. "Can you cook?"

"No," he admits. "But nobody opens a can better than me."

For some reason, I find that ridiculously charming. I laugh and immediately regret it when a battering ram hits my head. "Sit," Dante says, urging me to the couch. "Close your eyes. What kind of tea do you want?"

How does Dante know I want tea? "There's a blend called Serenity in my cabinet. Follow the brewing instructions on the tin."

"Got it."

Dante disappears into my kitchen and reappears with an ice pack. I take it from him with a whimper of relief and hold it to my forehead. The caffeine helped a little with the headache but did nothing for my nausea and light aversion. I shut my eyes, drape a throw over myself, and zone out in my darkened living room.

The delicious aroma of lemongrass wakes me up. I crack an eye open. "This doesn't smell like it's from a can."

"You only had tomato soup," Dante replies. "I wasn't sure if tomatoes were a trigger for your migraines, so I went to the Thai restaurant around the block and got you some chicken soup instead. Here's your tea."

I take the mug from him and hold it with both hands. "Thank you," I whisper. "This is very kind of you."

"Not really," he replies. "Anybody would do the same thing. Except, evidently, Enzo Peron." Disgust saturates his voice. "That fucking guy. Didn't he have the decency to bring you home?"

"It's not his fault." I sip the tea, letting its warmth fill my senses. "He doesn't know about the migraines."

"Because he takes no interest in your life." Dante's voice is low and furious. "You deserve better than him."

Enzo is an elaborate lie and nothing more. "I'll

cry if you yell at me."

He exhales in frustration. "I'm sorry. I'll drop it." He hands me a container. "Soup."

What do I deserve? That's such a complicated question, too complicated to deal with when my head feels like it's going to burst and my senses are being assaulted from every direction. But the lemongrass, ginger, and garlic in the soup are fragrant, and the tea is hot and soothing and steeped for exactly the right amount of time. And he's even brought me fresh spring rolls.

Why are you here, Dante?

"Zadie is going to take Angelica to school tomorrow. But can you pick her up in the evening?" The words tumble out of my mouth, and then I regret them. What am I thinking? Tomorrow's Friday. Dante undoubtedly has a date. "Never mind, I'll ask Rosa or Lucia, and if they can't do it, it's okay. Angelica isn't any trouble. She just freaks out when I'm sick."

"No need. I'll pick her up."

Okay then. I finish my soup and my tea. Dante sits quietly in the chair across from me, recognizing that I'm not up for conversation. The silence feels companionable, though. The tension that usually accompanies our interactions is gone, buried under a temporary truce.

My eyes keep drifting shut. "I should go to bed," I murmur when I'm done eating.

"Okay." He gets to his feet. "I'll get out of your hair then. There's more Thai food in your refrigerator."

"Thank you." Dante's the only person who's been around when I'm sick. My parents were great at extravagant gestures but terrible at the day-to-day stuff. Somehow, even as a kid, I knew I wasn't supposed to bother them when I didn't feel well.

Dante isn't acting like I'm a bother.

"It's nothing," he says.

No, it isn't. It's *kind*.

"It's always you," I mutter. The drugs are making me woozy and chatty. "In the hospital room, all those years ago. And now. You're making a habit of being around when I'm sick."

His face goes expressionless. "Two times is hardly a habit."

"Mmm." I bite back a yawn. "Good night, Dante."

I stagger to my bedroom, strip off my clothes in

the dark, and get under the covers. The soup, the coffee, the tea, the drugs have all helped to ease the pain. I didn't think I could sleep an hour ago, but now, rest feels possible.

It would be nice to be held. Not by Dante—he is, after all, my nemesis—but by someone else. A man I can lean on. One I can trust. Someone kind and protective, who will always watch out for my daughter. One that will bring me soup when I'm sick. "Maybe Enzo is right," I mumble to myself. "Maybe it's time to stop being scared."

DANTE

CHAPTER NINE

I swallow hard as Valentina strips off her clothes. I can see tantalizing glimpses of her body through the doorway to her bedroom. I avert my gaze until she gets under the covers and then release a breath.

Then she murmurs, "Maybe Enzo is right. Maybe it's time to stop being scared."

I wash her mug and tidy up her kitchen. Peron is right about what? Stop being scared of what? Or who? I straighten her cushions, fold her throw, and realize I'm looking for an excuse to stay.

She's fast asleep. I can hear her breathing, deep and even. I don't want to leave her alone, but she doesn't want me around. She's fine on her own.

I put the uneaten spring rolls in her refrigerator. Shutting the front door quietly behind myself, I leave.

Valentina's feeling better by the weekend. On Sunday afternoon, after a late breakfast of croissants and fruit accompanied by an espresso for me and hot chocolate for Angelica, I take my niece back home to her mother.

"Are you coming up, Uncle Dante?" Angelica asks cheerily, holding up the bag of pastries we brought for her mother. "You can give her the chocolate croissants."

"No, cucciolina." I'm strangely reluctant to see Valentina. Ever since she joined the organization, we've established defined roles. I stop her from following her more reckless instincts, and she hates my guts for it. But our truce on Thursday felt like a seismic shift in our relationship.

Until I regain my footing, it's best to avoid her.

"You go up by yourself," I continue. "Your mother is recovering from a migraine and will not want visitors."

Angelica rolls her eyes as if I've said the stupidest thing in the world. "You're not a visitor, Uncle Dante. You're family."

That fantasy died a death a long time ago. "I have to work." That's not a lie. My inbox is overflowing with the day-to-day minutia of the organization, and worryingly, Giorgio hasn't checked in. "I'll see you soon, okay? When's your dance recital?"

"That's *ages* away."

I check my calendar. "It's in three weeks."

"Yes, ages."

I smother a grin. "Well, I'll see you then. Off you go, kitten."

I'm walking back to headquarters when shit falls apart, and I get a phone call from the padrino.

"Where are you right now?" he barks.

Something's wrong. "I just dropped Angelica off with her mother. Why?"

"Head back there. I need everyone here for an emergency meeting. Joao, Tomas, Leo, and Valentina. You can serve as her escort."

The hair on the back of my neck prickles. "You want Valentina too?" I demand. This is bad. Valentina is a specialist—she doesn't attend regular meetings. It's safer for her to stay arms-length away from the nitty-gritty of our business. Whatever this emergency is, she shouldn't need to be at headquarters for it.

Not unless. . .

"Okay, the downstairs neighbor can watch Angelica for a few hours."

"No," Antonio says tightly. "Bring her too."

Ice drenches my spine. Antonio wants me to escort Valentina to headquarters and doesn't want me to leave Angelica alone. The precautions can only mean one thing.

Valentina and Angelica are in danger.

Agnese, Antonio's housekeeper, takes Angelica under her wing as soon as we arrive. "I'm baking a cake," she says. "You can help me, can't you, cucciolina?"

Valentina forces a smile on her face. She knows, as well as I do, that something is up. "That's a good idea. Thank you, Agnese."

We file into the padrino's office. He's already there, as are Joao, Tomas, and Leo. There are two empty seats, one on Antonio's right and one at the other end of the rectangular table.

Valentina makes a beeline for the far seat. I sit down and glance at Antonio. He's good at maintaining a poker face, but I've worked at his side for ten years and can read his emotions.

Antonio is worried. Badly so.

"I have some new information about Verratti," he says, "that confirms our suspicions. The Bergamo mafia has run out of money. Salvatore urgently needs to raise some cash. Without an infusion of capital, he won't be able to pay off his creditors, and worse, he won't be able to make payroll." He leans forward. "He needs his deal with the Russians to go through. He cannot survive without it. And I will not let it happen."

The padrino's worry makes sense now. He has a girlfriend, someone he cares about. Antonio has nerves of steel, but it's a lot harder to do what you must if you're putting your loved ones at risk.

"You think he's going to target you?" I ask.

"Not just me. Everyone in this room is in danger. Verratti will do everything he can to destabilize us. If we're in crisis, the Russians might be able to sneak their guns into Venice without us finding out." Antonio looks around the table soberly. "He's desperate, and desperate men do desperate things."

Across from me, Valentina's face is bloodless.

"Even in winter, Venice is teeming with tourists. It's a security nightmare." He straightens his shoulders. "Until this situation is resolved, everyone stays in Giudecca."

Giudecca is an island without many tourist attractions, with only one ferry in and out.

Securing it will be challenging, but Leo can handle it.

But Valentina and Angelica don't live in Giudecca. They live in Dorsoduro, a neighborhood awash with students and tourists—busy, noisy, and vibrant.

Dorsoduro is *impossible* to secure.

Antonio's thoughts are running in the same direction as mine. "Valentina, you'll have to move," he says. "You and Angelica can stay—"

His words cut through my fear. I lean forward, propping my forearms on the table. "With me," I say firmly. "They'll stay with me."

She stiffens. Antonio glances at her. "Valentina?" he prompts. "Are you okay with this?"

I glance at her, daring her to protest. For a long instant, she doesn't reply, and then she nods. "Yes, Padrino."

So much for avoiding Valentina.

My feelings don't matter. Whatever the cost, I will make sure that she and Angelica are safe. I failed once when I let Roberto hurt Valentina. *I will not fail again.*

She's never stepped foot inside my house. Now,

she's going to be living with me. Driving me to distraction with her glasses falling down her pert nose, her yoga pants hugging her round ass, the scent of her frankincense and jasmine hand lotion in my nostrils, her hair in every color of the rainbow. . .

I foresee a lot of cold showers in my future.

VALENTINA

CHAPTER TEN

I have a theory that the way you really get to know someone is through their homes.

Your home says a lot about you. My daughter is my priority, so my apartment is strewn with her toys and craft supplies. Rosa lives and breathes fashion, and her place is filled with fabric swatches, patterns, and half-finished garments. Her walls are covered with design sketches and old Vogue pattern envelopes, and stray pieces of thread cling stubbornly to the carpet. Lucia's apartment is empty except for a blowup air mattress and one solitary chair. Her space screams that she is here temporarily and is not planning on staying. However, given her relationship with Antonio, I predict that's going to change.

Dante's been a hovering presence in my life for almost ten years. I'm pretty sure I know everything important about him. He never loses his head in a crisis and is probably the most infuriatingly even-tempered person I know. He's terrifyingly competent. He pays more attention than I think he does. (Exhibit A, knowing coffee helps with my migraines.)

Women throw themselves at him all the time, but he doesn't take any of them seriously. He goes on dates every other month, but it's always with a new woman. No repeats. The last time he dated someone seriously was two years ago. Marissa was a baker, friendly and kind. I don't know why it didn't last.

But as much as I know about Dante, I've never been in his house. I have no idea if he's neat or messy. He told me on Thursday that he doesn't cook. Does he always eat out, or does he live on canned soup and sandwiches? No clue. He knew enough to bring me Thai food from my favorite restaurant when I was sick—more of that paying attention thing—but I don't even know what his favorite cuisine is.

And now, I'm going to find out.

Because we're going to be living together for who-knows-how-long.

I suppress my urge to scream out loud.

Moving in with Dante makes sense; Angelica's safety comes first. But that doesn't mean I'm not dreading the next few weeks. Being around Dante isn't good for me. There's too much history there, history that can't be overcome.

To Dante, I will always be a victim. Someone who needs protecting. When he looks at me, he sees the past and nothing else. He doesn't see anything but that broken girl on the hospital bed.

There's no point wishing for anything else because it's not going to happen.

Hating him isn't a choice. It's a matter of self-preservation.

Leo lingers to talk to Antonio when the meeting ends, but the rest of us head out. Dante stops me in the hallway. "Valentina."

There's a look of wariness in his eyes. I feel a brief moment of wistfulness for the version of Dante that brought me soup and made me tea, and then I banish it. "What?" I demand. "Let me guess. You didn't expect me to agree to stay with you. You thought I'd protest."

"Not really. You might take idiotic risks with your own safety, but you'd never endanger your daughter."

"Hang on a minute. That sounds suspiciously like a compliment. One wrapped in an insult, of course, but still. Am I dreaming?"

His lips tilt into a smile. For an instant, a dimple flashes on his chin, and then we're back to monotone. "Agnese is watching Angelica. We should sort out the details before we get her."

"Details?"

"What are we going to tell her about the move? School? The next sleepover with Mabel?"

Oh shit. He's right. Life would be infinitely easier if Angelica was a toddler, but she's not.

She's nine, old enough to ask questions.

"I don't want to worry her," I fret. "And she can't miss school, not now. She's just settling in and making friends. Her dance recital is in a couple of weeks. If I pull her out—"

"Valentina." He rests a steadying hand on my shoulder. "Take a deep breath."

He's right. I'm freaking out. I inhale, count to ten, and then exhale. Dante waits patiently as I get through a couple of breathing cycles, and then he says, "First things first, you won't have to pull her out of school."

"I won't?"

He shakes his head. "Verratti is not stupid enough to attack a school. If he does that, the Carabinieri won't arrest him. They'll hunt him down like a dog. I'll talk to Leo. One of us will walk her to and from school, and we'll make sure there's a team keeping an eye on her." When I open my mouth, he adds, "Unobtrusively. We won't do anything that makes her stand out."

It's stuff like this that makes it difficult to actually hate Dante. He genuinely cares for Angelica. He knows as well as I do that the last year has been rough, and if I pull her from school now, it will jeopardize the friendships she's slowly making. *He gets it.*

"And when she asks why we're moving in with you?"

His forehead furrows. "Apartment renovations?" he suggests. "A water main break caused some damage that you need fixing?"

I give him an exasperated look. "There was no damage when we left our place half an hour ago. She's not an idiot."

"True." He sighs. "This would have been a lot easier if she was still four."

An unwilling laugh tears out of me. "I was just thinking the same thing." I chew on my lip. "Okay, the renovation idea could work. What if I was thinking of selling my apartment and getting a bigger place? One that's big enough for a puppy?"

He nods, an appreciative glimmer in his eyes. "Using the puppy as a distraction. I like it. Do you have a renovation wish list? Email it to me, and I'll get a team on it so our cover story holds up. As for Mabel, I assume you've done a thorough background check on her parents."

"Of course. They're cool. But maybe we'll do the next sleepover at your house, just to be safe. If you can deal with two nine-year-olds wanting to watch Disney princess movies all night long."

"I'll manage," he says dryly. "You do realize you're going to have to get her a puppy at the end of this?"

I smile at him. "I'd probably have done it anyway." What do you know? Two truces in a week. What are the odds of that? "Okay, can you keep an eye on Angelica while I go pack my equipment? The rest of my stuff can wait, but I need my computers."

"Are you fucking kidding me?" he demands. "Did you not hear anything Antonio just said? No. You're not going anywhere without me."

And there goes that moment of peace, burst into nothing like a soap bubble. "Dante, you're being ridiculous. I'm perfectly capable of going to my apartment by myself. I'm really close to cracking that encryption. This is not a good time to stop."

"I don't care," he snaps. "I'm not letting you out of my sight until this thing blows over."

His phone chooses that moment to ring. He picks it up. "You're late," he snarls. The person on the other end says something, and Dante looks pissed. "Fine," he growls. "I'll be there in a couple of hours."

He hangs up and looks at me. "I'll accompany you back to your apartment so you can pack up your stuff and drop you and Angelica off at my place, but then I have to go out," he says. "No leaving my house until I get back. Got it?"

I swear to God—he drives me *insane*. "You want me to stay holed up in your house like a captive? Like some kind of prisoner?"

"Call it whatever you want," he replies. "But yes."

He is *such* a jerk. Irritation fills me, tinged with more than a little disappointment. For an instant, I thought he saw me as someone capable, but I was fooling myself.

It doesn't matter. Everything is electronic now, every business record, every financial transaction. Hacking is the new superpower, and I'm good at what I do. I don't need him to see me as an equal— I know my worth.

I just have to survive living with the infuriating, overprotective, hot-as-hell Dante Colonna.

But if his high-handedness is a preview of what the next few weeks have to offer, somebody better find me an alibi. One more order from Dante—just one more—and I'm going to have to kill him.

DANTE

CHAPTER ELEVEN

Angelica is perched on a stool in Antonio's kitchen, flour smeared on her cheeks and chin, beating some batter with a hand mixer under Agnese's careful supervision.

Valentina's lips curve into a soft smile as she takes in the scene. "She's growing so quickly," she murmurs, lifting her phone to take a photo. "Soon, she'll be a sullen teenager who doesn't want to talk to her mother."

I snort in amusement. "What a glass-half-empty person you are. Angelica has never had a sullen day in her life. I can't see her personality changing so dramatically."

"Mine did," Valentina replies. She stares at her daughter through the doorway before taking a deep breath and straightening her shoulders. "Might as well get this over with." She enters the room. "Hey, kiddo. What are you doing?"

"Agnese is showing me how to make the batter," Angelica replies.

"Looks like you had a little flour mishap." Valentina fishes a tissue out of her pocket and wipes her daughter's cheeks. The maternal gesture tugs at something in my heart. "I have a surprise for you."

Angelica's eyes flash to me and then to her mother. "What kind of surprise?"

"You know how you've been wanting a puppy?"

"Yeah. . ." Her forehead furrows. "But we don't have enough room for a dog."

"What if we sold our apartment and moved into a bigger place?"

My niece gives her mother a sharp look. "Really?"

"Yes, really. Dante has kindly offered to have us

stay with him until we find a new place."

I grimace. Valentina is a terrible liar. Truly awful. I'm waiting for Angelica to ask a thousand follow-up questions, but to my surprise, she doesn't say anything. She looks at me again and then at her mother. "We're going to stay at Uncle Dante's?"

"Yes." Valentina gives me a confused look—I'm not the only one surprised by Angelica's quick acceptance—and I shrug. "For the next month, probably."

"Okay." Angelica returns her attention to the bowl. "I have to finish making this cake."

Valentina's brow furrows. "And I have to pack our stuff. Do you want to stay here with Agnese while I do that?"

That's a good idea. The padrino's house is the most well-protected residence in Venice.

Angelica nods decisively. "Yes, please."

"What was that about?" I ask Valentina as we head back to Dorsoduro. "I thought Angelica would have a thousand questions, but she just went along with your story. That's not like her."

She makes a face. "I have a theory."

"One you're going to share with me?"

Valentina gives me a sidelong glance. "It doesn't concern you."

Valentina's tone warns me not to push. I open my mouth but think better of it. After what Roberto did to her, I've never understood why Valentina's allowed me to have a relationship with my niece, but she has. She's gone above and beyond to make me a part of Angelica's life. We have lunch once a week, and whenever Valentina has a migraine, Angelica stays at my house. I've been there for every significant milestone. Every birthday party, every Christmas.

It's a kindness I did not expect. One I do not deserve.

So, rather than push her, I keep my mouth shut. We ride across the lagoon in silence, each lost in our thoughts.

Valentina quickly fills two large suitcases with clothes and toys at her apartment. "I have my laptop," she says, zipping a suitcase shut. "But I'll have to come back for my computers." She looks up. "I forgot to ask. Is there a room in your house that I can use as an office?"

"You can take over mine." A pale pink lace slip peeks out from the open suitcase. The fabric looks like silk, soft and touchable. My throat goes dry as I imagine Valentina wearing it, moving closer to me, an invitation in her eyes. Then she lifts the garment over her head, let it drop to the floor. . .

What the fuck is wrong with you? Valentina is the mother of your niece, asshole. She's not the object of your sexual fantasies.

"Dante?"

I blink, dispersing the fantasy. "Yes?"

"Can you give me a hand with this?" She points to the now-closed suitcase. "It's too heavy for me to take down the stairs."

"Yeah, sure." I pick both suitcases up. Is it my imagination, or is she eyeing my muscles? Does she like what she sees? If I knew she had a thing for biceps, I'd get rid of my sweater and give her a better view.

Knock it off, idiot.

My house is skinny and tall, only twenty-five feet wide but four stories high. When I bought it nine years ago, it was falling apart. I could have afforded to have someone renovate it, but instead, I've spent every spare moment doing the work myself. It's remarkably satisfying to see the house regain its former luster because of my efforts.

I open the front door and gesture Valentina in. "You want to get Angelica now, or do you want to unpack first?"

"Unpack first, please." She rubs her temples. "I could use a minute."

Her head's starting to bother her. She needs to sit down. "Let me show you to your bedroom. I'll make you a cup of tea while you settle in."

"I didn't know you drink tea." She looks around the living room. "I'd love some, please. But could I get a tour first? I've never been here before."

Not by my choice. "Of course. This is the living room, obviously." I wave to the back. "And there's a small bathroom." I wonder what she thinks of my space. My walls are white and my furniture dove gray. Antonio's house looks comfortable and lived in. Mine looks starkly empty in comparison.

"Nice."

"The kitchen is one level up." I pick up her suitcases and start to walk up the stairs. "There's also an eat-in nook."

She follows me into the kitchen. "I like this," she says appreciatively. "It's very clean and bright." She gives me a teasing look. "This looks like the kitchen of someone who doesn't cook much."

"Guilty," I admit. "Do you like to cook?" It's a weird question to ask someone I've known for almost a decade, but I honestly don't know the answer. Valentina and I are usually too busy sniping at each other, which doesn't leave time for conversation.

"I do," she replies. "It relaxes me. And I won the kid lottery. Angelica is, thankfully, an adventurous eater. Mabel only eats food that's white in color."

"What does she eat?"

"White rice, pasta with butter, cauliflower, and bananas. There's probably more, but I'm forgetting. How many levels are there?"

"Four. Five, if you count the rooftop garden."

"Ouch. I'm going to be forced to get in shape, I see."

"There's nothing wrong with your shape," I reply on autopilot, only realizing what I said when Valentina stops and gives me the strangest look. "What?"

"You paid me a compliment. It's weird. Did the real Dante get abducted by aliens, and are you a body double? Quick, say something mean to me. Tell me my hair is too bright or that my glasses make me look like an owl."

An owl. Where does she come up with these things? "Your glasses are adorable, and your hair makes me smile." She looks taken aback as I continue. "If it wasn't for your stubborn insistence to do the most dangerous things imaginable—"

A relieved smile flashes across her face. "Ah, there he is, the Dante I know and love. For a second there, you had me worried. What's on the next level?"

The Dante she knows and *loves?*

It's just a figure of speech, asshole. Nothing else.

"Bedrooms," I respond. Once again, I lead the way up the stairs, pushing open the door to the right of the landing. "This will be yours." It's not much. There's a queen-sized bed in the room, and the mattress is comfortable, but the walls are empty, and the room lacks color. "Sorry about the sparseness."

She gives me a puzzled look. "What are you talking about? I like it. I have room to breathe." She enters the room and bounces experimentally on the bed. "This is great. Is this where Angelica sleeps when she's here?"

She's bouncing on the bed. I should have torn my eyes away from her naked body on Thursday, but I didn't, and now my imagination has even more material to work with. Before I can corral my thoughts, my mind has constructed a fantasy that involves Valentina on top of me, those gorgeous tits bouncing as she rides my cock.

She asked me a question. "No, she has her own room." I open the door that connects the rooms. "Voila."

Unlike the rest of the house, Angelica's room is a riot of color. There's a canopy bed with purple drapes because purple is Angelica's favorite color. Fairy lights twinkle from the ceiling, and the blackboard-painted walls are covered with my niece's chalk drawings. Disney princesses pose on the window ledge, fighting with Lego pirate ships. A dinosaur model is in the corner, and large fabric butterflies are perched on the walls.

Valentina blinks. "Oh wow." She stares at me. "Two years ago, all she wanted more than anything in the world was a princess bed. And then she stopped asking for one. I now realize why."

"Angelica didn't tell you about her bed?" She's perceptive—perhaps too perceptive. Even as a seven-year-old, she realized her mother didn't want to know anything about me. "I wanted her to feel at home here."

"You spoil her." She crosses the room and bends down to examine the Lego boat. I avert my eyes so I can't see how her jeans stretch across her perfect butt. "Did she do this herself?"

"We did it together."

Valentina looks up at me, her eyes starting to soften. "Thank you, Dante."

I can't take it. Not the tone of her voice, not the look in her eyes. Seeing her in my house makes me want things I can't have. Things like Valentina and Angelica living here with me. Being a proper family. Shared dinners around a dining table and nightly walks around the neighborhood with the puppy Angelica wants so badly.

When I walked into her hospital room, she cringed when she opened her eyes and saw me there. Flinched away from me. I introduced myself and told her I was sorry. That I'd never let it happen again.

And I've never forgotten what she said to me.

"I don't want your promises. Go away. Leave me alone. I want nothing to do with your brother, and I want nothing to do with you."

Valentina hates me. She always has. I can't allow myself to be swayed by the softness in her expression because hope is a fool's game.

The ghost of my dead brother will always come between us.

The tour is not done. I haven't shown her my

bedroom or the rooftop garden. But everything suddenly feels suffocating, and I can't breathe. "Leo can bring Angelica here," I say abruptly. "I have to go."

Giorgio called just after the meeting with Antonio. He sounded on edge and insisted he needed to see me. "Meet me in Mantua," he said, naming a city halfway between Bergamo and Venice. "I'll be at Il Mulino."

Il Mulino is a bar downtown on the edge of the Piazza Virgiliana. Giorgio is already there when I arrive, a negroni on the table. "You're late."

"I spent fifteen minutes looking for parking. You couldn't have picked a place on the outskirts of the city?"

"I trust the people here. You want a drink?"

He lifts his hand, and a dark-haired waitress in her forties winds her way over to the table. "Another negroni already?" she asks Giorgio in a scolding tone. "What is that, your third?" She turns to me. "What would you like?"

"Just an espresso, please." I wait for her to walk away before switching my attention to my informant. "You wanted to meet."

"Yeah." Giorgio looks like shit. His eyes are bloodshot, and his hand shakes as he lifts his glass. Something has him spooked. He gulps down half his drink in one sip. "I looked into the thing you wanted."

Verratti's list of employees. After Antonio's announcement today, taking over Bergamo has taken on new urgency. This is no longer just about keeping the region stable. The Russians want to smuggle their guns through northern Italy, and Verratti is prepared to get violent to make it happen. In a very real way, Valentina and Angelica's safety depends on me taking over Verratti's organization.

"And?"

"Salvatore has a secretary, Bianca Di Palma. She makes his appointments, controls his calendar, pays the bills. . . If there's anyone who has what you were looking for, it'd be her."

"And?"

"She wasn't home." He empties the rest of his drink. "Her house was ransacked, and there were signs of a struggle." He swallows hard. "I found bloodstains on the carpet."

"Someone took her? Who?"

"I don't know." He starts to lift his glass and then realizes it's empty. "This is bad, Colonna. Very bad. Signora Di Palma isn't the first person to go missing. Nobody has seen Romano Franzoni in weeks. Salvatore is spooked. He canceled the Christmas party, and he and his father are holed up in their mansion, surrounded by bodyguards."

Franzoni is Verratti's second-in-command. He's smart and wily. A survivor. "This partnership with the Russians would never end well. Maybe Franzoni took off because he sensed the way the wind was blowing."

"No." Giorgio shakes his head. "Romano spoke up against doing business with the Russians, but he wouldn't leave. He's loyal. If he's gone, it's not by choice."

I put aside the problem of Franzoni for the moment. "Bianca Di Palma would have had books. Payroll records."

"There was nothing," Giorgio says. "It was all gone." His voice has a distinct tremble in it. "Someone took her out. And if I ask too many questions, I might be next."

Earlier this week, I yelled at Leo for putting Valentina in danger. "I don't want my niece growing up without a mother," I told him. But if I tell Giorgio to keep looking, I'm risking his life.

His daughter Liliana is younger than Angelica.

I bury my guilt deep. "I don't pay you for theories, Giorgio." My voice comes out harsh. "I pay you for results."

The truth is, if it's a choice between protecting Giorgio and my family, my family will win every single time. I would make unfathomable choices to protect Valentina and Angelica. "I want the names of everyone on Verratti's payroll. Keep looking."

I drive back to Venice. Bianca De Palma was attacked, and the Verratti payroll records she maintained have been stolen. Romano Franzoni, the Verratti second-in-command, would have known every employee in the organization. He's disappeared.

Revenant is actively hiding his tracks, and if Giorgio is right, he's prepared to kill to keep his real identity secret.

I don't have a good feeling about this.

VALENTINA

CHAPTER TWELVE

For a long time after Dante's abrupt departure, I stand in Angelica's bedroom and stare at the shut door. My thoughts churn violently, but I can't pin down any of them. It's all static in my brain. The sun is starting to set, but the boats still speed by, the roar of their engines muted inside the house. I pick up a stray Lego from the floor and hold it in my hand, my fingers running over the plastic. My stomach rumbles, reminding me that breakfast was a long time ago, but I can't seem to make myself move.

It's been a long and confusing day, and I'm having a reaction to everything. This bedroom, decorated with a princess bed, Legos, and love, is more than I expected. Much more. I figured Dante loved Angelica. I guessed he indulged her too, the way I sometimes did because deep down inside, I still felt a smidgen of guilt about her growing up without her father.

But knowing he loves her is different from truly seeing it. Angelica has a purple bedspread at home, and she has one here. She owns far too many Disney princess figurines at home, and that's the same here. Her floor at home is strewn with Legos. Here, someone's made an effort to tidy up. The bed is made, and the carpet looks freshly vacuumed, but there's no shortage of toys spilling from the shelves.

This isn't a guest room where my daughter sometimes stays when my migraines become too much to bear. This is *Angelica's* room.

And then, there was the look in Dante's eyes when I packed my nightgown. I would swear in a court of law that he looked at me in a *sexual* way. As if he wanted me and was picturing me naked.

His predatory male desire should have sent me running, *but it hadn't*. My heart should have started hammering in panic, but it hadn't been fear that made it speed up.

He doesn't even like you, I remind myself.

But his voice intrudes to counter that thought.

There's nothing wrong with your shape.

Your glasses are adorable.

Your hair makes me smile.

My phone rings, startling me from my thoughts. It's Leo. "I'm going to bring Angelica over."

Shit. Angelica. I'm a terrible mother. For a minute there, I almost forgot about my kid. But she's the priority. She's been the priority from the day the nurse placed her in my arms, all red and wrinkly and screaming in outrage.

"Valentina?" Leo prompts. "Ten minutes, okay?"

Dante and I were supposed to pick Angelica up from Antonio's place before he left so suddenly. If Leo's curious about the change in plans, his voice doesn't show it.

"Yeah, that's good." I give myself a mental shake. It doesn't matter that when he smiled at me, it felt like the sun had emerged from behind a massive cloud. What matters is that Angelica is going to be here soon, and she's going to be hungry. I better find some food.

As promised, ten minutes later, Leo knocks on the door. I check the security camera in the kitchen and head downstairs—so many stairs—to open the front door. "Hey there, squirt."

"Hey, Mama." Without prompting, she turns to Leo. "Thank you for bringing me, Uncle Leo."

Leo's expression softens from his default scowl. "You're welcome, Angelica." He waits until my daughter enters the house, and then he frowns at me in disapproval. "You opened the front door, just like that?"

"I'm not an idiot, Leo. I checked the security camera first."

He grunts. "Better than nothing. Next time, wait for me to call with the code phrase."

Are we in a spy movie? Leo's paranoia is only

matched by Dante's. No wonder the two of them get along so well. "Will do," I say to placate him. "Want to come in for dinner?"

He sniffs the air. "You're making pasta sauce?" he asks. "Needs some garlic, if you ask me."

My cheeks heat. Did I deliberately omit the garlic? Yes, I did. Damn Leo's nose. "Are you a restaurant critic?" I demand, going on the offensive to cover my embarrassment. "You want food or not?"

"No, I have plans." He gives me a knowing look. "And so do you, from the smell of things. See you later, Valentina. Remember, no going out alone. No quick trips to the corner store, nothing. This is serious."

I'm well aware of the gravity of the situation. I wouldn't have moved into Dante's place if I hadn't been convinced the threat was real. "Trust me, I'm taking no chances with our security."

I head in search of Angelica once Leo leaves. She's in her bedroom, sitting on the floor, Legos all around her. So much for the clean carpet. "Hey, kid. How did the cake turn out?"

"It was delicious," she announces. "I ate two slices."

"Did you now?" I ask wryly. "Taking full advantage of the fact that I wasn't there to stop you? You'll have to eat some vegetables to counter all that sugar."

She looks up, a calculating expression on her face. "No zucchini."

I have to laugh. Angelica will eat almost anything, but she hates zucchini with the passion of a thousand suns. It doesn't matter if it's steamed or grilled—it's the one thing she refuses to eat. "No zucchini," I agree. "Spinach or broccoli?"

I knew Dante didn't cook, so I wasn't expecting much by way of ingredients when I opened his refrigerator. But to my shock, it was filled with meat and produce. I have no idea how he arranged a grocery drop-off, but he did. I don't know why I'm surprised. Dante is competent in everything he does. It's maddening, really.

"Broccoli," she replies instantly.

"Broccoli it is. Oh, I almost forgot. I packed a

suitcase for you. Dante put it in my room. Let me grab it."

"Did you pack Diny?"

Diny—rhymes with tiny—is a twelve-inch-tall velociraptor dressed improbably in a pink tutu. Over the last couple of years, Angelica has abandoned most of her soft toys, but so far, Diny has survived the purge.

"Yup, Diny's in there." I fetch the suitcase and place it on her bed. "Can you unpack while I finish dinner?"

"Sure."

"Before more Legos, Angelica."

My daughter looks exasperated but gets up without a complaint. She really is a good kid. "Are you okay with us living here?"

"Sure," she replies, unzipping the suitcase and burrowing in her clothes until she finds her toy dinosaur. "I like it at Uncle Dante's."

"You do?"

"Yeah." She moves her T-shirts into the dresser. "I can play with Katie. I can do Legos—"

"And you can sleep in a princess bed." The one she conveniently forgot to tell me about. I bite my lip, debating whether to bring up the topic. When I told Angelica we had to move here for a few weeks, she had suspiciously few questions. I'd seen the calculation in her eyes; I know my kid. She's planning a romance between Dante and me.

I need to dissuade her of that notion as quickly as I can. Nothing will come of her dream. Dante is Angelica's uncle; that's it. If she's imagining us being one happy family, I have to tell her it's never going to happen.

But do I rip away the hope like a Band-Aid? She was bullied relentlessly in her old school because she didn't have a father. And that was only a few months ago. Sure, things are much better in her new school. No teacher is going around proclaiming that the best kind of family is one that has a mother and a father, and I'm not the only single mother there. But maybe I should just let her grow out of this fantasy on her own?

"And when we go back home, I'm going to get a puppy." She fixes me with an intense look. "Right?"

"You are definitely going to get a puppy. Are

you okay on your own while I finish making dinner?"

"Of course, Mama."

Dante's not back in time for dinner. I'm a little disappointed and then annoyed at myself for feeling that way. What the hell am I doing? I don't even like him.

"Is there enough left for Uncle Dante?" Angelica hesitates over a second helping of broccoli. "I don't want him to be hungry."

I roll my eyes. "Your Uncle Dante is capable of feeding himself." I look at her worried expression and bite back a curse. "There's plenty here, but if you want, I'll make up a plate and put it in the fridge for him. He is capable of reheating it, right?"

Angelica giggles. "Of course. He's very good at using the microwave, Mama."

After dinner, she wants to build a complicated Lego set of the Mars Rover. "I started it yesterday, but I got stuck. Can you help me with it?"

"Sure. Where are the instructions?" Angelica looks blank. I contemplate a lecture about putting things away in their proper places, but it's been a long day. I don't have the stamina, so I head to the Lego website and download the PDF. "Angelica, this is a two hundred and sixty-four-page instruction booklet."

We work on it for an hour and a half, and then it's her bedtime. I'm expecting the usual bargaining, but she must be tired. It only takes one story before she's out like a light.

I shut her door and head downstairs. There's still no sign of Dante. I could call him to find out where he is, but that's ridiculous and entirely too needy. We're not living together—this is a temporary situation. For all I know, he isn't even planning to eat meals with us.

And besides, I have work to do.

Dante said I could take over his office, but he didn't finish showing me his home, and I don't know where it is. Well, that's not exactly true. With the process of elimination, I'm assuming it's on the level I haven't seen so far, but that's the same level as his bedroom, a room I'm wildly curious about and yet strangely nervous to see.

I could call him and find out where I should work, but that feels suspiciously like I'm looking for an excuse to talk to him. Anyway, all I have with me is my laptop, not my full computer setup. I take it downstairs to the living room and poke around the house until I find Dante's Wi-Fi password. This doesn't involve hacking—it's scribbled on a Post-It note on the refrigerator. Which is bad data security by the Broker, the second-in-command of our organization. Tsk, tsk.

I prop the laptop on the pleasantly worn leather couch and look for a music player to pair my phone with.

Of course, Dante has nothing. Music probably annoys the devil. And the audio quality on my phone is garbage. In the rush of packing, I must have forgotten to grab my wireless headphones, which work with my phone. All I can find are the wired ones that plug into my laptop's USB port. Gah. Reluctantly, I connect to the Internet, muttering curses under my breath the entire time. I plug in my headphones and load up my playlist.

Like I told Dante on Thursday, Revenant shouldn't have branded his work. Now that I know it's him, I have a way to find the weakness in this encryption. I know he's impatient and prone to shortcuts—I've seen it in his posts over the years. Most people do a combination of AES and RSA protocols, but not him. He never does more than one round of encryption, relying on the unbreakability of his key. And because he brags, I know enough details about his custom algorithm to provide a starting point.

Rosa calls me about an hour into my work. "Are you serious about the date?"

"What?" It takes a few seconds for my brain to switch contexts.

"The double date we talked about?"

Oh, right. When Rosa called to check in on me Friday, in a moment of headache-medicine-fueled stupidity, I revealed that Enzo and I were done, and I'd be willing to go on a double date with her.

It's only been two days since that conversation, but it feels like a lifetime ago. Maybe it's because I'm in Dante's house, surrounded by his things. Curled up on the leather couch he sits on, inhaling the gentle aroma of the pine candle I lit on the coffee table. Or maybe it's the strange expression on his face when he showed me to his guest bedroom. For ten years, the bedrock of our relationship has been sarcasm and barely contained dislike. But the ground is moving under my feet, and I feel dangerously off-balance. The idea of setting off on a date from Dante's house makes my stomach do a funny flip.

And what happens when Dante goes on a date? I'll have to see him leave the house, dressed in one of his fancy woolen suits, smelling like amber, sandalwood, and musk, knowing that before the night is over, another woman will wear his cologne on her skin. Another woman will undress him, slowly removing his tie and unbuttoning his shirt. Will she kiss each spot of skin as it becomes visible? Will she stroke her fingers over the curved lines of his tattoos?

Enough. I don't know why it matters if Dante goes out on a date. *It doesn't.* It's just weird for Angelica, that's all. That's the *only* reason I care.

Rosa's waiting for me to respond. "Yes," I say, ignoring the feeling of wrongness that fills me as soon as I agree. Enzo was right; I have to get over this phobia. Roberto was ten years ago. I refuse to let him impact my life from the grave. "When?"

"Are you free Saturday night? Cocktails and dinner, how does that sound?"

Ugh. That'll take up the entire evening, more commitment than I was prepared for. But I'm determined to go through this. "Sounds like a lot," I grumble, not bothering to conceal my grouchiness from Rosa. She knows my anti-social tendencies. "But fine, I'll cooperate. Does he have a name, this friend of Franco's?"

"Neil."

"Neil. He's not Italian?"

"Half-Italian. His mother's English."

"What's his last name?" I ask, opening up a search window.

"Smith."

"No way," I say in disbelief. Neil Smith. Could his name be any more common? I'm not going to be able to get very far searching for him on the Internet. "I thought you said his dad was Italian."

"I think he uses his mother's last name. Valentina, are you doing a search on this guy right now? *Come on.* It's dinner and drinks, and I will be right there, and so will Franco. We won't leave you alone with him, I promise. Can you just wing it?"

The thought of winging it feels like setting out on a tightrope without a safety net. But it is extremely kind of Rosa to arrange this dinner. "Okay," I say grudgingly. "Fine. You're right. I won't look this guy up on the Internet. I will come to the restaurant on Saturday not knowing anything about him."

"Just like we did in the days before the Internet," Rosa says encouragingly.

I roll my eyes. "Rosa, you're twenty-five. You weren't alive in the days before the Internet."

She laughs. "True. But I've heard about them from my parents. Okay, see you on Saturday. I'll meet you at your place?"

"No," I say hastily. "I'll come to your apartment." I don't want to explain living at Dante's to Rosa. She'll have a thousand questions about the arrangement, and I won't have answers to any of them. And she'll absolutely ask me if I have a thing for Dante. I definitely don't, but I don't want to get into it with her.

"Sounds good."

We chat for a couple of minutes, and then Rosa hangs up, saying something about needing to sew up a sample garment. Like me, she's a night owl. I go back to work. There are several random number generators that generate encryption keys. I just have to figure out which one Revenant used, and I'll be able to read this data. I compile a list of every random number generator the hacker has mentioned on the forums and get to work trying each one.

On my seventh try, I hit gold. I generate a key and apply it, and file after file starts to decrypt.

Yes!

I'm double-clicking on the first unencrypted file when, suddenly, my monitor goes dark, and a chat window pops up on the screen. "Nice try, Valentina," a cursor types. "But you have to work harder to get the better of me."

Fuck. Fuck. *Fuck.* I'm frozen for a split second, and then my brain starts to work. I lurch for the power cord. I need to... It'll take me too long to disconnect... Where is Dante's modem? I've got to... *Fuck.*

I power down the Wi-Fi, but it's too late. All the files I decrypted are gone. My laptop is completely corrupted. Everything is ruined.

But that's not the worst of it.

Revenant knew my name.

Not my hacker handle. *My real name.*

Dante is going to flip out.

DANTE

Chapter Thirteen

I head back to work after meeting Giorgio. It's almost midnight by the time I make it home. I have a faint hope that Valentina's already asleep, but she's not. She's in the living room, slumped over her laptop. I glance at the TV and realize it's just on for background noise. Unless her taste suddenly extends to blue cartoon dogs with Australian accents.

She raises her head when I open the door. I see the defeated look in her eyes, and a fist squeezes my heart. "What happened?"

"I fucked up." She pushes the laptop aside and wraps her arms around herself, the gesture oddly vulnerable. "I wanted to listen to music while I worked and couldn't find your sound system. So, I connected my laptop to the Internet and listened while I worked."

"Okay?" I'm not seeing the problem.

"I was online when I decrypted the files I found in the farmhouse, Dante. Revenant found out. I must have triggered an alert because he activated some malware and destroyed everything. My laptop is toast; I'm going to have to wipe it and do a complete reinstall. Your modem is compromised. Every device connected to the Internet needs to be reset to a factory default. Like I said, I fucked up." Her voice is bitter and self-loathing. "All because I couldn't work without music."

"Hey, hey." I settle next to her on the couch. "Stop that." She's being really hard on herself. "It was a mistake. We all make them."

"It was a dumb rookie mistake. I should be better than that."

"Again, will you stop that?" I look at her exasperatedly. "You were in bed with a migraine two days ago. Today, you found out that we're likely in danger, and you and Angelica had to move into my house in a hurry. You're in a new location; your routines are disrupted. You're human, Valentina. All of that takes a toll."

"You're being nice to me again. It's weird." She takes a deep breath and hugs her knees to her chest. "There's something else." She doesn't look at me. "Before everything shut down, the hacker opened a chat window to gloat that he caught me. But he didn't refer to me by my handle." She hands me her phone. "I managed to take this picture before everything got wiped."

I look at her screen. The photo is blurry, but the words are readable. *Nice try, Valentina. But you have to work harder to get the better of me.*

It takes me a second to clue in. Then I do, and I go very, very still. Ice hardens my spine.

The fucker knows her name, and he wants us to know he knows it.

He *threatened* Valentina. When I find him— and I *will* find him—I am going to make him regret it. *I'm going to make it hurt.*

"Interesting." I force myself to keep the rage

from my voice and hand her back her phone. Valentina is notoriously touchy about it. Andreas picked her phone up when it beeped one day and got the glare of death, one that sent him backing away hastily from her. "Cocky bastard."

"I don't know how he found me." She gives me a sideways glance. "Despite what you think, I *am* careful. I rarely post on the forums. I don't reveal any identifying information about myself. I'm painfully aware it's not just my safety I need to worry about. It's also Angelica's."

I'm still furious. But not with her. I'm furious with the bastard who threatened her. "You want a drink?"

She gives me a startled look. "A drink?"

"After the day we've both had, a shot of whiskey sounds like a pretty good idea."

"I'm too tired to attempt to fix the mess right now; I'm afraid I'll make more mistakes. Getting drunk seems as good a thing to do as any."

She gets to her feet and follows me up the stairs to the kitchen. She looks exhausted, and I should send her to bed. But I'm a bastard who's greedy for her company and this quiet, shared moment. "Sit,"

I tell her, pointing to the table. "What do you want to drink? I've got whiskey, as promised, or would you prefer wine?"

"A shot of whiskey is fine. No ice, please."

She sits at the table. I hand her the drink and take the seat next to her. For a few moments, neither of us says anything. Then Valentina breaks the silence. "Maybe I'm not as good as I think I am. Maybe I'm a liability."

"That's the dumbest thing I've ever heard," I say bluntly. Valentina's unshakable confidence in her hacking skills is one of my favorite things about her. "Enough with this nonsense. We couldn't do half the things we do without you."

"I fucked up an entire week's work. I have another copy of the data from Verratti's computer, but it's going to take me days to decrypt it. I have to recreate everything I did, and it doesn't matter that I've done it before. The computational time alone. . ." Her voice trails off. "I've lost my edge."

"You hacked into all our accounts last week with laughable ease. You made us all look like idiots. You are *terrifyingly* talented." She opens her mouth to argue. "Take the damn compliment, Valentina."

She gives me a faint smile. "Okay." She takes a sip of her drink and makes a face. "I'm shocked you have whiskey in your home," she says. "I don't think I've ever seen you drink. I thought you'd unwind with an espresso or something."

"I'll be up all night if I drink espresso now." I'll be up all night anyway, thinking of Valentina asleep in the bedroom on the level below, wondering if she's wearing that pretty pink lingerie I saw her pack or if she sleeps naked. "I don't drink very often."

"Why not?"

There are a thousand glib answers I could offer. "I'm painfully aware that Roberto drank too much and hit you under the influence of alcohol. I don't want to become my brother."

"There's very little risk of that happening," she responds immediately. "You're nothing like Roberto." I don't have time to dwell on what that means before she continues, "In any case, that was a long time ago, and it ended when Antonio killed your brother. The past has no bearing on the present."

Guilt sears through me. I've never told Valentina the truth. That Antonio didn't kill Roberto.

I did.

It was an accident. As furious as I was with my brother, I didn't shoot him in cold blood. I'm not that much of a killer. We got into an argument, and Roberto drew a gun. We grappled for it, and in the struggle, he got shot. To this day, I don't know if it was my finger on the trigger or his.

I've always concealed the details of his death from Valentina. Because there's a secret, shameful part of me that wonders if it really was an accident. On some level, did I want to get rid of my brother because Valentina was too good for him? Did my subconscious believe that she'd never be mine as long as he was alive, and that's why I've never told her how important she is to me?

Valentina thinks the past doesn't have any bearing on the present, but in this, she's wrong. Our pasts *define* our present.

"Dante."

"Sorry. My mind was elsewhere. It's been a long day." And I just want to sit here in this kitchen, which smells comfortingly of tomatoes and lemon, of cooking and love, with Valentina.

"Did you eat anything? I set aside a plate of food for you."

"You don't have to do that."

"Oh, I think I do," she says dryly. "Angelica insisted." Her eyes dance with amusement. "She *promised* me you knew how to work the microwave."

"That's definitely within my skill set." My mother wasn't much of a human being, and I never knew my father. A home-cooked meal isn't just about food. It represents something far more, something elusive and infinitely precious.

And now I'm just being a sentimental fool.

"Thank you for the meal."

I heat my plate. Valentina remains in the kitchen, showing no signs she wants to leave. "Why was your day shitty?"

"I have an informant inside the Verratti organization who I asked for a list of people on the payroll, hoping to find your hacker." I relay Giorgio's news—Salvatore Verratti hunkering down, Bianca Di Palma's abduction, and Romano Franzoni's disappearance.

She chews on her lip as she digests the information. "You think Revenant is connected to all of this?"

Her unconscious gesture sends a shaft of heat

straight to my groin. "More than that. I've been thinking about the money. Verratti shouldn't be broke, but he is. How did that happen?"

She sits up. "Revenant stole money from the organization?"

"It's extremely likely, yes."

"But if he has, why hasn't he disappeared? If I was stupid enough to steal from the mafia, I'd take the money and run. I'd cover up my tracks so that nobody could ever find me. Not Verratti's enforcers, not another hacker."

"I don't know. My gut tells me that that's where Franzoni comes in. It's an extremely well-kept secret, but Bianca Di Palma, the missing woman, is Romano Franzoni's mother. If Revenant—what a fucking stupid name—needed muscle, threatening Signora Di Palma is the easiest way to get Romano to fall in line. She's a seventy-five-year-old woman. Small, slight. Bad knee. She wouldn't have been able to put up much of a fight."

"Crap." She sips her whiskey. "Okay, here's what I'm thinking. Your informant Giorgio. How long has he worked for the Verratti organization?"

"All his life. He's one of their best enforcers."

"Okay, he's our way in, then." She straightens her spine, her eyes gleaming as she plots our next move. "Everything is electronic these days. Your pet enforcer will have a device that connects to the Verratti network. A phone, a computer, something. If I can get in, I can get their payroll for you, and we can use it to figure out who Revenant really is. Even better, I siphon off what's left of their money."

"The fastest way to dismantle an organization. Make the paychecks bounce."

"Exactly." Her tiredness has vanished. "Let's do it."

"I'll think about it. Can you get in without being detected?"

Her smile switches off. "Seriously?" she demands. "You're not even going to let me try to do my job?" She slams her glass down on the table. "Because it's not *safe?*" She says safe like it's an expletive. "There's protective, and then there's stifling. Do you know the difference, Dante?"

She looks furious, and I've never wanted to kiss her more. "This time around, it's not your safety I'm concerned about."

She opens her mouth to deliver another insult, then she shuts it. "What?"

"If your intrusion gets detected, your hacker friend will trace it back to Giorgio, who has a six-year-old daughter, Liliana."

"Oh."

"Yup."

"I leaped to conclusions, didn't I?" Her voice is rueful. "Sorry about that."

"You cooked dinner for me. It was delicious. There's nothing to forgive."

She rolls her eyes. "Don't get a swelled head; I cooked dinner for Angelica." A smile plays on her lips. "Thank you for the vegetables, by the way. I expected the worst when I opened your refrigerator, but it overflowed with produce. That was very considerate of you."

"It was nothing."

"Take the compliment, Dante," she advises, repeating my words from earlier. "It's not as if I hand them out that often."

I laugh. "Fair enough." I load the empty plate and our glasses into the dishwasher. "I never finished giving you the house tour. Want to see the rest of the place? While you're here, I thought you could work out of my office if you'd like. That's on the top floor."

"On the same level as your bedroom."

Am I picturing her in my bed? *Yes.*

Do I need a cold shower as soon as possible? *Also, yes.*

For fuck's sake, Colonna. Her daughter—your niece—is fast asleep. Get a grip.

I'd originally envisioned the top floor as a big open space with a bed in the middle and a desk on one side. But after living with the layout for a while, I decided I needed to be able to close the door to my office. So, I took the path of least resistance and simply installed a set of doors.

Long story short: You have to go through my bedroom to get to the office. Which would be fine if it's just me using the space but another thing entirely when Valentina's involved.

I show her around. "This late at night, you can't

see much from the window, but during the day, this room has the best view in the house. You can see the Salute from here. Will this work for you?"

She gives me an odd look. "Dante, this is right next to your *bedroom*. Are you sure you want me here? You do realize I work late into the night, right? I don't want to disturb you."

"It's fine. I'm a pretty sound sleeper. If I wake up, I'll just fall back asleep."

"What about if you have a guest?" Her cheeks go pink, and she avoids my gaze. "That would be beyond awkward."

It takes me a few seconds to figure out what she's talking about. "You think I'm going to bring a woman home while you and Angelica are living here? Give me a little credit, Valentina. I'm not going to do that."

"Umm, okay. As long as you're sure."

"I'm sure." I don't know where she gets the idea that I'm going to bring someone home. I haven't dated anyone seriously in... I can't even remember how long.

"I like your elliptical." She's looking at my bedroom. "It looks a lot nicer than mine."

"Feel free to use it. And the shower, too." I point in its direction. Great. Now I'm thinking of her sweaty and naked and wet. I need to get the hell out of this bedroom. "Want to see the rooftop garden?"

"Absolutely."

It's a clear, crisp night without too many stars in the sky—there's too much ambient light for that—and there's not a cloud in sight, so a full moon bathes us in its silvery glow.

Valentina shivers as she looks around. "I remember this building when you first bought it." A smile touches her lips. "I thought you were mad when you announced you were going to work on it yourself. Leo and I made a bet about how long it would take for the structure to simply fall down."

"Who won?" I take off my coat and wrap it around her shoulders.

She grips it with her fingers and pulls it closer. "Nobody. None of us could have predicted this."

She looks up at me, her eyes luminous. "This is beautiful, Dante."

She's so close. Her jasmine scent drugs my senses in a way the whiskey couldn't. There's a full moon night, and in the distance, a singer croons an old French love song, its lyrics seductive and yearning. *Give your heart and soul to me,* she sings. And I want to.

My head moves forward a fraction of an inch. *Do it,* the voice of temptation whispers. *You know you want to kiss her. You've wanted to kiss her from the moment you met.*

Her eyelashes are so long. I don't think I've ever noticed how lush they are. I trace the line of her jaw with my fingertip, and she shivers and takes a step closer, tilting her head up, her lips soft and full.

My head is spinning; I can't tear myself away from her. I dip my head lower, and my lips settle against hers, soft as a feather, for the merest fraction of a second.

And it feels like coming home.

She sucks in a breath. "Dante," she whispers.

What the fuck am I doing? "It's late," I say

harshly, drawing back. "I'm going to take a shower and go to bed."

"Yeah," she murmurs. The haze clears slowly from her eyes. "That's a good idea. Me too." She takes off my coat and hands it back to me. "Good night, Dante."

I watch her leave, only one thought in my mind.

I'm so fucked.

VALENTINA

CHAPTER FOURTEEN

D ante Colonna, my nemesis, the bane of my existence, was about to kiss me.

And worst of all, I wanted him to. If he hadn't stopped, I would have kissed him back. When his lips grazed mine, oh-so-briefly, a shock of need jolted through me.

Not just need. Standing in that moonlit garden, hugging Dante's woolen coat around my shoulders and my face tilted up toward him, I felt something far more dangerous than need.

It felt like *recognition*.

Like this is where I was *meant to be.*

Like every path and every detour I took in life culminated in *this.*

In him.

It felt like Dante Colonna was what I'd been searching for. He was my *destination.*

The whiskey has clearly gone to your head, Valentina. It's the only explanation. Alcohol-fueled temporary insanity.

The weird, sharp need still swims in my blood, in my veins. Dante said he was going to shower and go to bed. Is he in the shower now, water cascading lovingly down the taut muscles of his body? Or is he toweling himself dry, chasing stray droplets that cling to his skin? If I tiptoed up the stairs and peeked into his bedroom, would I discover that he sleeps naked?

"Enough," I say out aloud, my voice sharp. "Cut it out." It's one thing for me and Dante to have something of an extended truce while I'm at his house and tacitly agree that we don't want to bicker in front of Angelica. After the year she's had, I don't want to do anything to upset her, and if Dante and I are at war, it will only worry my child.

But it's another thing *entirely* for me to have lustful thoughts about Dante. Or worse, *romantic* thoughts. And it's another thing entirely for me to see the photo Leo took of the three of us at Angelica's ballet recital in January on Dante's dresser and let myself imagine us as a family. That road is paved in folly and heartbreak, and I will not subject Angelica to it.

Thankfully, whatever this madness is, it'll end soon. I'm pretty sure the moment I tell Dante I have a date on Saturday, our truce will come to an end.

Monday is a whirlwind. I hit snooze on my alarm three times before jumping out of bed in a panic. Angelica is going to be late to school.

But when I go into her bedroom, she's not there. I follow the sound of her voice to the kitchen, where she's eating breakfast with Dante. "Uncle Dante gave me cereal for breakfast," she announces when she sees me.

"Because you told me that's what your mother would give you." Dante gives her a mock glare. "Right, Angelica?"

"I have cereal for breakfast *sometimes.*"

My lips twitch. "She has cereal for breakfast *rarely,* on the days her mother oversleeps. Otherwise, it's eggs and toast." I can't be too mad. Angelica is awake, dressed, and ready for school, and I'm not the sort that looks a gift horse in the mouth. "Thanks for getting it, Dante."

"It was nothing."

I can barely look at him this morning. Like Angelica, he's already dressed for the day. He's wearing a black shirt, sleeves rolled up to the elbows, and a pair of russet-brown corduroy pants, and annoyingly, he's managing to make the casual outfit look like a million bucks.

I, on the other hand, look like I just crawled out of bed. Which I did. My hair is sticking out in a thousand different directions, my pajamas are faded flannel, my Pikachu T-shirt needs a wash, and I'm pretty sure my lashes have eye crud on them.

Argh.

"I can walk her to school if you want to go back to bed," Dante says pleasantly as if last night never happened. "You look like you could use a few more hours of sleep."

Asshole. And I'm never hitting that snooze button again. *Never*. I give him a saccharine smile. "Thank you for your concern, but I'm fine."

"Okay." He hears the edge in my voice, and the corners of his lips tilt up. It's *eight*. Nobody has any business being sexy this early. He gets to his feet. "If you've got the situation under control, I'll head to work. You want me to pick Angelica up this afternoon?"

"Yes, please." I turn to my daughter, who's pretending to be deeply absorbed in the cereal. "I need to bring my computers here, kiddo. After school, can you hang out at Aunt Lucia's apartment while I do that?"

"Will Uncle Dante be there too?"

Dante responds before I do. "Sure," he says easily. "I'm not doing anything else." He puts his bowl in the dishwasher. "The cleaners are scheduled for Tuesdays and Fridays, and while you're here, I've arranged for Marta to deliver groceries daily. She'll be here around noon." He picks up his phone and texts me her contact information. "So please tell her what you need. And if the cleaning schedule doesn't work for you—"

"It works great." Cleaners twice a week sounds *amazing.*

"Good. Marta and Paulina have been vetted, of course, but I've told them the office is off-limits. I figured you wouldn't want them in your stuff."

"Thank you." He's making it really hard for me to stay mad at him. Which is a problem. Because when I'm not annoyed with Dante, I notice things like the breadth of his shoulders. The way the muscles in his forearms flex as he drinks his espresso. I remember the calluses in his fingers as he stroked my chin last night, remembering the butterflies in my stomach as he moved closer to me. . .

"Mama, I need thirty euros for my dance costume." Angelica's voice tugs me back to reality. "And do you know where my math textbook is?"

"Probably in your school bag. Come on, I'll help you look."

Leo accompanies me to my apartment. "So," he says as I pack my computers. "You and Dante."

I give the security chief a death glare. "There is no me and Dante, Leo. Angelica and I are merely living at his place until the Verratti issue is handled."

"Of course. It's *perfectly* normal to make pasta without garlic." He places a monitor into a moving box. "Did he like it?"

He scraped his plate clean. And then we had an almost kiss in the moonlight. "I have no idea," I lie. "I didn't ask. Can we focus on the packing? Once everything is set up, I need to rebuild my laptop."

"The two of you," Leo says with a shake of his head. "Never seen a pair of more oblivious people." He tapes the box shut. "And what happens when Dante goes on his date on Friday?"

The breath leaves my lungs. Of course Dante's going on a date. The events of the weekend made me forget, but like clockwork, the Broker goes on a date every month. It's usually around the middle of the month, usually on a Friday night. It's always a different woman, but he always takes her to the same restaurant. My nemesis is a creature of routine.

Then why does it feel like someone jabbed a fist into my heart?

Leo's watching me, waiting for me to respond. I make myself speak. "I don't care if he goes out on a date, Leo. Because, and let me say this really clearly so you understand, nothing is going on between Dante and me."

He rolls his eyes, clearly unconvinced. "Whatever you say, Valentina. Whatever you say."

I will swear in a court of law that there wasn't a music player in Dante's home office last night, but there is one by the time Leo and I return with my computers. There's also a standing desk, a replica of the one I have at home, with a vase overflowing with daisies in one corner. My favorite flower.

To my everlasting gratitude, Leo doesn't comment.

It takes me an hour to get everything set up how I like it. After that's done, I get to work scrubbing Revenant's virus from every single infected system. The doorbell rings while I'm in the middle of that mess.

It's noon, which means Marta is here with groceries. I head downstairs to let her in. She gives me a bright smile as I open the door. "Signorina Linari, it's a pleasure to meet you."

"Please, call me Valentina." Dante forgot to tell me Marta is absolutely gorgeous. She's roughly my age, but that's where our similarities end. Marta looks like a young Sophia Loren. "You look like you have your arms full. Can I give you a hand with something?"

"Thank you." She hands me a paper bag. "Signor Colonna asked me to bring you lunch. He said you'd probably forget to eat."

My stomach rumbles loudly in support of her words. Dante strikes again, damn it. "Thank you."

Marta puts away the groceries, shooing my offers to help. She chats with me as I eat, and by the time I've eaten, I learn she's lived in Venice for three years, she never would have found her apartment if it wasn't for Dante's help, and the Katie person Angelica mentioned yesterday is her daughter.

Jealously raises its ugly head as I watch her wipe down the counters. She's an integral part of Dante's life, and I'm the outsider, and I don't know why that matters. And when she offers to bring me lunch every day, so obviously nice and sincere, I feel like even more of a jerk.

I'm in a terrible mood by the time she leaves. After that, rebuilding my laptop takes much longer than expected. Much, much longer. I've just installed the final program when Dante knocks on the door. "Hey, we're back."

I blink up at him. "What time is it?"

"Six-thirty."

"Shit." I scramble to my feet, ignoring my screaming muscles. "I didn't get dinner started."

"I figured you'd be busy, so I brought pizza." I open my mouth to say something, and he grins. "*And* salad, so we could pretend to eat healthy."

"You eat pizza? How? So unfair. If I eat bread,

it goes straight to my hips."

"And what's wrong with that?" His gaze slowly slides down me before he seems to catch himself. "Anyway. Come, eat while it's hot."

My stomach churns all through dinner. Angelica chatters about her day—the fight Anita and Pedro had during recess, Mabel's new iPad, and how Signorina Mason taught them all about insects— but I only half-listen. I need things to get back to normal between Dante and me. He can't tell Marta to get me lunch. He can't get us pizza for dinner. He can't take care of me when I'm sick. He can't take care of me, period.

I need to put an end to this truce. Because if I don't, I'm going to start wanting things I cannot have. I'm going to want Dante Colonna in my life. For real.

I wait until Angelica is in bed, then head to the living room. Dante is reading a book, his feet stretched on the coffee table. "How did the computer reset go?" he asks. "Is it safe to use the Wi-Fi again?"

"Yes," I say shortly.

He quirks an eyebrow at my tone. "Everything okay?"

"What are you doing Saturday night?" I demand, ignoring his concern. Yes, I know I'm being a bitch. "Can you watch Angelica, or should I ask Lucia?"

He frowns. "Why?"

"Because I have a date."

I'm trying to get a rise out of him. But even I am astonished at how well it works. "A date?" he explodes. He gets to his feet and stalks toward me. "Are you fucking with me, Valentina? You want me to take our already stretched resources and assign them to you so that you can go out on a Saturday night? You can't stay away from Peron for even a week?"

I should be thrilled at my success. I'm not. "Not that it's any of your business, but I'm not going out with Enzo." He's close enough that I can feel the heat radiate off his body. I step back to put some distance between us, and my back hits the wall. "I'm having a double date with Rosa and the guy she's seeing."

"No," he says flatly. "It's not a productive use of our resources."

My temper flares. "And there it is," I sneer, my chest heaving. "The Dante I know so well." He's not touching me, but his body is caging me in. I should be terrified. I'm not. "What about your date Friday night? Somehow, that's a productive use of our resources?"

His eyes narrow. "How do you know I have a date?"

"Because I work with you, and you have the most predictable schedule in Venice," I snap. "You go on a date once a month, every month, and take them to Grazie. Never the same woman twice, though. What's the matter, Dante? Can't bother being charming for more than an evening?"

"Are you watching me, Valentina?" His voice lowers. "Paying attention to my movements?" A seductive light fills his eyes. "Why is that, sparrow?"

He's close enough I could kiss that smirk right off his face. Kiss? No. Not kiss. *Never* kiss. What the hell is wrong with me? He's close enough that I could *smack* the smirk off his face.

"Tell me, Valentina." His voice is a hypnotic murmur. "Why do you care who I date?"

I've lost this round. That's fine; this is just one battle in a long war. "Let me go."

He steps back instantly, his eyes still amused. "Running away? You can dish it out, but you can't take it?"

I was willing to let it go. I was the one who walked into the trap, after all.

But then, the bastard does something that pisses me off.

He laughs mockingly after my retreating back.

It's the laugh that pushes me over the edge. So, later that night, I give in to my temper. I open my laptop, hack into Dante's account, and use his credit card to order Viagra on the dark web. I pay extra for a courier to deliver it to Dante at Grazie on Friday at eight p.m.

Ideally, when he's smack dab in the middle of his date.

It's going to be *glorious.*

Now, I just have to figure out how to plant a bug on Dante. Because I really, *really* want to listen to the train wreck.

DANTE

CHAPTER FIFTEEN

Dante:

"She's going out on a date," I explode. I'm still fuming from Valentina's revelation last night. Leo had the misfortune of calling me on my drive to Brescia with a question and, therefore, gets to hear me vent. "On Saturday. She and Rosa are double dating."

"What are you talking about?"

"Valentina is going out on a date on Saturday," I say through clenched teeth. "With some guy called Neil Smith."

"Oh." Leo digests my news. "Can I give you some advice, Dante?" He continues before I can decline. "You and Valentina have been circling each other like two boxers in a ring for *years* now."

"She hates me."

"Better hate than indifference, my friend," Leo shoots back. "But she is not indifferent to you, and you're *certainly* not indifferent to her. If you want to go out with her, then tell her that. Ask her out on a date. Take her to a nice restaurant, preferably someplace that isn't Grazie. Send her flowers, take her dancing. Woo her."

"We don't have that kind of relationship, Leo."

"But you want to. For two years, you've brooded in your office when the second Thursday of the month rolls around. You got lucky with Peron; that relationship didn't go anywhere. What if she hits it off with this guy, this Neil whatever?"

"Smith. Sounds like a fake name, if you ask me."

Leo ignores that. "How long are you going to sit on the sidelines? You want her, then tell her. Fight for her. And while you're at it, don't attempt to control her the way your brother did."

"What the hell is that supposed to mean?" I

nearly ram into the Toyota driving entirely too slowly in front of me in the left lane. Idiot. I lean on my horn to express my displeasure.

"Somebody's in a mood today." Leo's voice is amused. "Don't yell at her, and don't diminish her hacking skills. Roberto hated that she was good at computers, you know? He wanted her to be dependent on him for everything."

I keep forgetting that Leo's known Valentina for even longer than I have. He was one of the few people who tried to stop the abuse but got banished from Venice for his efforts. "I don't yell at her," I say defensively. "And I don't. . ." My voice trails off. I did discount her hacking skills, and she broke into my computer to prove me wrong.

"You yelled at her after the farmhouse," Leo contradicts. "Then you high-handedly forbade her to go on more field missions without your permission."

"Because it was an insane risk," I say, an edge in my voice. The Toyota finally gets out of my way, and I hit the accelerator. "My brother beat her, Leo. I keep her from being reckless. Those are not the same things."

"It wasn't an insane risk," Leo counters calmly. "It was a carefully planned operation. We had that farmhouse under observation for over a week. She had Andreas with her, *plus* I provided remote support. There was nothing reckless about what she did. She needed the files on that computer, so she came up with a plan to get it. She did her *job*. You would have done the same thing."

"It doesn't matter what I would have done. I am a trained killer, while Valentina has never fired a gun in her life."

"She didn't go in there alone."

"If she wanted that computer, she could have sent me in to get it."

"You wouldn't have been able to get past the lock," Leo points out. "She's not your brother's abused girlfriend any longer, Dante. She's a competent, capable member of our team. You're so hung up about what happened in the past that you're fucking up the present."

There's a measure of truth to Leo's words, but he's not entirely right. I don't see the broken girl in a hospital bed when I look at Valentina. I see *her*. She's smart and beautiful, and when she walks into the room, the air crackles with her presence.

And if something were to happen to her, it would *wreck* me.

"You said Valentina is not indifferent to me. Why do you say that?"

Leo laughs out loud, the bastard. "That's all you're going to get from me. If you want to know more, I suggest you talk to Valentina."

Usually, when I need to run a background check on someone, I ask Valentina. But I can't go to her this time—for obvious reasons—so I bite the bullet and Bruno Trevisani.

Trevisani is a sleaze and a dirtbag, and I hate dealing with him. But he's a cop, so he has access to an assortment of databases.

He picks up on the first ring. "Colonna. It's been a while. How are things?"

"Fine," I say tersely. I'm not here to make small talk. "I need a detailed background check on someone. A Neil Smith. I don't have his codice fiscale, but he's a friend of Franco Roberti, who works at Studio Tardino Comi."

"It won't be easy," the cop says. This is his standard answer, the opening salvo in a bargaining session.

"Two thousand euros. I need it by Saturday."

Two thousand for a background check is generous, normally enough to ensure Trevisani's cooperation. But not today. "I can't do that," he says, sounding genuinely regretful. "I think the chief of police is watching me. It'll take me two weeks, minimum."

Damn it. "Do what you can," I grind out. "Call me as soon as you have something."

While we're headquartered in Venice, our territory extends past the island. We control a swath of Northern Italy, including Padua, Verona, and Brescia. Ever since the Russians were spotted in Bergamo, I've been visiting these towns, reminding the people in charge where their allegiances should lie.

Today's meeting in Brescia is with Massimo Rinaldi. Signor Rinaldi is eighty-three and runs his city with an iron fist. He meets me in an osteria around the corner from his house. "Dante," he booms, kissing me on both cheeks. "What brings the Broker to my town? Sit, sit. Luigi, wine. Bring the Barolo, the good bottle." He turns to me. "At my age, you don't save the wine. You drink it."

"You'll outlive us all."

Luigi shows up with the bottle of Barolo and pours it into two glasses. I wait until Massimo takes a sip, then broach the topic at hand. "The Russians approached the padrino. They want to do business in Venice."

"What kind of business?"

"Gun smuggling. The guns would be shipped from Croatia into Venice, then follow an overland route to France. The padrino turned them down."

"Of course," Massimo replies. "The boy is many things, but he's not an idiot."

The boy. I have to work at keeping my expression neutral. I wish Antonio were here. I would pay serious money to see the look on his face.

"I'm here to suggest that if the Russians approach you directly, you decline. They will offer you a lot of money." I take a sip of my wine and hold his gaze. "It would be a shame if you took it."

Massimo is no fool; he hears the threat in my voice. But it slides off his back like water off a duck. "I would not take it," he says. "I don't want more money, Colonna. I'm eighty-three. I like my life. My only granddaughter is getting married in the summer. I want to live to see her children. You don't have to worry about me."

Luigi sets a platter of crostini in front of us. Massimo considers the plate and selects one topped with mortadella. "You won't get any trouble in Verona, Parma, and Piacenza. It's Bergamo you need to keep an eye on."

How does Massimo know the Russians approached Salvatore? That isn't public knowledge; it's a carefully guarded secret. "Salvatore Verratti?"

"No, no. Well, maybe the boy would deal with the Russians, but I was talking about the father, Federico. Federico would murder his own mother if he thought he could make a few euros from it." He shakes his head. "The man's a butcher. The affair with that girl. . ."

"What girl?"

"This was before your time. Thirty years ago, maybe forty? Federico cheated on his wife with their au pair, a student from England. The fool got her pregnant." His face has an expression of distaste. "His father-in-law, Elisabetta's father, was the padrino. Federico knew there'd be trouble if his wife found out."

The story's obviously troubling Massimo. He drains his glass of wine, and I refill it. "There are ways to handle these things. She wasn't planning on making trouble, that girl. She was nineteen, for fuck's sake. She shouldn't have gotten involved with Federico, but at least she was smart enough to flee when she found out she was pregnant."

"And then?" I prompt.

"It wasn't enough for Federico that she wasn't in the country any longer. He couldn't take the risk that Elisabetta would find out, so he sent someone after her. Had her killed in her home, stabbed to death. Butcher."

Ten years ago, Valentina almost lost her baby. The Carabinieri were asking questions about her attack. If I hadn't killed Roberto, would he have gone back to the hospital to finish the job? Would he have murdered her in cold blood? He might have. Or maybe that's what I want to believe to soothe my conscience.

"Was it before or after she gave birth? What happened to the child?"

"I don't know," Massimo replies. "I wouldn't have put it past Federico Verratti to order a pregnant woman murdered, and I wouldn't put it past him to kill a defenseless baby." He shudders. "They told me she was stabbed eight times. It haunted my nightmares for weeks."

This coming from the Butcher of Brescia. I make a mental note to hunt down the details. Something tells me it might be important.

"This was not an isolated event," the older man continues. "This is who Federico Verratti is. As for Salvatore. . ." He shrugs expansively. "The apple can't fall too far from the tree, can it?"

Massimo insists I stick around for dinner. "What's the rush? You have a wife waiting for you at home?"

"You know I'm single."

"Let me guess. You like your freedom." He frowns at me. "Can I give you some advice, Colonna?" Like Leo, he doesn't wait for my answer before continuing. "Find a nice woman and get married to her. You're young and think you have forever, but the years go by quick. Before you know it, you'll be as old as I am now. It's a lonely place to be without family."

Right now, Valentina's probably cooking dinner. A lavender candle will be burning near the stove because that's her favorite scent. Maybe she'll have brewed a pot of tea, and maybe she'll sip from a cup while she chops vegetables. Angelica will be sitting at the kitchen table, doing her homework.

If I join them now, I could eat dinner with the two of them. When we finished our meal, I'd clean because Valentina cooked. Then, after dinner, Angelica would insist I watch a movie with them, something with princesses because that's what she likes. When she's in bed, Valentina and I would sit next to each other on the couch and talk about our respective days.

My heart tightens in painful yearning. But as much as I want it to be, this dream isn't real. I've known Valentina for ten years, and before this threat, she never once stepped foot inside my house. They're only living with me because of the danger. As soon as it's safe, they'll move away.

It's a mirage.

I don't need Massimo's lecture to appreciate the importance of family. I want Valentina so much it's painful. But the sooner things go back to normal, the better. She's only been in my house for two days, and already, I'm starting to crave things I cannot have.

VALENTINA

Chapter Sixteen

On Tuesday, once I've dropped off Angelica at school, I make my second attempt at decrypting the data I took from Verratti's computer. This time, *without* the Internet.

I connect my phone to Dante's excellent audio system, load up my playlist, and get to work. I'm taking twice as many precautions as I did two days ago, but the decryption goes much quicker this time. By the time Dante gets home at eleven at night—he's such a workaholic—I've managed to crack the encryption. I've even made a start on analyzing the data on the computer.

I'm deep in Verratti's financials and focused on what I'm doing, so I don't hear the front door open. It isn't until Dante knocks on the office door that I realize he's back home.

"Sorry. Didn't mean to startle you."

I will my heart to stop racing. "I didn't hear you." I look up at my nemesis. He's leaning against the door frame, looking impossibly sexy. "You look tired."

He gives me a faint smile. "It's been a long day. And you look. . . *energized*. Let me guess—you've decrypted the data."

"Am I that easy to read?" I ask, a little offended.

"I didn't think it'd give you much trouble."

Oh. Warmth fills me at his compliment and, with it, a twinge of guilt about my upcoming attempt to sabotage his date. "Do you want something to eat? I made tom yum soup."

He quirks an eyebrow. "Marta knew where to buy lemongrass? Tell me you didn't leave the house and traipse all over the city for the right herbs."

Just like that, my guilt vanishes. "I didn't," I snap. "Contrary to what you think, Dante, I am not an idiot."

He grimaces. "You're right. I'm sorry. I shouldn't have said that." He massages his temples, the telltale sign of a headache. "Thank you for the offer, but I ate already. I went to see Massimo Rinaldi. He insisted I join him for dinner."

"In Brescia? That's a long trip."

"It is that." He undoes his tie, and I have to tear my gaze away from his fingers. My throat is dry. I'm suddenly very conscious of my outfit: a pair of old yoga pants and a T-shirt that's falling off my shoulders. "But Massimo isn't likely to switch sides on us, so it was a trip worth making. Find anything good in the files?"

"I've only just started looking, but yes. They stored their crypto keys on this computer."

"Help me understand why that's significant."

"If we have their private keys, we can steal their money. There's almost four thousand Bitcoins here." I give him a gleeful smile. "That's a hundred million euros."

I can see the wheels turn in Dante's head. "This

is Verratti's missing money, isn't it? Revenant hid the money from Salvatore in the Verratti server?"

"I suspect that's what he did. Verratti can't access his crypto because Revenant encrypted all the data on his server. But if he suspects Revenant is responsible—"

Dante starts to laugh. "Then the hacker can't get anywhere near the computer in the farmhouse to access the keys. It's too dangerous."

It's so nice to work with someone quick on the uptake. "Exactly. What do you think?" I already know what Dante's going to say. He's going to tell me it's too dangerous to steal this money. Revenant knows my name. We can't risk it. Blah, blah, blah. Days and days of effort, all of it for naught, because Dante Colonna will shoot me down. "If we take it, he'll know it's us."

"He will, yes." He smiles coldly. "He'll also be a hundred million euros poorer, which will hamper his ability to respond. Do it, Valentina. Take the money."

I gape, not sure if I've heard Dante correctly. "Did you just say—"

"You heard me." He removes his cufflinks and

rolls up his sleeves, exposing some of that glorious ink, and *I'm riveted.* "You did a great job, Valentina. Thank you."

Did my fairy godmother just give Dante a personality transplant? What's going on here? What am I missing?

VALENTINA

CHAPTER SEVENTEEN

Should I have canceled the Viagra delivery? *Yes.*

Did I cancel the Viagra delivery? *No.*

Okay, fine. *I admit it.* I want to ruin his evening, okay? The idea of Dante going out on a date turns me into a seething ball of jealousy. Imagining him bringing another woman flowers, holding her hand across a candlelit table, and sharing dessert with her before he kisses her good night makes me want to explode.

I'm a bad person. A bad, *terrible* person.

He said he wouldn't bring his date back here, and I believe him. But what if he goes to her place instead? What if he doesn't get back until two in the morning? What if he doesn't get back at all?

I don't even want to think about it.

After Tuesday's late-night excursion, Dante hasn't had any more long evenings in the office. Every day, without fail, he walks with me to pick up Angelica. He helps with her homework, eats dinner with us, and cleans up afterward. He's still fairly useless in the kitchen, but his knife work is impeccable. No surprise there; he is pretty damn good at stabbing people.

I have no illusions about his sudden desire to spend more time with us. Dante let me steal Revenant's bitcoins, and his presence at my side is more of his protectiveness. The security guards Leo has assigned to me apparently aren't enough; Dante needs to be here personally. It should irritate me, but *it doesn't*. I tell myself I'm tolerating the situation because of Angelica's safety, but it's more than that. I'm in the grips of a seductive illusion where Dante worries about my safety because he cares about *me*. One where he comes home early from work because he wants to spend time with *me.*

And it is just so, *so* tempting.

Then there's his bed. Every time I go into Dante's office, I'm forced to pass through his bedroom. During the day, before Marta comes to tidy up, his sheets are rumpled. It's impossible to resist burrowing my nose in his pillow. I've had to rearrange my working hours so I don't work late into the night because I am not capable of focusing when Dante is asleep in the next room.

And the flowers keep appearing in the office.

Every day, there is a fresh vase of blooms. Not always just daisies. Sometimes, there are roses in the palest shade of pink. Or bright, colorful lilies. But there's always a daisy tucked into the bunch.

I didn't even have to work that hard to plant a listening device on Dante. He leaves his phone lying around the house, and all I had to do was install a listening program on it. And I don't have to crack his passcode. The other night, Angelica was watching a video of lion cubs playing on Dante's phone, and when she needed to unlock it, he just told her what his passcode was. *In my earshot.*

I tell myself it's his own fault he's so damn trusting, but that doesn't do anything to smother my guilt. He trusts me, and in return, I've planted a listening device on his phone. Like I said, *I'm a bad person.*

All in all, I'm a mess by the time Friday evening rolls around.

Much to my daughter's delight, Mabel came over for the evening. They huddled in Dante's living room in a makeshift pillow fort, ate pizza, and watched *Encanto*. By the time Zadie picked Mabel up, Angelica was fighting yawns and didn't even protest when I told her it was time for bed. Now she's fast asleep in her room.

So it's just me, in his office, earphones on, listening to Dante on his date.

Ugh. I *hate* this. The woman Dante is out with is Lara Zambelli. She is twenty-six, has a master's degree in public policy, and works in the mayor's office.

She also has a laugh that drives me insane. Every time she giggles, it's like fingernails on a chalkboard.

Admittedly, I am not an impartial audience.

"You look good enough to eat." I can hear the lust in Lara's voice through the phone. *Down, girl.* She giggles. "Are women supposed to say that?"

You have a master's degree in public policy, Lara. You can do whatever you want. Own your horniness.

Dante sidesteps the question. "That is a lovely dress," he says smoothly. "You look beautiful."

I ball my hands into fists. Is that desire in Dante's voice? Does he find her hot? I don't have any video of this nauseating conversation, just audio, but I snooped on the city website earlier and found a photo of Lara, who has lustrous black hair cascading down her shoulders and white, even teeth displayed in a wide smile. She looked pretty and polished, charming and graceful.

I look down at my gray sweatshirt and my cargo pants. Ugh. The clothes are clean; that's about the nicest thing I can say about my outfit. And polished, I am not.

And why do I care?

Lara and Dante make small talk over drinks. An Aperol Spritz for her and an espresso for him. I learn that they met when Dante was visiting the mayor. Why was Dante in the mayor's office? Not a clue; I'm not privy to his every move. Although, given that his nickname is the Broker, he was probably making a deal of some kind.

"I love this restaurant," Lara says with another giggle. "It's so romantic." She giggles again, and I grit my teeth to keep from screaming. When is that damn Viagra showing up? I almost want to throw down the headphones and go take a shower. Scrub out the thoughts in my head with soap and shampoo. Why am I putting myself through this? Why am I torturing myself?

The waiter arrives and asks them if they're ready to order food. Dante orders a shrimp appetizer, and Lara suggests the two of them share. I roll my eyes. "Get your own damn food," I mutter grouchily. Dante probably has no idea—guys are clueless—but Lara's ploy is all too obvious. Share a plate of appetizers, reach for the same piece of shrimp as Dante, and make sure your fingertips brush against his? Oops, that was a total accident; I didn't plan that *at all*.

Where the hell is that delivery driver, anyway? He should be here by now.

He finally arrives just after the waiter has set down the mains. "Signor Colonna," a man's voice says, interrupting Lara's story about one of her co-workers. "I have a delivery for you."

This is my moment of triumph, but I can't go through with it. I tear off my headphones and throw them down on the desk. I can't hear any more of this. I shouldn't have fucked with Dante's date. It's none of my business what he does in his personal life. And if Lara is the woman he's meant to be with, then so be it. I'm not miserable; the ache in my stomach is probably just indigestion.

I'm so lost in my recriminations that I don't hear Dante come up the stairs. I don't hear him enter his bedroom. It isn't until he enters his office that I realize he's back home.

He stalks into the room, his dark eyes flashing, menace radiating from every line of his body. I rise from my chair on instinct, but it's too late to escape. Dante is between me and the door. There's nowhere to run. Nowhere to hide.

Not that I was planning to run.

I turn and face him, my chin raised. "Didn't like my present?" I taunt. "What's the matter? Did

Lara run away when she found out about your *problem?* She wasn't understanding about your little blue pill?"

"Listening in on my date?" He moves closer, caging me between his body and the window. My ass presses against the cold glass, and I shiver. Dante notices, and his nostrils flare. "You never answered my question, Valentina," he says. "Why do you care?"

"Don't flatter yourself," I shoot back. "I don't."

"Is that so?" He laughs, his voice low. "You planted a bug on me because you don't care? You hacked into my credit card and sent Viagra to a restaurant because you don't care?" He strokes my lower lip with his thumb. Heat flares through my body, a sudden flame that almost makes me moan aloud.

"Such a pretty mouth." His tone is hypnotic. His touch, even more so. "Such a pretty, lying mouth. Try again, Valentina. Why do you care?"

I want him. I want him so damn much. But it's Dante Colonna. My nemesis. Angelica's uncle. Can't let myself forget that.

"You go out on so many first dates," I say

sweetly. My breath feels like it's coming in ragged gasps. "Never see the same woman again. You obviously have a problem." I stare into his darkly inviting eyes. "I'm just trying to help."

"Mmm." He slips his thumb between my lips. I lick it, just a little, and his eyes darken. "So, according to you, the reason I'm not planning on seeing Lara again is because I can't get it up? That's what's keeping me from being in a relationship."

"Exactly." Don't suck his thumb into your mouth. Do not suck his thumb into your mouth. Do not wrap your lips around it and lick it like a popsicle. And whatever you do, *definitely* don't think about doing the same with his cock. "What other reason could there be?"

The pulse in my neck beats like the wings of a caged bird. Dante lowers his mouth to that spot, his tongue a live current of heat and desire. I've kept this feeling contained for almost ten years, but Dante's skillful lips set the genie in the bottle free.

He presses his body against mine. I feel his erection touching my stomach, a hard bar that makes a liar out of my words. "Because she's not you," he says, anger and frustration coating every syllable. "That's why I'm never going to see Lara again. That's why I never see any of those damned women again. Because none of them *are you*."

And then Dante Colonna, my nemesis, the bane of my existence, kisses me.

On Saturday, when Dante showed me his moonlight rooftop garden and grazed his lips across mine, I felt tingles everywhere. But that was only a preview of the real thing.

The real thing is. . . fireworks. Heat. A raw current of desire. He slides his tongue into my mouth, his hand cupping the nape of my neck. My heart thumps erratically. It's been ten years, but that's not the only reason for the shiver that runs through me. Underneath the lust, underneath the drugging desire that fills my blood, is something far more dangerous. It's the feeling like this is where I was always meant to be. It feels like coming home.

Dante kisses me like I'm a cold glass of water on a hot summer day. No, that's not quite it. He kisses me like a man who's been dying of thirst, aching need in every swipe of his tongue, in every nibble of his lips. I kiss him back, a thrill shooting up my spine. "You think I need Viagra?" he growls into my ear. "I only have to look at you, and I'm hard."

There are a thousand reasons this is a bad idea. I can't remember any of them now. All thought has fled my brain, and what's left is pure, potent desire.

Dante nibbles a path down the side of my throat, slow and heated, and this time, I can't hold back my gasp of pleasure. A fire ignites in me, and I press into him, my breasts smashed against his muscled chest, my nipples swollen with need, my fingers bunching in his cashmere sweater.

Then a piercing scream tears through the house.

Angelica.

VALENTINA

CHAPTER EIGHTEEN

Angelica had a nightmare. The two of us burst into her room to find her sitting in her bed, tears streaming down her cheeks. "They were mean to me," she sobs. "They told me I didn't belong. And the teacher laughed at me."

Dante's lips tighten. "You're not in that school any longer," he says. "And if someone's being mean to you, kitten, tell me, and I'll punch them in the nose."

Angelica giggles. "You can't punch people,

Uncle Dante," she says. "Hitting's not allowed." She gives me her most adorable look. "Will you read me a story, Mama?" She pats her bed. "You listen too, Uncle Dante."

This is more of her matchmaking. I'd call her on it, but it's obvious her nightmare really bothered her. We settle on either side of her, and I read her a story. And when she's asleep again, we tiptoe out of her bedroom.

"Valentina." Dante runs his hands through his hair. "We should talk."

His words echo through me, over and over, like a stuck record.

She's not you.

That's why I'm never going to see Lara again. That's why I never see any of those damned women again.

Because none of them are you.

Dante hasn't dated anyone seriously in... I don't even remember how long. Forever.

Because of me?

But that can't be. That's crazy.

My body sizzles with remembered heat, and my mind spins in confusion. Talking is the last thing I want to do right now. Avoidance sounds like a much better strategy. "It's late," I blurt out, avoiding his gaze. "I should get to bed. Good night, Dante."

I dart into my bedroom and shut the door. I hear him on the other side for a long minute before he climbs back to his bedroom.

Sleep is a very long time coming.

Rosa calls me at noon the next day. "Hey, I just wanted to give you a heads-up. Evidently, we're going to a fancy restaurant with a dress code." She sounds mildly exasperated. "Wear a cocktail dress."

Shit. I *totally* forgot about the double date. After the events of last night, can you blame me? "Umm, Rosa. . ." I begin, not sure how to proceed.

"Tell me you're not bailing, Valentina."

Dante isn't even home. He was gone by the time I woke up. Angelica, propped in front of the TV with a bowl of sugary cereal, told me he was going to work. "He said to tell you he'll be back before dinner."

I heave a sigh in response to Rosa's question. "Can I?"

"No," she replies instantly. Then her voice softens. "When we talked last weekend, you seemed really determined to try dating again. Is your change of heart because of Enzo? Valentina, I don't think—"

"What? No." It's because Dante kissed me yesterday. He haunted my dreams all night long. His words still ring in my ears. *Because none of them are you.*

"It's just drinks and dinner. Do you even own a cocktail dress, by the way? Apart from that black dress I made you three years ago."

The black dress that Rosa's so dismissive of is hanging in my closet back home. I didn't pack it; why would I? "Nope."

"I figured. Come over early. You can borrow something of mine."

"Thank you." Rosa is a fashion designer, and her wardrobe is the stuff of dreams. She always looks amazing. I make one last-ditch attempt at getting out of the date. "But we're not the same size."

"We're close enough; worst case, I can alter the dress. I can sew, you know."

"Where are we going for dinner?"

"Vetrano," she replies. "And before you ask why, it's because Neil insisted. According to Franco, he knows the head chef."

Ugh. Vetrano is a two-star Michelin restaurant. I'm sure the food is lovely, but it's also extremely expensive. It's the kind of place you go to for an anniversary dinner, not a blind date.

And judging by Rosa's exasperated tone, she's not exactly thrilled at the choice either.

It's just one evening, Valentina.

"Okay, I'll see you at seven."

I stare at my phone for a long time before I text Dante.

> My date is tonight. Can you watch Angelica, or should I ask Lucia?

He takes almost five minutes to reply.

> I'll watch her.

Did I expect him to say something snide? Did I want him to protest and forbid me from going? Yes, I admit it; I was bracing for an explosion. Instead, I get this terse reply. I probably deserve it.

> I have to be at Rosa's place at seven.

There's no reply.

> Evidently, we're going to Vetrano. I have to dress up. Ugh.

I don't know why I keep texting Dante. I want him to say something to me. Anything. I wish he was here. I wish we could have talked this morning.

If he was here, what would you say?

> Anyway, I'm going to borrow a dress from Rosa.

He finally writes back. It's another terse message.

> I'll be home at 6.45.

I take a deep breath. Evidently, we're both going to pretend last night's kiss didn't happen. That's fine. It doesn't bother me *at all*.

My next difficult conversation is with Angelica. "I'm going to be out tonight," I tell her, trying to keep my tone casual. This stupid date. So much angst and I don't even want to go. "Uncle Dante is going to be here, though."

She doesn't look up from the screen. I can't compete with Saturday morning cartoons. "Where are you going?"

"I have a date."

That attracts her attention. "With who? Can I meet them?"

"No." I wish I had other single mother friends so I could ask them how much they let their children know about their dating life. "It's a first date. I have to get to know them a lot better before I introduce them to you."

My daughter fixes her serious gaze on me. "Uncle Dante is nice."

Sigh. This again. "That's good," I tell her. "I'm glad you like him. Because you'll be spending the evening with him."

Leo walks me to Rosa's apartment. "So, you're going on a date," he says. "This is a terrible idea."

"More people weighing in on my every decision. That's *exactly* what I need in my life, Leo."

"Sarcasm is the lowest form of wit," the big security chief replies.

"Oscar Wilde." I recognize the quote and give Leo a surprised look. "Really?"

"What? As astonishing as it may seem, I read."

I roll my eyes. "Who's being sarcastic now?" Trading insults with Leo takes my mind off the awkward moment when Dante walked into his house. We both stared at each other for a long moment. Neither of us said anything. I chickened out, okay? Rather than talk about last night, I murmured something about not wanting to be late and fled. "I know you read. I just didn't know you read nineteenth-century Irish poets."

We arrive at Rosa's before Leo can respond. He waits while I knock on the door.

Rosa answers the door wearing a tiny jade green slip. "You wouldn't believe what happened. I tore my—" She realizes I'm not alone, and her face turns beet red. "Umm, hi. My zipper broke."

"Yes." Leo's expression is deadpan, but I've known him for a long time. He's *totally* checking Rosa out.

Well, well, well.

"Rosa Tran, meet Leonardo Cesari. Rosa was in school with me and designs clothes. Leo works with me."

"Nice to meet you." Rosa holds out her hand, and the strap slides down her shoulder. "Umm," she says again, grabbing it before her breasts fall out of the skimpy garment. "Sorry about the strip tease. My clothes don't usually fall to pieces on me."

"No apology needed," Leo says, a wicked glint in his eyes. "I enjoyed it." He nods at me. "See you later, Valentina."

Rosa makes wide eyes at me when the door shuts. "That's the Leo you work with? You never told me how hot he is."

"Leo isn't. . ." I reconsider that statement. "If you like the type, I guess. He's too old for you. Besides, you're dating someone. I thought you liked Franco."

"He's okay." She doesn't sound terribly enthusiastic. "Last week, he told me that fashion is frivolous."

I wince. Why on Earth would you tell a fashion designer her work was frivolous? Franco's an idiot. "Why are you still seeing him?"

"That's a question I've asked myself more than once." She tucks a strand of hair behind her ear. "Anyway, let's get your dress sorted, and then I'll deal with my zipper mishap."

Vetrano is only a ten-minute walk from Rosa's place. We've arranged to meet our dates there, so we walk over after we get ready. One of Leo's team is tailing me, I'm sure, but whoever it is stays out of sight.

Normally, I would be freaking out about the

impending date. Instead, my mind replays last night's kiss and today's disastrous aftermath. I check my phone ten times on the way to the restaurant.

Rosa notices. "What's going on with you? Why are you so fidgety?"

"You know me," I say vaguely.

She gives me a sideways look. "I *do* know you. You're not usually glued to your phone."

No, I'm not. Tonight, though, I keep checking to see if Dante's texted me. Of course, he hasn't. "Just checking to see if everything's okay with Angelica."

I shouldn't have mentioned my daughter. "Who's watching her?" Rosa asks. "Lucia?"

"No," I admit reluctantly. "Dante."

I must not be very good at keeping my voice neutral. Rosa stops walking and pivots around to face me. "What's going on?" she demands. "Why do you sound like that?"

"Sound like what? I'm fine." I force a smile on my face. "Oh, look, we're here."

Neil Smith is not great. Okay, that's a little unfair. There's nothing particularly *wrong* with Neil. He's not bad looking. He's average height and has curly black hair and piercing blue eyes. His suit fits him well enough.

He's just a little too much. I don't know how to describe it. When he talks, his voice is a note too loud. When I take off my coat and he sees me in Rosa's pink cocktail dress, his gaze lingers a shade too long. His smile is a bit too broad when he asks me what I do.

But the biggest thing wrong with Neil?

He's not Dante.

"I work as a web developer," I say in response to his question. "Freelance work, mostly. I did Rosa's website." I give Franco a challenging look. "Have you seen it?"

Franco is oblivious to my subtle disapproval. "No," he replies. "Fashion isn't really my thing. With the world in the state it is, I think people should focus on something more important."

Dump him, Rosa.

"Like what?" I ask sweetly, making a superhuman effort to keep the rage out of my voice.

"Well, I donate money to a variety of worthy

causes." Franco sets off on a long and pompous spiel about his charitable donations. If he sees the irony about dining in a restaurant where the average check per person is *three hundred euros*—I googled it—he doesn't register it.

The waiter arrives with menus. Neil immediately reaches for the wine list. "I'll order a bottle for the table," he announces. "Ladies, please don't worry about the prices. Tonight's on me."

Forget giving Neil the benefit of the doubt. That pompous announcement seals it. *I don't like him.*

"Thank you," Rosa murmurs. She holds up her menu to cover her face and mouths, "Sorry" to me.

Neil orders a hideously expensive bottle. I mentally shudder at the waste. I make good money—Antonio Moretti pays me well for my expertise. But I have difficulty spending it. Maybe it's because I grew up poor. Or maybe because money was a big part of why I couldn't leave Roberto—I didn't have enough to flee. We could have moved into a larger place three years ago, and Angelica could have got her puppy, but I'm frozen, afraid to make the move.

Maybe I've been frozen for a very long time. If

so, then Dante's kiss *definitely* woke me from my slumber.

At Neil's urging, we all order the tasting menu. I'm secretly afraid we'll get nine courses of flavored foam, but thankfully, we get actual food, and it's delicious.

The tasting menu is definitely the best part of the evening. When the bill shows up, things get a little unglued.

Neil places a credit card down. The waiter takes it away ceremoniously, only to return a moment later. "I'm sorry, sir," he whispers discreetly. "The card did not work."

"Did not work?" Neil splutters. He glares at me when he says that, as if it's my fault. "There's plenty of room on it."

"I'm sorry, sir," the poor waiter says again. "We tried twice. Perhaps a different card?"

Gritting his teeth, Neil pulls another credit card from his wallet and practically throws it at the man. "Try this one," he snaps.

It doesn't work either.

It's only when the third card doesn't work that I clue in. This can't be an accident. This has to be

Dante sabotaging my evening. This is payback for the Viagra.

But my prank only targeted Dante; it didn't involve Lara. I might not like her, but she's an innocent bystander. Dante, on the other hand, seems to think Neil's fair game.

Not cool, dude. Seriously, not cool.

I pull out my purse and pull out a card. "Here," I say to the waiter. "Use mine."

I'm fuming by the time I get back to Dante's house. "You made my date look like a fool," I hurl out the moment I open the door. Dante is on the couch, his legs stretched out on the coffee table. "Deliberately."

Dante shrugs. "If he can't pay for a bottle of Chateauneuf-du-Pape, he shouldn't order it." He lifts a glass of wine in my direction. I glance at the bottle, and it's the same wine Neil ordered for the table.

Asshole.

"Why did you sabotage my date?"

"How did your new friend handle his credit card issue? With good grace, or did he throw a tantrum? You learn a lot about people from watching how they handle a stressful situation."

He looked like he wanted to punch the waiter. And when we left the restaurant, Neil insisted we go to an ATM, where he withdrew enough money to pay me back. He practically threw the notes at me. As Dante obviously knows. "You were watching my date?"

"I was here with Angelica like I said I would be," he replies. "But yes, I was having you watched."

"What the hell, Dante?" All of a sudden, the adrenaline drains out of me. "It's hard enough as it is. If I want to see Neil again, I'll do it without your interference. Just leave me alone, damn it."

"What about Peron? Are the two of you done?" My words sink in, and he looks up, his eyes narrowed. "What do you mean, it's hard enough as it is?"

I sink onto the couch. "Enzo and I were never a thing," I say wearily. "It was all a pretense. We never actually dated." I lift my chin at him, fighting the urge to cry. "There, are you happy now?"

DANTE

CHAPTER NINETEEN

I go still. "You and Enzo were never a thing. Explain."

"It was a lie, all of it." She sounds drained. Flat. "I'm afraid of intimacy. I haven't had sex in ten years, and I freeze up when I'm on a date. When someone has a drink, I wonder if he's going to get wasted and hit me. I pretended to have a thing with Enzo so people wouldn't worry."

Shock ricochets through me. Ten years. There's been nobody since my brother did a fucking number on her. Rage ignites in my gut. If I could go back and kill him all over again for what he did, I would. Ten years, and she's still afraid. All because of him.

She takes off her coat and tosses it on the couch. "Roberto's dead. Antonio killed him a decade ago. But he left a long shadow." She forces a smile. "I miss the intimacy sometimes, but on the bright side, I have Angelica, and she makes me happy every single day. So what if I can't have sex? That's what vibrators are for."

But Antonio didn't kill Roberto. *I did.* The words are on the tip of my tongue, but I bite them back. Valentina is already upset. Now is not the time to burden her with my secrets.

"For the last two years, when you've been meeting Enzo at Casanova—"

"Have you been watching me, Dante?" She throws the accusation—a repeat of my words from earlier this week—with a flash of her customary spirit. "Why do you care?"

"Answer the question, Valentina."

"Or what?" She glares at me and then relents. "Two years ago, Rosa set me up on a blind date with Enzo. The waiter had barely taken our drink order when I had a panic attack." She doesn't meet my gaze. "I hated myself for it. You were seeing Marissa—"

"What does that have to do with anything?"

Marissa had been the straw that broke the camel's back. She was lovely. Kind. Easy-going. Any man would have been lucky to have her, but when I looked at her, I didn't see the woman in front of me. I saw Valentina, the woman I couldn't have.

"Nothing," Valentina replies, avoiding my gaze. "Everyone around me was living their lives, and I was stuck in the past. I tried telling myself to get over it. I tried therapy, but nothing worked. I felt like a failure. So I hatched this plan to keep everyone off my back, and Enzo kindly went along with it."

I can't decide if I'm grateful to Peron or if I want to punch him in the face.

"You didn't freeze up yesterday when I kissed you." Of all the things to say, why that? "You didn't panic."

She looks up. "You're right; I didn't." A wondering note fills her voice. "Huh. Imagine that." She shrugs it away. "I guess it makes sense."

"Why?"

"Because I know you," she says, throwing up her hands in exasperation. "You're not a stranger that I have to risk trusting when the last time I trusted someone blew up in my face. I've known you for ten years, Dante. I know *exactly* who you are. Annoying and bossy and overprotective—"

She trusts me. My heart starts to beat very fast. For ten years, I've told myself this isn't my life. I've convinced myself I don't get to be with Valentina. Then she went on that date tonight, and I was forced to face the truth. If I don't fight for Valentina, I will lose her. If not to Enzo Peron, then to Neil Smith. If not to Neil Smith, then someone else. I sat in the dark, fighting the urge to drown my sorrows in a glass of whiskey, and I stared into the abyss of a life where I never told Valentina how I felt about her.

Not going to happen.

I feel like I'm walking on ice, and any moment now, it's going to crack, and I'm going to drown in the cold waters below. I'm about to take the biggest risk of my life, *and it's worth it*. "You're doing it wrong."

"Doing what wrong?"

"Sex. You're going on dates with strangers, and it hasn't worked. So, try something else."

"Like what?"

I take off my tie and offer it to her. "It's basic exposure therapy. If you're afraid of something, you expose yourself to it in a safe environment." I hold out my wrists to her. "Tie me up."

Her head jerks up. "What?"

"It's a safe environment. I can't hurt you if I'm tied up."

She rolls her eyes. "Dante, I've seen you fight."

"Your father was a sailor," I counter. "Surely he taught you to tie a knot I can't get out of."

"Not with a tie."

"There's some cotton rope in the kitchen." She raises an eyebrow, and I add, "It's for a clothesline."

"It'll shred your skin."

"Only if I tug free. I won't."

She looks at me for a long time. "Does your bedroom door have a lock on it?"

"Yes."

And then, *shockingly*, she gets to her feet. "Let's continue this conversation there."

Triumph surges through me. She hasn't told me to fuck off. She hasn't laughed in my face. She's actually giving my suggestion serious thought.

Fuck, yes.

I hurry her up the stairs and into my bedroom before she changes her mind. I lock the door behind me, then turn to Valentina and look at her properly for the first time. I noticed her dress when she took off her coat downstairs—I'm not blind—but it didn't seem right to leer.

For the first time in my life, I let myself drink in my fill. The cocktail dress is pink and short and tight, Valentina's breasts spilling out of the plunging neckline. I'm torn between twin urges to rip it off her body and feast on her, and I want to beat Neil Smith bloody in a jealous rage.

I do neither. "This is a very sexy dress, Valentina."

"And you want to stab Neil in the face because he directed most of his remarks to my breasts?"

I did *not* know that. Funny how Leo's report left that part out. "Who, me? I would never."

She laughs out loud and perches on the foot of my bed. "Liar. How does this exposure therapy work? You're going to give me homework?" She flushes pink. "Sex homework?"

She says sex homework and all the blood rushes from my brain straight to my cock. I want to pinch myself. I still can't believe this is happening. I'm waiting for her to change her mind. "Something like that."

She doesn't respond, not immediately. Instead, she examines the rope we retrieved on the way up and gives me an appraising look. "What's my first assignment? I'm going to tie you up, and then what?"

"And then you're in charge."

She gives me an exaggeratedly shocked look. "Hang on. Am I hearing you correctly? Dante Colonna, control freak extraordinaire, is *voluntarily* offering to give up control."

"I do have a suggestion for your first assignment," I continue, ignoring her sarcasm.

"What a surprise." She flashes me a grin. "What is it?"

I join her on the bed. "Tie me up and lose that pretty dress, sparrow. I'm going to lose my mind if I don't taste your sweet little pussy."

She inhales sharply. For a long moment, she doesn't say anything. She stares at her hands in silence, and I wonder if I've pushed too hard, too fast. I'm about to ask her if she's okay when she says, her voice low, "I've never done that before."

"Sat on a man's face?" The man in question is my dead brother, and it should be weird, but I'm far more concerned about Valentina's reaction.

She finally looks at me. "I mean oral. No one's ever gone down on me."

"You're kidding me."

She rolls her eyes. "Yes, Dante. I'm joking. I find my non-existent sex life *hilarious.*"

Okay, I deserve that. "I don't know what to say," I tell her honestly. "It's a fucking travesty." I crook two fingers at her. "Come here, sparrow. I've never known you to be bashful— don't start now. Get naked, then come here and sit on my face."

"Bossy," she chides. "I thought I was tying you up." She rises to her feet and moves closer, turning around and standing between my legs. "Help me

with the zipper? It sticks a little, and I don't want
to tear Rosa's dress."

This is actually happening.

I ease the zipper open, and her dress falls to the
floor. She steps out of it and turns around, and I
swallow hard. She's wearing a cream lace bra, a
pair of lace panties, and nothing else. Her breasts
are round and full, her hips luscious and curvy. I
clench my hands into fists, fighting the urge to pull
her closer. Given what Valentina told me, I'm
awed by her trust. I don't want to do anything to
erode it.

She clears her throat. "It's your turn. Take off
your shirt."

I unbutton it and toss it aside. She surveys me
with hot, hungry eyes. I *like* that look. "Lie down
on the bed."

I do as she asks. My heart is beating so fast I
think I might pass out. I've wanted Valentina for
ten years. I've tried to deny it until I'm blue in the
face. But now she's actually here. In my bedroom,
in her underwear. Looking at me like she's seeing
me for the very first time.

It feels *unreal*.

"And now I tie you up." She straddles me, a blue-haired goddess, and my mouth waters. Her plump breasts are practically falling out of her bra, the dark pink outline of her nipples visible under the lace. "Hold still, please."

She ties my wrists together and loops the rope around the headboard. I flex my muscles, testing the bonds. She knows what she's doing; I'm not getting free any time soon. Then again, why would I? I'm exactly where I want to be.

"And now, your ankles."

When she's done, I'm spreadeagled on the bed, restrained, my heart racing in my chest, my cock so hard it hurts. "Take off your bra and panties, Valentina."

"That sounds suspiciously like an order."

My lips twitch. "It's a request. *Really.*"

"Is it?" She unclasps her bra and tosses it aside, then pulls her panties down her hips. God, her magnificent breasts, her rose-tipped nipples. She's *delectable.* A work of art, a Botticelli painting come to life, all curves and temptation.

"Come here." I can't *wait* to taste her. My cock strains against my trousers. "Kiss me."

She shimmies over to me and straddles me. I kiss her, nibbling on her lower lip, pushing my tongue into her mouth. *Mine.* She hums in pleasure and kisses me back. I lift my hips, trying to grind my hard cock against her pussy, wishing I had my hands free. Her swollen nipples are begging for my fingers, my mouth, my teeth.

I'm panting by the time she pulls away. "You're killing me here, Valentina," I grit out. "At this rate, I'm going to come in my pants, and I haven't done that since I was a teenager watching porn on the Internet. If you don't get that sweet little cunt on my face, I'm not responsible for what happens."

She smiles at me, a bright gleam in her eyes. "Well, we can't have that, can we?" I stare, mesmerized, as she moves into position. She takes her time, her progress excruciatingly slow. My cock feels like it's going to explode, and my balls ache. My little sparrow is teasing me, and I *love* it.

Her hips sway above my face. If my hands were free, I'd pull her down on my face and feast on her. I strain upward, ignoring the ache in my shoulders and my biceps. She hovers above me, leaning on the headboard to support her weight.

The intoxicating scent of her fills my nostrils. "So wet," I say through gritted teeth, greedily licking every sweet drop. "So fucking wet. You like teasing me, don't you, sparrow? You like me tied up?" I strain up and swipe my tongue through her slit. She tastes like a feast, *and I'm starving.*

She moans and grinds into me. I lick up her center and circle her clit with the tip of my tongue, and she jerks above me, her thighs quivering with the strain of staying still. "Dante," she groans. "Please."

"Please, what, sparrow?" I lick and suck and tease her. Each moan from her sends an arrow of need straight to my groin, but I ignore my cock with determination. It's been a very long time, but tonight isn't about me and what I want. Tonight, it's about Valentina. About making her come on my face, her juices smearing on my chin, her scent filling my every breath.

She tangles her fingers in my hair. "Dante," she groans. "Please. . . *fuck.*" That last word comes out as a wail. "I can't. . . I'm going to. . ."

Her thighs grip my face, her clit grinds down, and she comes on my face, long and hard. I keep tonguing her until she finally goes slack and pulls off me.

The whole episode couldn't have lasted ten minutes. But these ten minutes have done what the last ten years haven't. They've changed everything.

I've had a taste of Valentina, and it only confirms what I've always known. She's a drug in my blood, and I'm never going to be able to let her go.

For a long time, she lies next to me, staring up at the ceiling, not saying anything. "Are you going to untie me?" I ask her finally.

"Oh, right." She jumps up. "Sorry."

"You okay?"

"Never better." She sits up, her eyes resting on my straining cock. "Can I. . ."

"Yes."

She laughs softly. "I didn't finish asking the question."

"Whatever you want to do, I'm okay with it."

"And if I want to find out if the great and powerful Dante Colonna is ticklish. . ."

"Evil." My lips twitch. "Just the soles of my feet. But that's not exactly what I had in mind." I stop talking as she unbuckles my belt and unzips my fly, lifting my hips so she can take off my pants. She tugs them down past my hips. . .

Then she goes still.

Shit. The tattoo.

"Dante," she whispers, her voice strained. "There's a tattoo of a sparrow on your hip." Her finger traces the small line drawing.

This isn't the conversation I wanted to have right now. Ah well. Too late for that. "Yes, I know."

"It looks exactly like the tattoo I have on my hip."

"Mmm."

"When did you get it done?"

The day after I killed my brother. But that's another conversation we don't need right now. Not when I can still taste her on my lips.

I take a deep breath. "I was selfish and self-absorbed. I knew Roberto had a girlfriend. He would call to brag about you. The way he talked about you. . . it should have set off alarm bells, but I wasn't paying attention. Then he put you in the hospital. You paid the price for my carelessness. The tattoo acts as a reminder of what my priorities should be."

"When did you get it done, Dante?"

"Ten years ago."

She sucks in a breath. "Dante, I can't. . . First you tell me you aren't going to see Lara again because she's not me." She keeps her face averted as she undoes my bonds. "And now this?"

I make a desperate attempt to lighten the tension. "For what it's worth, after the Viagra delivery, I'm pretty sure Lara doesn't want to see me again, either."

"This is too much," she continues as if I haven't spoken. "I don't know what I was thinking." She undoes my bonds, then grabs her panties and pulls them on with shaking fingers. "This was a mistake. You're Angelica's uncle. We don't even like each other. When this ends in disaster—*and it will end in disaster*—we'll still be bound together by her." She pulls the dress over her shoulders, not bothering to zip up the back. "We shouldn't have done this." She finally looks at me. "If Neil asks me out again, I'm going to say yes."

I watch her get dressed, my heart sinking. She's wrong about me not liking her. My problem isn't that I don't like her. It's that I like her too much.

But her last words hit a nerve.

"No," I snap. "We're not going to do this, you and me. For a change, we're going to stop pretending."

"I don't know what you're talking about."

"Bullshit. Yes, it's overwhelming the way I feel about you. You think I wanted to go on a date every month, knowing that none of those women would be enough? You think I *liked* watching you go to Casanova? That I *enjoyed* seeing you with Peron?"

I stare into her eyes. "You told me you panic before every single date, yet you rode my face and came on my tongue. Because you *trust* me." I crowd her against the window with my body. "Tell me that's worth walking away from."

She stays silent.

"Exactly. Here's what we're going to do, Valentina. We're not going to run away, either of us. Yes, this is complicated. Yes, it could fail. But

I'm not pining in silence anymore; I'm done with that. I want you, and I'm going to fight for you."

"Let me go, Dante."

I take a deep breath and step aside. What the hell else am I going to do? Refuse to let her leave my bedroom? And if I do that, what's next? Beating her because she doesn't want me?

I'm not Roberto.

I get out of her way and watch her walk out the door.

VALENTINA

CHAPTER TWENTY

L ucia and Antonio are now officially in a relationship. My friend tells me this over drinks on Wednesday, her face glowing, and I'm *thrilled* for her.

My childhood was always rocky. My parents got married because my mother was pregnant with me, but they hated each other and ended up resenting me for the way their lives turned out. But Lucia, she was *loved*.

And then, when Lucia was eighteen and away at college, her mother got a terminal cancer diagnosis.

Inexplicably, she hid the news from her daughter. I didn't know either. Had I known, I would have told Lucia. Instead, she kept her secret to the grave. Lucia never got a chance to say goodbye.

Then, the night she died, her father shot himself.

Lucia buried both her parents on the same day, and then she left Venice. I didn't hear from her for over a year. I never thought she'd come back home again, and I didn't believe she'd heal from that wound the way I didn't think I'd ever heal from Roberto's damage.

But I was wrong because here she is, practically incandescent with happiness. And I'm not jealous. Really. Okay, maybe I'm a little. . . not jealous, but wistful. Lucia's joy makes me *want* things I've never let myself desire.

It makes me want *Dante.*

That orgasm. . . Poetry should be written about it. Sonnets.

I was playing with fire, and I knew it. But when he looked at me, smoldering invitation in his eyes, and told me to tie him up, to use him for my pleasure. . . What woman could resist that offer? Not me.

At first, I'd been self-conscious, painfully aware that this wasn't a stranger. This was *Dante, and he mattered*. But then I took off my clothes, and his gaze drank me in, and desire overtook my nerves.

I wasn't sure what to expect. When he licked me, my first thought was—this isn't like my vibrator at all. It was a light, almost teasing touch, so light that it barely registered. But then his tongue flicked over my clit, *and I was lost*.

Dante Colonna is always so controlled. But on Saturday, he ate me out with abandon and relish, growling with pleasure, his chin sticky with my juices, his thick cock straining against his trousers.

I haven't let myself think about it. About him. About the sparrow tattoo on his right hip. If I were to lie on top of him, the two birds would touch. I haven't let myself wonder about its significance, and I haven't allowed myself to replay his pronouncement.

I want you. I'm going to fight for you.

I feel *safe* with Dante. And not because he was tied up. If it was anyone else in the same situation—for example, Neil Smith—I wouldn't have felt the same way. Not even close. No, I felt safe precisely *because* it was Dante.

Ugh.

To keep my mind occupied, I've thrown myself into work. We stole over a hundred million euros from Revenant, and I've been braced for retaliation. So far, the efforts have been rather uninspired. Phishing attacks, mostly. Tomas was sent an invoice from a cleaning company that looked legit. Thankfully, he was on high alert after my demonstration, and he checked the books and realized the cleaning company had already been paid. Had he clicked on the link, the resulting malware would have installed a key logger on every one of our networked computers. I've been working long hours shoring up our defenses against cyber-attacks. Because of that, I've had no time to research Revenant. I'm no closer to finding out who he really is.

I get back home at ten after drinks with Lucia. The house is silent. Angelica is at Mabel's, her second sleepover in as many months. Dante isn't back, either. He sent me a text earlier telling me he'd be late. I make my way to my office and start coding.

I'm making a virus. I haven't forgotten Giorgio Acerbi. So far, Dante's informant hasn't produced the payroll information we need, causing Dante no end of frustration. He still hasn't decided whether we use Acerbi's devices as a way into the Bergamo network, but I want to be ready when he gives me the go-ahead.

I don't need to start coding from scratch; I've made similar viruses. I start modifying the algorithm, my mind wandering as I work. It's been more than a week since I moved into Dante's place. Things have gone a lot better than I thought they would. I feel comfortable here, and I know why. When I open the cupboard, it's stocked with my favorite teas. The desk in this office is identical to the one in my house. There is always a vase of flowers in my room, a daisy tucked in the blooms. It's a thousand little things he does to make me feel at home.

And, of course, Angelica loves it here.

My phone rings, startling me out of my reverie. I glance at the screen, wondering who's calling so late. It's Whitney, Angelica's dance teacher. She's about my age, friendly and bubbly, and passionate about dance. "Valentina," she says, sounding stressed. "I'm so sorry to call you this late at night, but I have a problem. I just got the costumes for next Thursday's recital, but unfortunately, the company has screwed up Angelica's outfit. It's too small for her."

"But the recital is just a week away," I protest. "Is there time to order another costume?"

"That's what I was calling you about. I just got off the phone with the vendor. They have a warehouse in Padua, and they have Angelica's size in stock. Unfortunately, they close on Friday for three weeks for Christmas. I'm so sorry about this, but is there any way you could pick it up tomorrow?"

Padua is friendly territory. And besides, Angelica really needs her costume. "Yes," I reply. "I can do that."

"Oh, thank heavens." Whitney exhales in relief. "Again, I'm so sorry about the mess, Valentina."

I assure her it's not a problem and then hang up. Standing up, I massage the back of my neck. My muscles are killing me. With everything going on, I've been slacking off on working out and taking care of myself, and my body is letting me know it's extremely unhappy with me. I go into Dante's bedroom and do a quick ten-minute stretching routine.

The massive king-size bed is right there. The linens are rumpled, and the pillows are scattered. Marta doesn't come in until tomorrow to clean. A sweater is carelessly tossed on the mattress. I pick it up. It smells like Dante—sandalwood and musk, with a hint of pine. It makes me think of wide-open spaces, lazy summers and hot, passionate sex.

Sex homework. I wonder what Dante's assignments would have been. Going by the first one, I would have enjoyed myself. *A lot.*

Instead, I ran away.

I'm not a safe person. After all, I'm a hacker for the mafia. Being adventurous, taking risks—it's in my blood. But I have Angelica to think about. If Dante and I hook up and things end, I don't think I'll be able to be in the same room as him again.

And it's definitely going to end. This is a guy who owns seven cars. Each one is his favorite until he buys the next. Sure, I have no proof he has the same attitude toward women, but I also have no proof it's not. I can't take the risk; I can't do that to Angelica. My daughter *adores* Dante, and I need to prioritize what's best for her. I can't let my desire drive my decisions.

Dante hasn't pushed. He hasn't tried to kiss me again, hasn't tried to get me into his bedroom. But he watches me, and I'm painfully aware of him. Every time his gaze meets mine, my heart thumps in my chest. A repeat of Saturday night seems inevitable, and the prolonged anticipation is almost unbearable.

That's the moment Dante opens the door. A spark lights in his eyes when he sees me next to his bed, his sweater in my hand, and my nose buried in the cashmere.

"What are you doing, Valentina?"

DANTE

CHAPTER TWENTY-ONE

I f I'm not mistaken, Valentina is clutching my sweater and sniffing it. A shock of primal male satisfaction jolts through me. *She's interested.* She's still deciding if she is going to do anything about it, but she's definitely interested.

I can work with that.

She lifts her chin in the air. "You're very messy," she says rebukingly. "This is a cashmere sweater, and I found it on the floor."

"Really?" I tilt my head to the side. "I thought I left it on the bed."

She flushes pink. "I just got a call from Angelica's dance teacher. There was some kind of mix-up with the costumes for her upcoming dance recital, and Angelica's costume was too small. I have to go to Padua to pick up a new costume tomorrow. I can take the train—"

I'm about to ask her if she's insane but think better of it. "I'll drive you," I say instead. "When do you need to go?"

"They're open until five tomorrow."

"After breakfast, then?"

"That'll work. Thank you, Dante."

"See? Progress. I didn't call you reckless, and you didn't call me an overbearing asshole. You're welcome." I wink at her. I probably shouldn't provoke her, but what can I say? I like to live dangerously. "Can we get back to talking about my sweater?"

She flings it down on the bed, gives me a death glare, and marches out of my bedroom.

I store my cars in Mestre. From the outside, the building looks like a nondescript warehouse near the docks. Inside, it's a shrine to Italian automobile design. I hold my hand to the fingerprint scanner, and the lock opens. The lights flicker on, my cars gleaming under the spotlights.

Valentina rolls her eyes. "Single-handedly keeping the Italian car industry afloat, I see," she remarks wryly.

I laugh. "What else am I going to do with my money? It's this or get Angelica a pony."

"Do not buy my daughter a pony, Dante," she says repressively. "Which car are you going to take today?"

"The '54 Spider." The 1954 Ferrari 500 Mondial Spider Series dates back to the early years of the racing company. This particular car was sold by Enzo Ferrari himself. It's the crown jewel of my collection.

She gives me a strange look. "Your newest acquisition? This is the car you bought at auction last year, isn't it?"

"Yes." It might be new to my collection, but I've wanted this car for a very long time. They only built thirty-two of them, and I couldn't believe my luck when this one came up for sale. Even though it was fire-damaged and needed a lot of work to restore it to its original form, I hadn't hesitated. "I've had my eye on this beauty forever," I say fondly, running my hand over the hood. "Haven't I, sweetheart?"

"Oh, great. You're one of those guys who talks to their cars."

She might sound grouchy, but her eyes keep returning to the Spider. "Would you like to drive her?"

Her head jerks up. "You're going to let me drive your car. The one that cost half a million dollars."

It was closer to a million, but I'm not going to tell her that. "It's just a car." I hand her the keys. "The accelerator is very jumpy. Be gentle with my baby."

"Has anyone ever told you you're crazy?" Valentina shakes her head, but there's a smile playing about her lips. "Okay, let's go."

It's a sunny day, and there's no traffic on the A4. We make the drive to Padua in good time. Valentina is beaming widely by the time we pull up at the warehouse. "That was great," she says enthusiastically. "Although, for the sake of your nerves, I'm going to let you drive on the way back. You looked *green* when I was getting on the highway."

"I did not. I have my restoration shop on speed dial."

She laughs as she opens the door. "There's going to be an explosion of tutus inside this store. You want to wait in the car?"

As if I'm going to let her go in there alone. "No. I'll come with you."

I'm waiting for her to bristle at my overprotectiveness, but she just shrugs. "Don't say I didn't warn you."

Nobody is inside. Valentina rings the bell, and we wait. An old lady eventually shuffles to the front. "Some threat," Valentina whispers under her breath before smiling brightly at her. "Buongiorno, Signora. I'm here to pick up a ballet costume for my daughter. I called this morning?"

She blinks in confusion and consults the notebook in front of her. "Angelica Linari, yes?"

"That's her."

"One minute."

It's a lot closer to five by the time the woman returns with Angelica's hot pink tutu. "How old is your daughter?"

"Nine."

She peers at us. "But you're so young," she exclaims. "The two of you married early, and you're still together?" Valentina opens her mouth to explain that, no, we aren't married, but she doesn't get a chance. The woman continues, "That doesn't happen too much in this day and age, does it? A shame. My husband and I, we've been married for sixty-eight years. A good, long time." She beams at us. "I wish the same for you."

"Thank you," I say politely. "Come on, *wife*." Calling her wife feels surprisingly satisfying. "We should get back."

We get in the car, and I start the drive back to Venice. Valentina doesn't say anything. I'm wondering if she's thinking about the old woman's words. Does she want to get married? Roberto would have married her—he was old-fashioned that way—but it would have been a prison sentence, not a relationship, and she would have been his possession, not his partner. Valentina knows that as well as I do. But she seems lost in thought. Would she like to try being in a relationship again with someone who isn't an abusive asshole?

Someone like me?

She glances at me from the corner of her eye. "So, the sex homework you mentioned," she says. Her cheeks are flushed, but she plows ahead determinedly. "What would my next assignment be?"

Okay, she wasn't thinking about a relationship at all. "I haven't had time to devise a curriculum." I think frantically. "Do you watch porn?"

"Do you?"

"Umm, is this a trick question? Am I going to get into trouble if I say yes?"

She rolls her eyes. "No, of course not. Just answer the question, Dante."

"Yes. I watch porn from time to time. Do you?"

"Sometimes," she admits. "My bedroom door at home doesn't have a lock, though, and I'm always nervous about Angelica barging in, so I tend to read more than watch."

"My door locks. And Angelica goes to bed at eight." I hold her gaze in mine. "That's your next assignment. Tonight, once Angelica is asleep, come on up. Bring your laptop and a clip that turns you on, and we'll role-play it."

I'm bracing for her to turn me down, so it's almost a shock when she smiles. "It's a date."

There are a thousand things to worry about. We were able to steal a significant sum of money from Revenant, and Valentina was able to decrypt every file we took from Bergamo, but it doesn't have the payroll information we need to track down the hacker. Then there's Giorgio. My informant should have checked in with me today but didn't. Either he's gone underground, or something bad has happened to him.

But right now, none of that can bring me down. Because I've waited for Valentina for ten years, and she finally said yes.

VALENTINA

CHAPTER TWENTY-TWO

I'm a distracted mess for the rest of the day. A distracted, *horny* mess. It's a good thing the virus I'm building doesn't require a lot of attention because my mind refuses to stay on task.

Dante offers to pick Angelica up at school. "We'll pick up pizza on the way," he says. "That way, you don't have to make dinner."

"Thank you."

True to his word, when the two of them get back home in the afternoon, Dante's holding three large pizza boxes. "How much pizza are the two of you planning on eating?"

Angelica giggles. "We couldn't decide what kind to get, so we got everything. Uncle Dante said you like to snack in the middle of the night."

Uncle Dante is too observant for his own good. It's a little scary. He puts together a quick caprese salad while I plate the pizza and help Angelica with her homework.

"The virus is almost done," I tell him in a low voice when she's bent over her notebook. "Have you decided if I'm going to deploy it?"

"Not yet." A troubled expression flashes over his face as he halves the bocconcini. "I'm worried about Giorgio. I can't reach him, and he's not the disappearing sort."

I look up, concerned. "Romano Franzoni and Bianca Di Palma are also still missing. You think Revenant took Giorgio, too?" A sudden thought strikes me. "Retaliation for the money we stole from him?"

"I hope not. There shouldn't be anything to connect Acerbi to us."

"But it's a possibility." I feel sick. Dante said Acerbi had a young daughter. If something's happened to him because of the money I stole. . . "I shouldn't have—"

"Hey, hey." Dante shakes his head. "None of that. I told you to do it. I bear the responsibility, not you." He glances at my daughter and then at me. His message is clear: Not in front of Angelica. "Salad's ready. Let's eat some of this pizza before it gets cold."

After dinner, Angelica declares that she wants to watch *Encanto*. "Again?" I ask her. "Didn't you just watch it with Mabel?"

"Uncle Dante's never seen it, Mama," she replies. "We're going to watch it together."

"But does Uncle Dante *want* to watch it?" I give the Broker a skeptical look. This is the man who stabbed three people in a farmhouse less than two weeks ago. I cannot imagine him enjoying a Disney movie.

"Of course," he replies with a wink. "Angelica said it's her favorite movie. I'll make popcorn, kitten. Valentina, want to join us?"

If I see the two of them together, their dark heads bent over a bowl of popcorn, my ovaries might explode. "No, I have to work." And then I flee.

Time is weird. During the day, it felt like the hours were crawling by, but then everything speeds up. But before I know it, Angelica is in bed, fast asleep, and it's time for Sex Lesson 2.

Pretty lingerie is an indulgence, considering the generally sorry state of my love life, but I'm grateful for my weakness tonight. I dress in the pale pink chemise Dante couldn't take his eyes off when I was packing, put a matching pink robe on over it, grab my laptop, head up to Dante's bedroom, and knock on his door.

"Come in," he says, his voice deep.

I open the door, my heart beating very fast. "Hey." I wet my lips. "I'm here."

Dante's sitting on his bed, computer in his lap. He's shirtless, his taut abs on glorious display. A sheet covers his lower half, so I can't see if he's naked under it. Next to him, the cotton rope we used on Saturday is coiled into a neat bundle.

He sees me, and heat flares in his eyes. He looks

like he's imagining what's underneath the robe. He doesn't have to try too hard; I'm going to get rid of it soon enough. As soon as I can stop my heart from racing.

"You look like I'm going to eat you," he observes. He winks at me, a comical leer on his face, and pats the mattress next to him. "Come into my parlor said the spider to the fly. . ."

His leer makes me laugh. "You're being ridiculous." And I'm grateful because it's dampened some of the tension I'm feeling. Some, but not all. My stomach is still doing cartwheels, and my pulse is a jackhammer. I enter the room, shutting the door behind me. "Lock it," Dante reminds me. "Just in case."

"Right." I turn the key in the door's lock and walk up to him. "You have your laptop out. Already looking at porn?"

"Just work." He shuts the computer and sets it on the floor. A wry smile crosses his face. "I don't need to look at porn when you're here, Valentina. My imagination is already working overtime."

A thrill goes through me. "Are you imagining me naked?"

"Naked," he says. "Clothed. Half-dressed. I imagine you in the shower, water cascading down your body. In bed, your hair damp, your skin smelling like the jasmine lotion you love, your vibrator tucked between your legs." His cock hardens noticeably. "I imagine you masturbating while I watch, then handing me a remote control and putting me in charge of your orgasms. . ." His lips twist. "When it comes to you, my brain is very creative."

Oh God. I'm flushed, hot, and turned on, and he hasn't even touched me yet. I set my laptop on the bed and take off the robe. His sharp intake of breath sets me ablaze. "Whatever my imagination offers," he says, his appreciative gaze roaming my body, "the reality is a million times better."

"You're flattering me." I sit down next to him, leaning against the headboard I tied him to just a few days ago. "What's the rope for?"

"If you want to tie me up—"

"I don't." I want him to touch me today. Everywhere. I want to feel his hands roam over me, pinch my nipples, squeeze my breasts. I want them to trail down my body and dip into the cleft between my legs.

"Are you sure? I want you to feel safe."

"I do feel safe," I insist. I scoot closer so our shoulders down to our thighs touch. "If I didn't, I wouldn't be here." I open up my laptop. "I did my homework assignment. I found a clip that turned me on. Do you want to watch it with me?"

"Do you even have to ask?"

I press Play.

On my screen, a dark-haired man walks into what seems to be a very expensive hotel suite. His suit fits him perfectly; he looks rich and powerful. The concierge accompanies him. "We've arranged for your every need, sir," he says as he opens the door.

The large living room windows show a city skyline outside. Either New York or Toronto, I can't tell which one, but in either case, this is a high-budget shoot. The room is decorated in shades of cream and gold, with tall flower vases on every table surface. The concierge shows the man the room service menu and offers to make him a reservation at any restaurant in the city. Then he stops in front of a closed door. "And through here is the bedroom."

It's another beautiful room, but the camera doesn't linger on the furnishings. No, it zooms directly to the king-size bed. A woman is kneeling in the middle, wearing a pair of black lace panties and nothing else. Her hair cascades down her shoulders in lustrous waves. "The special item you ordered," the concierge says. "I hope she is satisfactory."

I sneak a glance at Dante. "She's hot, right?"

Dante shrugs. "She's pretty enough, in a pornstar kind of way." He tucks a strand of my hair behind my ear. "But she's not you."

"You're flattering me again."

The man circles the bed. His eyes take in the woman, lingering on her mouth and full, pouty lips. Her pert nipples stand to attention, ready to be enjoyed. He flicks one with his thumb, an inscrutable smile on his face, and she bites her lip to stifle her moan. "I believe she'll do," he says to the concierge. He slips the man a hundred-dollar bill. "Leave us alone."

Dante's fingers trail over the neckline of my chemise. A light touch, barely there, and then he waits. I suck in a breath and nod. "Yes," I whisper. "Please. More."

He runs his fingers over me again, just inside the lace, raising goosebumps on my skin. His touch is leisurely, maddeningly so. Meditative. I shiver. My skin feels too sensitive to touch, but wild horses couldn't pull me away. I can't get enough.

"Eyes on the screen," Dante reminds me.

"I've seen it before. You're the one who hasn't."

He pinches my nipple in reply through the silk, and a moan tears out of my mouth. "Watch it again," he says, his tongue tracing the edge of my earlobe. His hand slides up my thigh in a slow, teasing motion.

On the screen, the man takes off his jacket and tosses it on the plush armchair. He stalks closer to the woman and puts a thumb against her mouth. "Open," he orders. The woman obediently opens her mouth, and he rests his thumb on her tongue, his gaze assessing.

Dante's fingers trace light circles on my thighs, nudging the hem of my chemise higher. "What turns you on about this scene?"

I flush. It's one thing to be half-naked in front of Dante. But telling him my fantasies involves a level of trust that—

But you do trust him.

"She's a gift for him to use," I mumble, my cheeks flaming. "She's there to please him. It's not a scenario I'm going to endorse in real life, obviously, but since it's a fantasy, it's hot."

"Are you my gift for the evening, Valentina?" He pushes the strap of the chemise down my shoulder. The fabric falls away, exposing my breast to his hot gaze. "Very nice," he murmurs, his voice a low, husky rumble. He glides his thumb over my nub and watches it swell. "Very nice indeed."

We're barely paying attention to the porn on the screen. The man walks to a sideboard and pours himself a drink. He takes a sip, fishes the ice cube out of his cut-glass tumbler, and runs it over her nipple.

I suck in a breath.

Dante smiles at me, feral, hot, and hungry. "I think that's a yes." He gets up, and unfortunately, he's not naked under the sheet. He's wearing a pair of pajamas, the flannel faded, the waistband hanging low on his hips, the trail of—

"You're staring, Valentina." He grins a satisfied

male smile. "And I'm flattered. Stay right here. I'll be right back."

He returns in record time with a glass of whiskey. "None for me?" I quip.

He shakes his head. "You haven't earned it, sparrow."

Fuck, yes. It's like he looked inside my mind and dragged my naughtiest fantasy out of there. "How can I earn it?" I ask, looking up at him through my eyelashes. "Can I earn it on my knees?"

I only caught a glimpse of Dante's cock on Saturday before the tattoo freaked me out, and I ran away. Have I been thinking of it ever since? *Of course, I have.* Eight inches of thick, rock-hard male flesh, and all of it for me. I can't wait. The most frustrating part about the last ten years is that I loved sex. To take the thing I love and make it the subject of fear. . . But I'm here now, and I'm not afraid. I'm very, *very* turned on.

"Not yet," he denies me calmly. He stands at the foot of the bed and examines me. "Get on your feet."

His voice is sterner now, and the sternness sends a wave of arousal shooting through me, like an arrow to my pussy. I fight the urge to squirm. "Do you like me with my glasses or without?"

I'm talking about how he wants me in this fantasy of ours. But Dante misunderstands, either deliberately or by accident. He laughs softly. "With or without, sparrow, it doesn't matter. I like you." Before I can react, he gives me his next order. "Stand by the window, facing out."

I'm *starved* for him. Saturday did nothing to take the edge off my appetite.

I take my glasses off and stand where he wants me to. The outside world softens to a blur, the lights across the lagoon shimmering into a kaleidoscope. The only thing that remains in focus is *Dante*.

He moves behind me. I can see his reflection in the mirror, looming over me like a dark shadow. He kisses the curve of my neck. "I'm going to unwrap my gift now."

I hesitate. There's not much risk of being seen. We're looking out over the water, and Dante's bedroom is dimly lit. Someone has to be right outside the window to see me. But paranoia is part of my job description.

His hand is on my lingerie strap. "Valentina," he says. His voice jerks me from my indecision. Dante wouldn't do anything to put me in danger, quite to the contrary. He's infuriatingly overprotective. I have nothing to be concerned about.

I take a deep breath and let reality bleed away again. I'm Dante's gift, here to do whatever he wants me to. And if he wants me to get naked, then that's what I'm going to do.

"Yes." I slip the straps down my shoulders, and the chemise falls to my waist. Dante slides it down past my hips, and it falls to the floor, pooling in a fluid puddle. "Step out of it."

I move free, and Dante picks my lingerie up. "Like liquid silk," he says. He drinks me in, his gaze openly possessive. "Keep your hands on the window. Spread your legs wide."

The Broker is good at giving orders.

I comply. Dante puts a hand around my waist and tugs me back until my ass is pressed against his cock. "Wider," he demands. I obey, and he nods in approval. "Good girl. Hold that position for me."

He moves away. A flush creeps up my cheeks as

I look at my reflection. Naked except for the tiniest scrap of lace covering my pussy, my breasts are in full view of the window, my ass is lewdly thrust toward him, and my legs are spread wide. I look ready to be mounted from behind.

Dante returns. "You've been a good girl," he says. His glass is at my lips. "One sip."

I drink, and the heat of the whiskey slides all the way down my throat. Perversely, it makes me shiver. "Cold?" Dante asks. "You're about to get colder, sparrow."

I expect the ice. I brace for it. But Dante doesn't slide it over me, not right away. First, he runs his hands all over my body. He pushes his finger into my mouth like the man did in the clip we watched. He cups my breasts and plucks my nipples, grips my hips and squeezes my ass. Every inch of me is carefully assessed. Inspected as if I were on sale, and Dante wants to make sure he gets his money's worth.

It sets me on fire.

"Beautiful," he says, stroking the insides of my thighs. "Do you know how hard it was to be tied up when my fingers itched to glide all over you? To touch you, to feel the pulse beat beneath your skin?" He licks that throbbing spot in my neck. "And then you ran away." Imitating what we watched, he fishes the ice cube out of his glass and glides it in a circle over my nipple.

I gasp. I can't help it. The ice is so cold it hurts, but the sharp pain immediately dissolves into pleasure. "One taste of that sweet, sweet pussy, and I'm an addict." He wraps his arm around my chest to hold me in place and trails the ice cube over my nipples. When the cold becomes almost too much to bear, he replaces the ice with his fingers, pinching my nipples to warm them up.

Then, he repeats the cycle all over again.

Ice and fire until the two sensations merge into one.

I throw my head back against him and moan, the twin stimuli overpowering. I start to move my hands from the window—I need to touch him—but he shakes his head in disapproval. "Did I give you permission to move?"

Why is this so hot? Why am I so turned on when he snaps orders at me? I don't know, and I don't care. Not when my need is molten hot lava threatening to burn me alive.

Dante kisses my shoulder even as he trails the ice down my spine. I know where it's going, and a shiver of arousal runs through me. I want to tell him to stop, and I want him to keep going. A tsunami of sensation swirls through my body. It's all too much, but I never want it to end.

"Did he touch her clit with the ice?" Dante asks. "In the video you like so much?"

"Yes."

He kneels between my legs. "Don't move," he orders with an evil smile. "If you move, I stop." He pulls my panties aside, too impatient to pull them down my hips, and rubs the ice between my folds. The sharp cold shocks me, but then his mouth is on me, wet and warm, and I can't stop the whimper that escapes from my lips.

On Saturday, it was just his tongue. Today, it's his tongue and his fingers, and that's even better. He tongues my clit until I'm almost about to come, then shoves two fingers inside me.

It's the first time in ten years that someone has touched me so intimately. The first time in ten years that the object inside me isn't a plastic dildo.

I've forgotten what a difference a man's touch makes. Dante twists his fingers around, stretching me, a pleasure so sharp it's almost painful. The ice cube drips water, mingling with my juices, and Dante licks it all up.

My body spirals tight. I keep my hands on the window as ordered, but I can't stop my hips from rocking. Dante's not the only addict in the room— I need this, *I need him.* My muscles clench, and my clit aches, and before I know it, I'm coming with a shout, my pussy gripping his fingers, shuddering out my climax on his tongue.

"Now," Dante says. "Now you can earn the whiskey with your mouth." He grabs a pillow from the bed and tosses it on the floor. "On your knees, sparrow."

Finally.

I get down on my knees. Dante frees his cock. It's beautiful, thick, and long, with a drop of precum beading on the head. I lick my lips in anticipation, and he groans. "Valentina," he growls. "If you keep doing that, I'm going to come the instant your pretty lips are wrapped around my cock." He sounds ragged, his usual calm control nowhere to be seen. A hot thrill fills me. I made the Broker lose his composure.

I wrap my fingers around his erection and lick the length of him, lightly, delicately, as if he's a feast to be savored, not rushed. He groans in pleasure. "Fuck, yes."

His eyes turn smoky, and his fingers tangle in my hair. He's not tugging me forward or making me gag on his cock, but he's reminding me he could. Another shudder of arousal runs through me. I flick my tongue around his tip, then take him in my mouth, looking up at him through my lashes. He's leaning back against the wall, looking at me on my knees, and his expression is hot, possessive, and male.

I slide my hands up his thighs, open my mouth wide, and take him deeper. He thrusts, and his cock hits the back of my throat, and I should be afraid, but I'm not. My heart races, and my pulse pounds, but this is desire, not fear. I hollow my cheeks to increase the suction and bob my head up and down his cock.

His breathing is shallow and uneven, his face etched with arousal. I'm so turned on that I snake my hand down my body to find my clit.

Dante notices. "No," he says, his voice threaded with displeasure. "Tonight, it's my fingers that make you come. My mouth, my cock. Do you understand, Valentina?"

I almost come right there. I redouble my efforts on his cock. His fingers clench in my hair, encouraging me to take him deeper. He's thrusting forward now as if he can't help himself, each stroke hitting the back of my throat and making me gag. My eyes leak tears, but my nipples harden into bullets, and my pussy demands more. He's unraveling; I can feel it in the tension of his muscles and hear it in the unevenness of his breathing, and that just makes me hotter, makes me take him deeper until he's in my throat, my nose buried against the base of his cock, and then he erupts in my mouth with a growl of hot satisfaction.

We make it to the bed. I don't get there on my own, though; my legs seem to have lost the ability to walk. Dante sweeps me into his arms and deposits me on his bed before joining me there. His hand slides up my ankle, caressing my calf, stroking my knee. He glances at me. "More?"

"Don't stop." I haven't had my fill, not even close. Sucking Dante's cock has ratcheted up my arousal. I need his cock in me. *Now.*

He skims his fingers over my mound before dipping them into my aching, swollen heat. I gasp in response. "I can't get enough of you," he says, promising me all the pleasure I want. "I've waited so long for you, and here you are, a drug in my blood, a thirst that can't be quenched." He rolls a condom on and then notches his cock at my entrance. "Yes?"

I'm wound so tight that if he doesn't fuck me now, I'm going to burst into tears. "Please," I beg, though I don't need to. This isn't roleplay anymore. This is real. Shields down, walls shattered, just the raw aching connection that's always existed between us. "Dante, please."

He thrusts into me in one long stroke. I bite my hand to muffle my scream and lift my hips to meet him. It's been so long since I had sex that it feels like the first time again, and this time, it's with Dante. All my fears about intimacy, all the pain and the trauma that have kept me from seeking this for ten years, tear away as Dante pushes inside me, and I'm impaled on his hard length. "You're going to scream my name over and over tonight," he growls, squeezing my breasts and pinching my nipples. "I'm going to make this so good for you, Valentina."

"It's so good," I sob. I'm unraveling. Hearing my name on his lips sends a surge of possessive pleasure through me. *Mine.* He holds me open and slams into me, deep and hard and perfect. The two tattooed sparrows collide, and my toes curl. Each thrust stretches me in a way that's almost painful. This is better than any of my fantasies. His breathing is harsh, and his eyes are glazed with pleasure. His fingers find my clit, and he rubs that swollen button until I'm gasping, shuddering, dancing again at the edge of an orgasm.

"Come with me," he rasps. "I want to feel you come all over my cock."

Yes, yes, yes, oh god, yes. I wrap my legs around his hips, urging him deeper into me. He groans out loud. Each thrust claims me. Marks me as his. He's close; his muscles are taut with the strain of holding back. My body shudders uncontrollably underneath his as he coaxes another orgasm from my clit. Then, as my muscles clamp around his cock, his control shatters, and he explodes inside me with a hoarse groan.

"Fuck, Valentina," he breathes, slumping next to me. I don't even have a moment to feel awkward before he pulls me into his arms and kisses the crook of my neck. "That was—" He shakes his head. "I don't have words." The hunger in his eyes is satiated for the moment, and what's left is a tenderness that makes my heart turn over. His fingers stroke me gently. "Are you okay?"

"Better than okay." I push his hand firmly away from my pussy and sit up. "I should probably go. I don't want Angelica to wander into my bedroom and find I'm not there."

He kisses me again. "Stay a little," he murmurs into my mouth. "Just for a little while."

The bed's soft and warm, and the room is cold, and if I stay here, I can snuggle against Dante's warm body and cuddle. "Okay," I agree. "Just until

I recover. You wore me out."

"Did I?" He sounds smugly satisfied. "Then you should rest and recover. Because I haven't had my fill of you, sparrow. Not at all."

DANTE

CHAPTER TWENTY-THREE

It's a clear, moonlit night when I pull up at the farmhouse and turn off my engine. It's quiet—almost eerily so. The building appears deserted. No cars parked in the driveway, no sign of the caretaker who lives here.

There's no cause for alarm, but I have a premonition that something's about to go very, very wrong.

A gunshot rings out.

Backup is on the way—a few of Leo's guys coming in to provide support. But I can't wait. I slam my shoulder against the front door, and it gives. I raise my gun and step in, my heart pounding like a drum against my chest.

The room is awash with blood. Crimson streaks are splattered on the walls, a macabre imitation of a Jackson Pollock painting. The sharp copper tang fills my nostrils, the smell of decay lingering underneath. The smell claws at the back of my throat, and my stomach heaves. It's a close thing, but I regain control with an iron will and advance into the room.

Then I see the lifeless body on the cold stone floor. It's a man. His arm is thrown out, as if begging for help against an unknown assailant. I approach the corpse and turn it over.

It's my brother, Roberto. His eyes are open. Accusing. *You killed me,* they seem to say. You murdered me in cold blood, and then you stole my woman. My child. *You're living the life I was meant to have.*

"You didn't deserve it," I say aloud. I make myself stand up. I back up the way I came and step out of the desolate farmhouse. . .

Only to find myself in another dark room. Here,

the air itself carries a weight, thick and oppressive. With each passing moment, it seems to close in around me, a suffocating embrace that threatens to swallow me whole. Fighting the urge to flee, I let my eyes adjust to the dimness.

Two bodies are sprawled on the floor. The larger corpse cradles the smaller one, a futile attempt to protect her from the oncoming storm.

I don't want to look.

I don't want to know.

Keeping my face averted, I turn the bodies and immediately recoil.

Mother of God, it's Giorgio and his six-year-old daughter, Liliana.

I turn away and lose the contents of my stomach on the floor. Someone has slit their throats, the killer tossing the blade carelessly to the side. Averting my gaze from the child's dead eyes, I pick it up. . .

My throat goes dry.

It's my knife. *I'm the killer.*

I don't have time to feel guilt or be violently ill. I don't have time to weep in regret. Just as I pick the knife up, a scream punctures the quiet.

Angelica.

I race in the direction of her voice. I smash through a door and enter another blood-splattered room. Giorgio is there, alive this time, even though I just saw his dead body. He's holding a knife—my knife—to Angelica's throat.

"You killed my daughter, Colonna," he says to me, low and vicious. "You didn't slit her throat, but you killed her anyway the moment you set me on this path." He presses the blade into Angelica's skin, and she whimpers in fear. "You knew that, didn't you, Colonna? But you did it anyway."

"She's just a child," I whisper, desperation coating every syllable. "Please. . ."

"A child?" Giorgio snarls. "Like Liliana was?"

"Please let her go," I beg him. Angelica looks terrified, and I can't bear it. "Take me instead."

Then, because this situation could not get any worse, Valentina appears next to me. Her eyes are red, her face streaked with tears. "Dante," she begs, clawing my sleeve. "Please. *Do something.* Save my daughter."

I search for a weapon. Anything. But my gun is missing, and the knife in my hand is gone. Giorgio's holding it. He lifts it up to me in a mocking salute, then brings it to Angelica's throat. . .

"Dante." Valentina shakes my shoulder. "Dante, wake up. Dante."

Everyone I love is dead. Valentina. Angelica. I fall to the floor, curl into a ball and scream. It's just me in the room, along with the corpses of the people I care about the most in the world. I couldn't protect them. I couldn't keep them from harm. I start to shake and shake and shake. I couldn't—

"Dante. You're having a bad dream. Wake up."

I force my eyes open and sit up. "Valentina?" I reach out and grab her hand. My fingers shake, my heart not ready to face my worst fear, but she's warm. She's flesh and blood and here. She's alive.

I'm drenched with sweat. I brush my hands through my hair. The nightmare was so fucking vivid. I can still smell the heavy copper tang of blood in my nostrils and the acid taste of bile on my tongue.

"What happened?"

"Bad dream." I take a deep breath and wipe my palms on my sheet. My heart is still racing. I focus on Valentina. "You're dressed."

"I wanted to get back to my bedroom." She sits next to me and gives me a slight smile. "Just in case Angelica wakes up." She rests her head on my shoulder. "Want to talk about it?"

I only have to close my eyes to see her body on the icy floor. "I was in the farmhouse in Bergamo," I say quietly. I don't want to let her hand go. "I found Giorgio's body there. He was dead, as was his daughter." I stare at our interlaced fingers. "Her throat had been slit. With my knife."

She sucks in a breath, and her grip tightens. "Dante. . ." Her voice is soft. "I'm so sorry."

"Then Angelica screamed." I don't know why I'm telling her this. I shouldn't. I don't want to put the nightmarish images in her head, but I can't seem to stop talking. "Giorgio had her. He told me I killed his daughter. And then he—"

"You didn't kill his daughter," she interrupts. "It was a nightmare, that's all. Anyway, if we're placing blame, I'm the one—"

"No." I cut her off. "I asked Giorgio to find Verratti's payroll information, knowing full well that my request put him in danger. I feel like shit about it, but I would make that call again. It's not even close. I would trade his safety for yours *every single time.*"

She kisses my cheek. "You don't have to protect me all the time, Dante. This started back in the hospital, I know, but I'm not a victim."

"You think that's why I protect you?" I shake my head. "I'm protective of you because you're precious to me, Valentina. You've been precious to me from the day we met."

Her eyes go wide. "Oh," she whispers. I've shocked her, though I don't know why. I thought the way I felt about her was obvious. *But she doesn't let go of my hand.* "Dante, I don't know how to—"

"You don't have to respond."

"That's good." She gives me a wry smile. "Because I don't know what to say." She wraps a strand of her hair around her finger. "I got nightmares for months after Roberto died. It was always a variation of the same theme. Angelica would be crying in her crib, and I would be asleep, and he would burst into my bedroom and hit the baby to shut her up. I don't think I got a good night's sleep that first year."

"I didn't know that."

"I didn't tell you. I knew you were different from your brother, and I've always felt like I could trust you. You're a good person, Dante. But in those early days, fresh off his abuse, I didn't trust my judgment very much. Anyway, I would wake up from my nightmare and remind myself that Roberto was dead. Antonio killed him. The threat was taken care of, and nobody could hurt my baby."

Tell her. Tell her the truth. Tell her it wasn't Antonio.

"Anyway," Valentina continues. "That's all over now." She snuggles closer to me. "I owed Antonio a debt, and I've paid it. It's all in the past."

I go ice cold. "That's why you went to work for Antonio? Because you were grateful he killed Roberto?"

She looks surprised. "Wasn't that obvious? After Roberto, I didn't want anything to do with the mafia. That first year, I wanted to do what Lucia did and move far away from Venice and never come back." She laughs softly. "Of course,

Lucia is back home now, so that didn't work well for her."

God, but the fates are cruel. I feel sick. She's only a hacker for the mafia because she thinks Antonio killed Roberto. All this time, I've tried to keep her as safe as possible, even if it resulted in her hating me when all I had to do to protect her was to tell her the truth.

"What would you have done if you hadn't become a hacker?"

"I've always been a hacker. But if I didn't go to work for Antonio, I would have probably worked in a bank or something. Something boring. Assuming I could even find a job, which wasn't guaranteed. It's not easy for single mothers with newborns to find work."

"Your debt is paid. That option is still open to you."

"Not really," she replies. "I can't talk about the work I did for the mafia, so there's a giant gap in my resume. Nobody is going to hire me except for the lowest-level jobs. Besides, I might not have picked this path if I had other options, but I love what I do. This is my life now." She moves so she's sitting astride me, her ass pressed against my crotch, and her lips meet mine. "I can't say I have complaints about how any of it turned out."

I kiss her back, but I can't focus.

The irony. The *fucking* irony of our damned pasts.

Valentina thinks I'm a good person. She trusts me. She shouldn't. Because it's not Roberto's abuse that has affected the course of her life.

It's the secret I hid from Valentina.

The secret I'm still hiding from her.

VALENTINA

CHAPTER TWENTY-FOUR

Getting up on Friday is a struggle. I wake Angelica up, feed her breakfast, get her ready for school, and then walk her there, all in a bleary haze.

I didn't get any sleep last night. I fell asleep in Dante's arms. We woke up at midnight to have sex again, and then at three, just as I was getting ready to leave, he cried out in the grip of a nightmare.

And then we *talked*.

The conversation with Dante in the middle of the night felt *intimate*, even more so than the sex.

He didn't try to pretend that everything was okay. He was vulnerable, and in return, so was I.

As early as two weeks ago, I would have never told Dante I had nightmares about his brother long after his death. He already saw me as a victim, or so I thought. Why would I give him more ammunition?

But without being conscious of it, something has shifted in the last two weeks. Dante's protectiveness doesn't feel stifling. It makes me feel. . . cherished.

I haven't given myself permission to think about the changing nature of our relationship. But if everything he's told me is true, he's wanted me for a very long time. And, if I'm being perfectly honest with myself, I've wanted him for almost as long.

Leo once said that the opposite of love isn't hate, it's indifference. And I've never been indifferent to Dante Colonna.

Love is a four-letter word, one I am not yet ready to say. But I can admit that I enjoyed last night and would like to do that again.

Dante is still at home when I get back from dropping Angelica at school. "I thought you'd be at work," I tell him, reaching around him to help myself to a cup of coffee.

He stretches lazily. "I'm having a slow start to my morning." He glances at his watch and makes a face. "I should probably speed it up. What do you have going on today?"

I take a sip of coffee. Yuck. When I'm sleep-deprived, coffee always tastes bitter in my mouth, and that's what's happening now. There's only one way to fix this.

"I'm going to start by taking a nap," I announce, stifling my yawn. "Thanks to a certain someone, I didn't get much sleep last night." He chuckles unrepentantly. "Unless there's something you need me to do?"

"No." He touches my cheek, a tender gesture that does something to my heart. "You've been working really long hours. You look tired. Get some rest."

"Yes, that is *exactly* what you should say to a woman."

He rolls his eyes. "That is not what I meant, and you know it."

As tempting as it is to give him grief, I'm too wiped. "Will you wake me up in a couple of hours? I'll set an alarm, but I'm afraid I'll hit snooze and ignore it."

"I can do that." He brushes a kiss over my lips. "See you this evening."

"Will you be home for dinner?" *God.* The moment I say those words, I wish I could take them back. I sound so domestic. I wouldn't blame Dante for freaking out a little.

"I will," he replies instead. "But don't make anything. I'm going to cook tonight."

"Somebody pinch me, I'm dreaming. You know reheating takeout in the microwave doesn't count as cooking, right? Or are you planning to open a can of soup?"

"Brat." He bops my nose gently and gets to his feet in one fluid motion. "Want me to carry you to bed, Valentina, or can you make it on your own?"

I picture Dante sweeping me into his arms and

carrying me up the stairs. He'd toss me down on the bed and look down at me, his dark eyes heated. *Take off your clothes*, he'd order as he undid his belt buckle.

Then we'd fuck again, and as hot as that sounds, I need my nap. "I can manage, thanks," I say hastily. Then, before temptation can swallow me whole, I flee.

The ringing of my phone wakes me up. "Rise and shine, sleepyhead," Dante says, sounding entirely too cheerful. "And turn on your camera."

"Why?"

"I've thought of another homework assignment for you."

I'm instantly awake. "Aren't you at work?"

"Yes, but my door is locked, and I'm using the secure app you told me to install on my phone."

"You listened to my warning. Shocking."

His voice lowers to a sexy purr. "I listen to everything you say, Valentina. Now, turn on your camera."

I do as he says and accept his video call request. Dante's face appears on my display. "Good girl."

Heat prickles through me. "What's my assignment?"

His lips lift in a half-smile. "Do you own a dildo, Valentina?"

I shiver. "Yes."

"Is it in your bedroom right now?"

"Yes," I say again.

"Interesting set of priorities," he says, amusement coating his voice. "You only had a few minutes to pack, and in that time, you remembered to pack your dildo."

My cheeks flame.

"Nothing to say?"

I give him a sweet smile. "I'm waiting for your instructions, *sir*."

Heat flares in his eyes. "So obedient. Bring it here."

Is the toy conveniently within reach in the bedside table drawer? I admit nothing. I pull it out and show it to Dante. His lips twitch. "Impressive girth."

"Mmm." You're bigger, I want to say, but that'll

make him too unbearably smug. "What do you want me to do with it?"

"Run it over your breasts," he instructs.

Not what I thought he was going to say. I take off my T-shirt, and his eyes turn hot. "You're so beautiful." Heat coils through my core at the raw desire in his voice. "So fucking gorgeous. Pinch those pretty little nipples for me."

I obediently pluck my aching tips until they're swollen and throbbing. Then I glide the thick fake cock over them, moving from one nipple to another.

"How does it feel?"

Dante sounds calm and controlled, and I'm unraveling. "I'm hot and wet," I whisper. "For you."

"Show me. Spread your legs."

I lose my panties and part my thighs, opening myself to his gaze, lust shuddering through me. I was never big into homework as a child, but I *like* this assignment.

Dante sucks in a breath. "So pretty," he says. "Now touch yourself. Lightly."

I part my lips and stroke my clit. The merest

touch of my thumb, but it makes me jump. I lick my lower lip as my orgasm spirals closer. "Dante, I—"

He's not done giving instructions. "Put two fingers in your pussy. Thrust once, twice. . . That's good. Pull them out."

Stopping is so hard I almost want to cry. My fingers glisten with my juices. I hold them up to the camera. "Please, Dante."

A smile creases his face. "The dildo now. Close your eyes, pretend it's my cock in your tight little pussy. Thrust it deep."

I've never done anything like this in my life. I've never even thought about it. But Dante's watching me, his gaze intent, waiting for me to obey, and I'm going to give him the best show in the world.

I line up the dildo and push it in, just the head. My pussy is soaked, aching for the feeling of being filled by a thick cock. I pull it out slowly and then go deeper, gasping at the burning stretch.

"Good girl." Dante has his cock out now. As I watch, he wraps his fingers around his length and slowly fists himself. "I didn't give you permission to stop."

I nearly climax at the sight, at his words. I keep my eyes on my phone, transfixed by Dante's hand rhythmically pumping his erection. I thrust the dildo in and out, matching his pace, muscles quivering, my skin covered with goosebumps. My breathing is shallow and uneven, and I feel *feverish*.

My toes dig into the mattress. I clench my eyes shut and throw my head back. Dante's voice sounds in my ears, praising me, calling me his good girl, his precious sparrow. And then ecstasy takes me. My muscles spasm around the dildo, and I explode.

It takes me a few moments to regain my wits. Finally, I sit up. "This is a *great* way to wake up," I tell Dante with a satisfied smile.

"I agree." He uses some tissues to clean up his cum and tosses them in the trash.

"What time is it?"

"One."

"Shit." I need to shower, check in on our firewall, and then pick up Angelica. "I'm late."

"I'll let you go then." He smiles at me, a warm, happy smile that lights up his face. "See you this evening, sparrow."

I pick up Angelica, and we walk to the dock. "How was school?"

"Okay," she replies. "Mama, Mariana walks home by herself, and she's my age."

"Mariana is *ten*."

"That's the same thing," my nine-year-old daughter replies with a roll of her eyes. "Can I walk back by myself?"

"No."

"Why not?"

Because I stole a hundred and ten million euros from a hacker, and he knows my name. And until we catch him, I'm in danger, and by extension, so are you.

Guilt fills me. Last night, I told Dante that I love what I do. That's true, but there are moments when I can't help feeling like a terrible mother. For Angelica's safety, maybe I should quit being a hacker. Maybe I should work as a bank teller or something.

Angelica is protected, I remind myself. There are three bodyguards around us, staying discreetly out of sight. If trouble breaks out, they're only a moment away. I don't know how they can distinguish between a threat and a tourist, but Leo assures me they can, and he's very good at his job.

"Maybe next year." She looks like she's going to protest, so I hastily add, "What kind of puppy would you like? A little one, like a Chihuahua?" Shamelessly using Angelica's favorite topic to change the subject? I am awful.

The bait works. "No, not a Chihuahua."

"A poodle?" I ask hopefully. "Something small and manageable?"

"No, Mama. I want a rescue dog."

"You do?" I'm not surprised. I took Angelica to the animal rescue on the mainland in August when my father died, and she was having a hard time processing his death. Playing with the puppies there helped her a lot.

"I already know which one."

"Show me." I hand her my phone. She navigates to their website and pulls up the picture of the dog she wants.

I glance at the picture. "Angelica, there are two dogs here." Two dogs with sweet eyes and adorably floppy ears.

"They're brothers, Mama," she says. "Nobody wants them because there's two of them. They've been there for *months*. Can we get them?"

"I don't think we have enough space for two dogs, honey," I say gently, feeling like a jerk for breaking my daughter's heart. She looks shattered. "What about if we—"

"There you are." A man's voice makes me jerk my head up. "You're a hard person to get a hold of," Neil Smith says, smiling widely at me. "How are you, Valentina?"

Oh, God. After the disaster that was the date with Neil last Saturday, he sent me an email saying we should get together again. Rosa must have given him my email address, but thankfully, she knows not to give out my phone number. I replied that I was really busy at work, but maybe sometime in January or February. I thought it was a polite way to let him down easily and that he'd get the message.

Evidently not.

My security guards start to close in. I give them an 'I'm okay' hand sign and smile pleasantly at the man in front of me. "Neil, what a surprise. What are you doing here?"

"I work in this neighborhood," he replies. He looks down at Angelica. "And this must be your daughter."

I didn't tell him about Angelica. The hair on the back of my neck stands up. "Can you go sit there for a minute, please?" I ask her, pointing to a bench at the edge of the piazza.

Angelica gives me a curious look and says, "Yes, Mama." I glance surreptitiously at my bodyguards. Yes, Silvio's already moving toward Angelica. Perfect.

Once she's out of earshot, I look squarely at Neil. "I didn't tell you I had a daughter."

"No, Rosa did." He laughs awkwardly. "I didn't realize it was a secret."

I'm probably being prickly for no reason. "I've been good," I reply. "Busy. You know how it is."

"Tell me about it," he says. "It's the end of the year, and payroll is a nightmare. You think the managers would know how much bonus money they want to give their employees, but no. They wait until the last possible minute to figure it out." He gives me a disarming smile. "I'm glad I ran into you. I wanted to apologize for last week. I wanted to make a good impression and then. . . Well, you know. When the machine kept glitching on my credit cards. . . I'm afraid I wasn't at my best."

That's actually a half-decent apology. And I can relate to first-date nerves. "Stuff happens." Specifically, Dante Colonna happened. "It's not your fault."

"Yeah." He runs his hands through his hair. "Anyway, I like you, Valentina, and I'd really like to see you again."

I hide my grimace. Ugh. He's being nice, and I don't want to hurt his feelings—it feels like kicking a puppy. But even if I wasn't in love with Dante, nothing would happen between Neil and me.

"I'm just really busy, you know? My calendar is jammed." His face falls, and I add, "Maybe sometime in the new year?"

And why did I say that? I don't want to go out with him. I should have just said that.

"Absolutely." He reaches out and plucks my

phone from my hand. "Why don't I give you my number, and we can figure out when?"

He starts navigating to my contacts. I stare at him in bemusement. Did he just grab my phone out of my hand? He did. I'm so astonished by the intrusion that I don't say anything for a few seconds; I just gape at him.

And then, I react. "Please don't touch my phone without my permission."

"Relax," he says with a laugh. "I'm not looking at your photos or anything. I'm just adding my number—"

Out of nowhere, Dante materializes at my side. "I believe she told you not to touch her phone," he says, his voice glacial. "Give it back before I break your wrist."

"Break my—" Neil splutters, puffing his chest out. "Who the hell do you think you are?"

"Somebody you should be afraid of if you know what's good for you." Dante gives the other man a dismissive nod. "Coffee break's over. Give Valentina her phone, Mr. Smith, and get back to work."

Neil gapes at Dante and finally seems to realize

it would be a bad idea to cross him. He thrusts my phone at me. "I'll text you," he snaps. He gives Dante a poisonous glare, then pivots on his heel and marches away.

I glance at the Broker. "Break his wrist, really?" I ask lightly. "Isn't that a bit dramatic?" Then I notice the look in his eyes. "What happened?"

"Giorgio was attacked," Dante says. "I don't know if he's alive or dead. I need to head to Bergamo immediately."

This is his nightmare coming to life. Poor Dante. I squeeze his hand. "Do you want me to come with you?"

He shakes his head. "No. I don't know what the situation is, and I don't want to worry about you. Can you stay at home with Angelica? Whatever happens, don't open the door, and don't leave."

"Yes," I promise, fighting to keep the fear out of my voice. Dante needs to focus, and he can't do that if I'm freaking out. "I can do that."

DANTE

CHAPTER TWENTY-FIVE

Giorgio is in surgery. Someone—probably his wife Mara—wisely took him to the hospital in Milan. That move might have saved his life. Milan is Ciro Del Barba's territory, and unlike Verratti, Ciro can be reasoned with.

Leo refuses to let me go to Milan alone. "Take Goran and Benito," he says. "I insist."

We take Antonio's helicopter there. We race to the hospital as soon as we land, and I burst into the waiting room. Mara is there, as is Liliana, fast asleep, her head on her mother's lap. "What happened?"

Mara lifts her head up. When she sees me, relief fills her face, followed quickly by anger. She knows Giorgio acts as my informant and blames me for what's happened.

She's right to do so.

But she doesn't voice her recriminations. "He got a message on his phone," he says tonelessly. "He went to meet someone."

"Who?" I demand.

"I don't know. He didn't tell me." She exhales shakily. "I had a bad feeling about it. I begged him not to go."

"He went anyway."

"He said he had to." She swallows. "But he promised me he'd call me every ten minutes. When he didn't, Liliana and I went out to investigate. I was tracking his phone, you see."

Smart. "You found him."

She nods. "He'd been shot. His stomach was torn up." She swallows a sob. "I loaded him into the car and came here. The hospital in Bergamo was closer, but—"

"You made the right call. As soon as he's stable, we'll move him to Venice. You and Liliana, too.

Bergamo isn't safe for you anymore. I'll arrange an apartment."

"Thank you." She strokes Liliana's pale blond hair absently. "They said the surgery would be at least four hours long. They told me I didn't have to wait, but—"

Tears well up in her eyes, and she averts her gaze. "You want a cup of coffee?" I ask her. "Something to eat?"

"Coffee, please."

I signal for the guys, who are hovering just outside the waiting room. "Benito, wait with her," I order. "Goran, watch the doors. No one goes in or out."

"Yes, sir."

I head outside and call Del Barba. He picks up immediately, almost as if he's been expecting my call. Knowing him, he probably has. "Colonna," he says. "I hear you've been making the rounds. You know, I'm a little disappointed you haven't visited Milan to warn me away from the Russians.

Antonio Moretti controls a wide swath of territory, as does Ciro Del Barba. The two men have come to an understanding. Both organizations are evenly matched, and it would be ruinous if they went to war. And so, we're allies of a sort.

"I didn't think I needed to."

"You don't. Unlike Verratti, I haven't lost my mind. Why are you in my city?"

So much for flying under the radar.

"I'm visiting a friend in hospital. I'm quite anxious that nothing happens to him or his family."

"You want them protected. I'm not sure I can do that."

I grow cold. Is Milan enemy territory now? "Why not?"

"Because of the auction. I'm still quite irritated, you know. I really wanted that Spider, and you snatched it away from me."

I exhale in relief. The '54 Spider is a beautiful car, and I've wanted it for a very long time. But a man's life hangs in the balance, and this is not a tough decision to make.

"The car you bid on was a wreck. It's been painstakingly restored. I want five favors."

"Three."

"Done," I say promptly. "Pleasure doing business with you."

"Likewise. I'll send my men around. Acerbi, his wife, and his child will be safe in Milan. I guarantee it."

I don't even bother to ask him how he knows who I'm visiting. "Someone shot him. Do you know who ordered the hit?"

"No." Frustration coats his voice. "Unfortunately. Let me know if you find out, and I'll make it worth your while."

"Nice try. I don't work for you, Ciro."

"No," he agrees. "You don't. A pity."

I hang up and head to the small cafeteria, where I buy coffee for Mara and hot chocolate for Liliana. Who could have attacked Acerbi? It could be Verratti, but neither Salvatore nor his father had left their compound in days. It could be the Russians, but I think they'd pause before resorting to violence on Italian soil.

It could be Revenant. I have no proof that he's part of this attack, but my intuition tells me he's involved.

So far, the hacker has done an excellent job evading detection. He's thwarted every attempt we've made to determine his identity.

And I haven't forgotten that he threatened Valentina.

When I find him—and I will—I'm going to make him regret it.

After five hours, the surgeon comes out into the waiting room. Mara jumps to her feet. "How is Giorgio? Is he going to make—"

"It's too soon to tell," the woman replies soberly. "He lost a lot of blood, and the next forty-eight hours are going to be critical. But he went through surgery well, and I'm optimistic."

"Can I see Papa?" Liliana pipes up. She woke up an hour back, drank her hot chocolate, ran around the waiting room in a sugar frenzy, and then Mara bribed her with a cartoon so she'd sit down. Is she aware of the magnitude of what's going on? I don't know. Every time I look at her sweet round face, I see Angelica, and guilt eats at me.

"I'm sorry, piccola." The doctor smiles down at the child. "Your papa needs to rest. You can see him tomorrow." She turns back to Mara. "He's in post-op recovery, but he's sedated. You can have a minute in the room."

"Go," I tell her. "I'll watch Liliana."

When Mara comes back, her eyes are red. But her voice is steady as she confronts me. "Are you going to make this right?" she demands. "Are you going to put a bullet in the brain of the person responsible for this?"

"Yes," I promise. My guilt has crystallized into icy fury. "But to do that, I'm going to need Giorgio's phone."

I wait until Mara and her daughter are settled at a hotel arranged by Del Barba's team before heading back home. It's almost three in the morning when I unlock my front door. "Thank you for your help today," I tell Benito and Goran, who insisted on accompanying me there. "Have a good night, what's left of it."

I let myself in and tiptoe upstairs past Valentina

and Angelica's bedrooms. The adrenaline has worn off, and I'm drained. I open my bedroom door. . .

Valentina is asleep in my bed.

For a moment, I'm overwhelmed. I stand in the doorway, and it feels like someone punched my heart. She's here because she knew I would be upset and didn't want me to be alone.

Everything I've dreamed about is here, laid before me for the taking.

It's based on a lie. If she finds out the truth about Roberto's death, it will be over.

I step into the room. "Valentina," I say softly. "Hey."

She wakes up. "Hey," she says sleepily, remembering why I left, and concern fills her eyes. "Is Giorgio alive?"

"For the moment. The doctor said the next forty-eight hours are key."

She sits up, the sheet falling to her waist. She's wearing one of my T-shirts. "Where is he? He's not in Bergamo, is he?"

"No, Milan."

"Ah, the King Maker's territory. What did Del

Barba want in return for protection?"

"My Spider."

She winces. "I'm sorry, Dante. I know you loved that car. I've never seen someone turn as green as you did when I merged onto the A4."

I shrug out of my jacket and unbutton my shirt. "You're so sure I gave it to him?"

"Of course you did," she says as if there's not a doubt in her mind. "Underneath that murderous exterior, you're a good person." She flashes me a teasing smile. "Annoyingly overprotective, though. *Touch her phone again, and I'll break your wrist.* I'm pretty sure Neil almost peed in his pants."

I know what she's doing; she's deliberately dragging my mind back to a happier place. "He deserves it. He grabbed your phone."

"He does seem to have a problem with boundaries," she agrees. "You coming to bed?"

She's staying the night. *And I didn't even have to ask.*

It's been a long, hard day. But right now, everything feels right again.

Tell her about Roberto. You can't keep this

from her. She would see it as a betrayal of her trust.

If I tell Valentina his death was an accident, she'll believe me. She won't blame me; that's not who she is.

But if I tell her the truth, things will change.

I've waited for this moment for ten years. Call me an asshole; call me a coward. When it comes to Valentina, I'm both. Because she's here. In my bedroom. Curled up on my bed. Wearing my T-shirt. Waiting for me to come home.

This isn't about sex. This feels like *a relationship*. Everything I've ever wanted is mine for the taking, and I won't do anything to risk it.

I can't.

When she finds out, she'll realize how many opportunities you had to tell the truth. And then she'll never be able to forgive you.

"As soon as I take a quick shower. I smell like the hospital." I toss my shirt aside and reach for my belt, and her eyes follow my hands. My cock reacts, the horny bastard. "Stay in bed. I'll just be a minute."

"How are you feeling?" she asks me softly.

"I'm angry. Furious. The more I think about it, the more I suspect it was Revenant." I wrap my arm around her waist, and she snuggles against me. "He couldn't hack into our network, so he shot my informant. This is war." My lips tighten. "Revenant's about to realize I make a very bad enemy. I got you something." I reach for my jacket and pull out the device Mara gave me. "Giorgio's phone."

"You shouldn't have," she quips. "We're a go then?"

"Yes. We're going to end this, once and for all. Verratti is broke; his paychecks are going to bounce. This is a perfect time to act. Get me the names of everyone on his payroll—I'm going to approach them with a better proposition." I bare my teeth in a grim smile. "We're going to take over Bergamo with Verratti's own money. As for Revenant," my voice hardens with resolve, "We're going to find his real identity. By the time we're done, there's going to be no money for him to steal and nowhere for him to hide."

No violence, just like I promised Antonio. I don't need blood in the streets to pull this off. . .

I have Valentina.

VALENTINA

CHAPTER TWENTY-SIX

Was I aware I was sending a signal when I waited for Dante in his bedroom? Yes, of course I did. I'm not an idiot.

This isn't about sex any longer. It isn't about steamy homework assignments. When I wore Dante's T-shirt because I wanted to keep his scent close to my skin, I did it knowing full well what it meant.

I have feelings for Dante.

But then he gives me Acerbi's phone, and he

makes it clear that we're doing this thing *together*. He says, "By the time we're done, there's going to be no money for him to steal and nowhere for him to hide."

By the time *we're* done.

We're a team, Dante and me. And because we're a team, I don't freak out when I realize I've fallen in love with him. I'm just. . . happy.

Dante rests his hand on my stomach. "Are you too sleepy for sex?"

Is he kidding? "You remember when I confessed that I haven't had sex in ten years? That's a lot of pent-up desire, Dante. I don't think you understand when I say—"

"I understand," he says wryly. "Trust me."

Hang on. What's he saying? I prop myself up on an elbow. "What's that supposed to mean?"

"What do you think? There hasn't been anyone for a long time."

"How long?" I demand.

"Really? We're going to have this discussion at three in the morning?"

"You're avoiding answering my question."

He trails his hand down the curve of my breast.

"I slept with Marissa once," he says. "Two years ago. It was a mistake." His fingers hook in the waistband of my panties. "When I was with her, I closed my eyes and imagined it was you. That's when I broke things off with her. Before Marissa, it was a three-year drought. After her, there's been no one."

I do the math. Dante's telling me he's had sex once in the last five years. *Once.* He wasn't traumatized like I was. He wasn't afraid of sex, wasn't terrified of intimacy.

It was because he wanted me.

Joy bubbles up in my chest. "How long have you had your eyes on the Spider you gave Ciro Del Barba?" I tease.

"Valentina, if you're attempting to draw some kind of parallel between my feelings for the Ferrari and my feelings for you, I'm going to be blunt and call you an idiot. Chalk this up to sleep deprivation."

I laugh at his disgruntled tone and wrap my arms around his neck, allowing the joy to consume me. "Shut up and kiss me, Dante."

We make love. No rope, no toys, no gimmicks. It's slow and unhurried, interspersed with a lot of kissing. Dante doesn't order me to masturbate while he watches. He doesn't command me to ride his face. He isn't tied up, and my heart isn't racing with nerves.

When he pushes into me, filling me with his thick cock, it feels *right*. He thrusts, and I dig my nails into his back, wrap my legs around his hips, and rise to meet him. When he fingers my clit, his face buried in my neck and says, "I want you to come when I do," I feel like I'm in the place I was always meant to be. And when we fall asleep together, it feels like. . . You know when you hold up your phone to take a picture, but the image is blurry? Then the lens adjusts, and everything comes into sharp focus? That's what it feels like.

The next couple of weeks are pretty great. Angelica's recital is a triumph. She's the prettiest and most graceful ballerina on stage, and I'm not just saying that because I'm her mother and biased.

Giorgio doesn't die. He makes it through the first forty-eight hours, but then, just before the transfer to Venice, he gets an infection, and the doctors are forced to pump him full of antibiotics and sedatives. He's unconscious most of the time and seems to have no memory of the events that led to his shooting, but it's not all bad news. His doctors seem reasonably confident that he'll live.

Dante and I spend our nights together, which is amazing. I set my alarm for five, and every morning when it goes off, I trudge downstairs into my own bed before Angelica can wake up. Got to admit—that part is less than great.

During the day, I make progress on dismantling the Verratti organization. It takes me five days of poring over source code to find a weakness in the communication app the Bergamo organization uses. From there, it gets easier. Seven days after getting Giorgio's phone, I have a list of everyone on Verratti's payroll.

"There are five people here that could be Revenant," I tell Dante. "But there's a complication."

Dante is reading my screen over my shoulder. "These cash deposits," he says. "Five cash deposits, two million each. You think Verratti paid his hacker in cash?" He looks grim. "You're saying it might not be any of these guys, then."

"I'm afraid so." The hacker isn't invulnerable—we hurt him badly when we stole his crypto—but every search for his identity has ended in a roadblock. "If he's not one of these five, I'm out of ideas." I exhale in frustration. "I'm sorry, Dante. I know you—"

"Hey, hey." He kisses my neck. "Don't be sorry. It's frustrating, I know, but we don't need this guy's identity to stop him. A lone hacker with no resources can only do so much. I've been talking to Verratti's lieutenants, sowing discord in their ranks."

He's right, of course. I'm so caught up in failing to find Revenant's identity that I'm missing the big picture. I smile up at him. "Tomorrow's payday. Given the time of the year, everyone will be expecting Christmas bonuses."

"You're ready to empty Verratti's bank accounts?"

"I am."

He smiles at me, his eyes sharp and focused. "Let's do it."

The plan works better than we could have imagined. Verratti's people *lose* their minds. Furious messages fly around, and angry recriminations are everywhere. People accuse Salvatore of mismanagement, of gambling their finances away, and of being unfit to lead. They question his judgment in allowing the Russians a foothold in their city. When they demand to know where Bianca Di Palma and Romano Franzoni are, they openly speculate if Salvatore has killed both of them. The Bergamo leader tries to restore calm in vain, promising that everyone will get paid as soon as his banking issues get sorted. But by the time the week ends, the damage is done.

On Saturday night, Dante and I open a nice bottle of prosecco to celebrate. It's midnight, and I've spent the evening watching the Verratti employees type increasingly angry messages to their boss.

This morning, we met with the padrino to update him on our progress. Antonio was delighted. "Salvatore is going to get arrested any moment now," he said. "Jail will be a relief. His people are furious, and frankly, I'm shocked nobody's tried to kill him."

There was a vicious smile on his face. Sometimes, it's almost possible to forget that Antonio Moretti's rise to power was bathed in blood. He murdered Domenico Cartozzi, killed the handful of soldiers that were loyal to the old padrino, and out of the ashes of the old organization, he forged a new Venice.

And, of course, he killed Roberto. I've never let myself forget that.

Dante pours the wine into two flutes and hands me one. "To the dismantling of Verratti's organization," I say, holding up my glass.

"To the hacker who made it possible," he replies. We're about to take our first sips when Dante's phone rings. It's Leo, and I can hear his panicked voice through the phone. "The padrino's been shot," he says. "You need to get here. Now."

He reels off an address. I have only a second to meet Dante's shocked eyes.

Then he runs.

DANTE

CHAPTER TWENTY-SEVEN

The worst night of my life was when Roberto put Valentina in the hospital ten years ago. I sat vigil in her room, waiting for her to regain consciousness, guilt bubbling through me like hot lava.

The night Antonio gets shot is the second worst night of my life.

Leo gives me an address not too far from la Piazza. I race there and push my way inside. Simon, one of Antonio's assigned bodyguards for the night, is hovering at the door. A relieved expression fills his face when he sees me. "He's bleeding from his shoulder," he reports. "A minor wound. I've called an ambulance just to be on the safe side."

Fear leeches out of me. "Well done. Where's Leo?"

"He went after the shooter. Andreas and Goran are on their way here."

"Did you recognize him?"

"No, sir. I didn't."

"Okay. Tell Leo to call me when he gets a chance."

I go inside, and Carlo, the other bodyguard, pivots to the door, his gun raised. He lowers it when he sees me, a sheepish expression on his face. "Sorry, sir."

"Not a problem." He's on edge, and I don't blame him. Antonio got shot on his watch.

Speaking of Antonio, the padrino's rising to his feet. Lucia is at his side, looking like she's on the verge of panic, but Antonio is calm. Well, as calm as you can be when you've just been shot.

"It's nothing," he says impatiently. "Just a scratch." He notices my presence. "Good, you're here. It was Marco."

Marco? Marco is the old padrino's nephew. Dumb as a rock but mean, one of Roberto's best friends. Someone who stood by and watched my brother beat Valentina. Ten years ago, he tried to knife Lucia when she was wandering alone on the docks late at night, but Antonio was there to stop him. As punishment, he banished Marco from Venice. Evidently, the man held a grudge.

I don't like this at all.

My phone beeps. I glance down at the display. It's a message from Leo, who has found Marco. "We have him in custody," I read, then glance up. The padrino is swaying on his feet, looking pale and ill. He keeps looking at Lucia, and I can interpret his expression. He's put her in danger, and it's making him sick with guilt. "Antonio, sit down. I've got this."

"Are you telling me what to do?" he snaps. "Because the last time I checked, I'm still the padrino."

I let his accusation wash off my back; he's hurt and lashing out. He sends Lucia away, which makes no sense at all because it's obvious to everyone here that they're in love with each other.

I open my mouth to protest, but then. . .

He falls to the floor in a dead faint.

And it turns out it wasn't a scratch after all.

Fuck.

We rush Antonio to the hospital. They take one look at him and wheel him into surgery. I call Valentina to give her an update. She listens in silence and says, "Lucia needs to be there. If you were in surgery, nobody could keep me from the hospital."

"I know," I breathe. She's telling me that she loves me. Not in those exact words, but I can read between the lines. I'm in love with Valentina, and she's in love with me. "Let's go get her."

Leo arrives at the hospital. His face is ashen. "Dante, I—" He breaks off, takes a deep breath, and plunges forward resolutely. "I failed. I don't know how Marco slipped into Venice undetected. He must have been watching Antonio's movements, biding his time, and we somehow didn't spot him. This is my fault. I'm responsible for these intelligence failures. Please accept my resignation."

Of all the— "Leo, you don't work for me."

"The padrino is incapacitated," he replies. "Until he's up and about, you're in charge."

"Antonio is in surgery. He's not dead," I say violently. Fuck. I don't want this. Not this way. Antonio is my friend, damn it, and he's going to make it. He has to.

Leo opens his mouth to protest, and I lift my hand. "Fine, I'm in charge. I don't accept your resignation. Here's my first order. Valentina and I are going to find Lucia and get her here. Can you protect Angelica while we do that?"

"You would trust me with her safety?"

"Yes, of course," I say impatiently. This situation isn't Leo's fault. Antonio refused to move Lucia to Giudecca because he wanted her life to be as normal as possible. Leo's been spread thin trying to secure multiple locations with limited resources. Something was bound to go wrong.

"Thank you, Dante," he replies, looking like a man who expected to die and has been given a new lease on life. "I won't let you down."

I've been in a hospital twice in the last two weeks. The waiting, the uncertainty, the fear that my friend might not make it—I hate everything about it.

It's a long night. But eventually, six harrowing hours later, the surgeon comes out and tells us Antonio will be okay.

After that, things just start falling into place.

Salvatore Verratti is arrested by the Direzione Investigativa Antimafia for tax fraud, racketeering, and the murder of his father. Evidently, Federico's body was discovered outside their compound with multiple stab wounds. The tax fraud and racketeering charges don't surprise me, but I didn't think Salvatore was capable of killing Federico.

On a less pleasant note, I interrogate Marco while Antonio is recovering. Leo has stashed him in the attic of one of our safehouses. I walk in there with death in my heart. "Talk," I say flatly.

"I've got nothing to say to you," he spits defiantly. "Go to hell."

I ignore his words. "I know you, Marco. You're as dumb as a rock and have as much imagination. So let me paint you a picture. You shot the padrino; you're going to die."

I pull out my knife, and his eyes jump to it.

"I'm not going to kill you, of course. He's going to want to do that himself." I run my finger along the blade. "I'm afraid it's going to hurt a lot."

"Moretti's going to torture me? He doesn't have the stomach for it."

"Is that what you think?" I shake my head. "Marco, Marco, Marco. You made a fatal mistake. You aimed your gun at Lucia, the woman the padrino loves. He's not going to forgive that." I bare my teeth in a vicious smile. "I'm afraid he's going to make an example of you."

Marco swallows. Sweat beads on his forehead. It's finally sinking in. *Good*.

"Unless. . ."

He looks up. "Unless what?"

"Answer my questions, and I'll ask the padrino to give you an easy death." He hesitates, and I add, "This is a one-time offer. It expires in thirty seconds."

"Fine," he yells. "Fine, I'll answer your goddamn questions."

There's only one thing I want to know. "Who sent you here?"

"Verratti."

Damn it. Frustration fills me. "Which one? The father or the son?"

He scratches his ear nervously. "The son. Salvatore."

"Are you lying to me, Marco?" I ask. "Because that would be a very bad idea."

"I'm not, I'm not. It was just weird, that's all. I was working in a restaurant in Lecce when, out of the blue, Salvatore Verratti texts and asks if I want to get even with Antonio."

"He texted you? You didn't talk to him?"

"No, never. I'm telling the truth, I swear. Check my phone."

"Oh, I will."

"It's not Verratti," Valentina says, throwing Marco's phone down in frustration. "Look at the timestamp of this text. Seven-fifteen in the morning, four days ago." She clicks a window on her laptop. "And this is the conversation Salvatore is having with his security chief. Spot anything?"

I notice it at once. "The messages have been sent at the same time."

"Yes. Someone pretended to be Verratti, sent Marco money and Antonio's location, and set this up."

"Revenant again?"

She nods somberly. "Who else could it be? Here's what I don't understand. How did Revenant find out about Marco? From all accounts, he was in southern Italy, living a quiet but impoverished existence. He hasn't stepped foot in Venice in ten years. He's never been on Antonio's payroll or Verratti's."

"Salvatore knew about the incident on the docks." I search my memory. "Marco approached Verratti for a job after he got kicked out of Venice. Salvatore called Antonio to find out why."

"But why would Salvatore tell Revenant about Marco?" she asks skeptically. "Revenant's been stealing from Verratti. The two of them aren't working together."

"None of this makes sense." I take a deep breath and squeeze her hand. "But Verratti is in jail, and his employees now work for us. Thankfully, all of this will be over soon."

But we still haven't found Revenant, and I can't shake off my lingering unease.

Trouble always comes in threes, my mother used to say.

First, Acerbi was shot.

Then, Antonio.

And the third?

I've learned to listen to my intuition, and right now, it's screaming a warning. This isn't over. Not by a long shot.

VALENTINA

Chapter Twenty-Eight

My first reaction when Dante says this will be over soon? I'm skeptical. It feels like we've been in danger for so long that I've forgotten what normalcy feels like.

But as the days go by and nothing happens, I exhale.

It's the week before Christmas. While the padrino recuperates in the hospital, Dante systematically dismantles the Bergamo mafia and integrates Verratti's team into our own, and Angelica and I go shopping for presents.

"It feels surreal to worry about Christmas shopping," I tell Dante late at night, tracing circles on his muscled chest with my fingertips. "I keep checking my phone to see if there's another network incursion attempt, but there's nothing. Revenant's just *gone*. He's not trying to hack into our systems and hasn't posted on the forums. For all intents and purposes, he's disappeared."

"Mmm."

I prop myself up on an elbow. "What do you think? Are we in the clear?"

"I don't know," he confesses. "I want to believe that Revenant's cut his losses. That would be the rational thing to do. But—"

"But people don't always act rationally," I finish.

He nods. "There are a couple things that don't make sense. Federico's murder, for one. Salvatore claims he didn't do it, and I'm inclined to believe him." He rolls over on his back and stares at the ceiling. "Then there's Bianca Di Palma and Romano Franzoni. Nobody's heard from them."

"What if Franzoni found out the Carabinieri were closing in on Verratti? Maybe he fled, taking his mother with him?"

"It's a good theory, except Giorgio swore that Bianca Di Palma's house had been ransacked. Maybe Franzoni faked an abduction, but why?" He exhales in frustration. "Life is messy. Things don't always slot neatly and tidily into place. Sometimes, there are loose ends that never get resolved." He shrugs. "My brain tells me this is over, but my gut says something different."

"I'm surprised you were okay with our shopping trip."

"It was a relatively low-risk undertaking. It's the holiday season, and the stores are crowded with shoppers. If Revenant were to attack in public, it would set off a huge outcry, and the Carabinieri would hunt him down." He smiles at me. "What did you buy Angelica?"

I sigh heavily. "I asked her what she wanted for Christmas, and she said she wanted the two dogs she saw at the rescue. I was hoping she'd forgotten all about it, but no. She really has her heart set on them. And we just don't have enough room for two dogs."

"I have the space," he says casually. "If you lived here, you could get her the dogs she wants."

I go still. "Dante, did you just ask us to move in with you?"

"I did." His expression is wary. "I've waited for you for ten years, Valentina. I don't want to wait any longer. I'm shamelessly using Angelica as an excuse. I might have even shown her those dogs— I admit nothing." He laces his fingers in mine. "It's soon, yes. But this thing between us. . . It *works*. And I can't let you go."

It does work. And I can't let Dante go, either. "I'm going to think about it," I tell him. "I need to talk to Angelica as well. But. . ."

"But?"

"I'm leaning toward yes."

Christmas arrives, and Angelica opens her presents. She's been interested in painting recently, so Dante bought her an easel and a paint set that would not be out of place in a professional painter's studio. "You spoil her," I tell him, and he flashes me a grin. "Hey, at least it's not a pony."

I get Angelica clothes, Legos and board games, new ballet flats, and baking supplies. No dogs. I tried adopting Lupo and Orso from the shelter, but the woman in charge had very firm feelings about pets under the Christmas tree. "No," she said firmly. "I've had too many pets given as presents and returned by the new year to let you have them. Come back in January if you still want them."

She looked so fierce that I hadn't argued with her any further. "I'll see you on the second," I said mildly. "Please don't let anyone else adopt them in the meantime."

I wracked my brain about what to buy Dante, finally settling for tickets to the Grand Prix. "You told me I didn't have to buy you anything," he accuses me when I hand him the envelope.

"You don't." This day, with Angelica playing with her Legos and Dante leaning against the couch, his legs stretched out and his face lighting up when he sees the Formula One tickets—this is the gift I need.

He hands me a flat box. "It's a good thing I didn't listen."

I open the lid. Nestled inside is a pendant

hanging on a thin gold chain. A golden sparrow perches on a hoop set with small diamonds. My eyes go wide. This isn't something he bought in a store. This is custom-made.

And it's perfect.

"What do you think?" he asks.

"It's beautiful." Angelica is too busy looking up Lego instructions on my laptop to pay attention to us, but I'm okay with her overhearing me. "I love you."

His eyes are very soft. "I love you too, sparrow."

Lucia calls me the day after Christmas to tell me that she and Antonio are getting married. "The wedding is in two weeks," she says. "Will you be my maid of honor, and will Angelica be my flower girl?"

"She'd be delighted, and so would I."

We chat for a long time about the various details. Rosa's going to make the wedding dress; the first fitting is scheduled for tomorrow. Neither

Antonio nor Lucia is religious, but they're still getting married at Il Redentore, the church in Giudecca that dates back to the sixteenth century. Lucia's hired someone to do the flowers and the decor but wants me to supervise, a task I'm glad to take on. I'm thrilled for my friend. She's been hurting from her parents' deaths for a very long time, but she finally seems healed and at peace. Antonio dotes on her, and it's obvious that he makes her very, *very* happy. Almost as happy as Dante makes me. The two of them are going to have a lifetime of joy together.

I'm working in Dante's office two days later when the doorbell rings. It's just me at home. Dante stepped out to the store, and Angelica is in Antonio's palazzo, where Agnese is teaching her how to bake.

I'm wearing sweatpants and a T-shirt, no bra. I have three bras that fit, and all of them are in the laundry basket, waiting for me to handwash them.

I pull on Dante's sweater to hide the visible nipple situation and head downstairs to investigate.

It's Silvio, and next to him is a stranger, a man in his forties with slicked-back hair. "I'm sorry to bother you, Valentina," Silvio says apologetically. "But Signor Trevisani insists he needs to speak with Signor Colonna."

"He isn't here. He just stepped out for some bread." Marta has the week off, so we're doing our own grocery shopping. It's amazing how quickly you get spoiled.

"I have the information he asked for." Trevisani looks around nervously. "Can I wait inside?"

I look at Silvio, and he shrugs. I consider the situation. Trevisani must be on Leo's authorized list because otherwise, the guards would have stopped him before he knocked on the door. It still feels weird to let a total stranger into the house, especially so close after our state of high alert.

"I'm an officer in the Carabinieri," Trevisani says urgently, showing me his badge. "I can't be seen outside Colonna's house. If someone recognizes me—"

Fair enough. "Come on in," I invite. Silvio looks

like he wants to join us, but it's only him on duty today. "I've got it, Silvio."

He comes inside and takes a seat on the couch. "Would you like something to drink?" I ask him politely.

He stops jiggling his leg long enough to answer. "No, thank you." He gets to his feet and holds out his hand to me, his gaze snagging on the sweater. "I didn't introduce myself properly. My name is Bruno Trevisani."

"Good to meet you. I'm Valentina—"

"I know who you are," he interrupts, the smile on his face very close to a leer. "You're the girl from the hospital, the one Colonna killed his brother for." He smirks. "Judging by your sweater, it looks like it all worked out for him."

I jerk as if shocked by a live wire. *You're the one Colonna killed his brother for.* Killed his brother. "What did you say?"

"You're the brother's girlfriend, aren't you? I kept the details out of my report as a favor to Dante, but what a mess that was. You know, he swore it was an accident, but now that I see you. . ." He laughs expansively. "Can't say I blame the man."

Bile fills my mouth. The room sways around me, and I grip the couch for support. "I'm going to have to ask you to leave," I say through nerveless lips. "I'll tell Dante you came by."

"What the—"

"Leave now. Please."

For ten years, I've believed that Antonio Moretti killed Roberto.

But if this cop is telling the truth, it wasn't the padrino.

It was Dante.

DANTE

CHAPTER TWENTY-NINE

When I get home, Valentina is huddled on the couch in the living room, hugging a pillow to her chest. "The bakery was closed," I tell her. "I'm afraid you're going to have to make do with grocery store bread. Sorry."

She doesn't look up. Doesn't reply. Her gaze is focused on the blank screen of the television. A whisper of fear goes through me. "Valentina?" I prompt. "What's wrong?"

For a long moment, she doesn't reply. "I have a

question for you," she says finally, still not looking at me. "And I want you to tell me the truth. Did you kill Roberto?"

My heart stops. She knows. I don't know how, and I don't know who told her, *but she knows.*

"Yes."

Valentina lifts her head. There's so much torment in her eyes that I reel back, stricken. I take a step toward her, instinctively wanting to ease her pain, but she flinches.

She's never once flinched from me. She does now.

I should have told her myself, but I didn't, and now it's too late to make amends. She looks *betrayed,* and it's my fault. "Valentina, I'm s—"

"Why didn't you tell me?"

I thrust my fingers through my hair. "I don't know," I say, aware of how inadequate it sounds. "The shooting was an accident, and I didn't think you'd—"

"You didn't think I'd understand?" she cuts in. "You thought I would assume you killed your brother in cold blood? Or did you think I would be angry that the man who abused me for a year and a half was dead?" She takes a deep, shuddering breath. "I've been sitting here in your living room, waiting for you to come back home, and I realized something. I trusted you, but you didn't trust me."

"That's not true. I trust you with my life."

"But you didn't trust me with the truth." Her mouth twists bitterly. "You had ten years to tell me, but you never did." She tightens her grip on the pillow, her knuckles white. "The night we slept together for the first time, you had a nightmare. I sat on your bed and bared my heart to you. I confessed that Roberto haunted my dreams for a year after Angelica was born, but he couldn't hurt me because Antonio killed him." Her voice is so low it's a whisper. "You listened to me, but you didn't correct me. You had every chance to tell me, and you didn't."

"I'm sorry." Her expression tells me my apology is too little, too late. "I should have told you."

"I told you the only reason I went to work for Antonio Moretti was that I owed him. You could have told me then. Antonio knew all along. Lucia probably knows by now." She shakes her head despondently. "I feel like such a fool."

Each word out of her mouth is an accusation that stabs me in the heart. Because she's right. I've had so many opportunities to tell her, and I've taken the coward's way out every single time.

"Two days ago, I told you I loved you. You could have told me then," she continues relentlessly. "But you didn't." She looks straight at me. "This isn't about protecting me; this is about respect. You don't respect me enough to trust me with the truth. You didn't treat me like a partner, Dante. You treated me like a child."

"Valentina," I start helplessly. "I fucked up. But please listen to me. I respect the hell out of you. I never intended for—"

"I have only one more question. Were you ever planning on telling me?"

She's offering me a tiny sliver of hope. I could seize it. I could lie and assure her I would have told her about my encounter with Roberto. I could do whatever is necessary to salvage our relationship.

But she deserves so much better than that.

She deserves so much better than me.

"No." I clench my hands into fists. "I've woken up every day this last month, wondering if I'm dreaming. You were here, you and Angelica, and I had everything I ever wanted. I'd like to pretend I would have told you about Roberto, but the truth?" God, it hurts to keep going. Each word widens the chasm between us. "The truth is, I didn't want anything to disrupt what we had."

"Everything we had," she whispers, "and everything we were was built on a foundation of lies." She lets go of the pillow and raises her head. "I think Angelica and I should leave. We'll go back to our apartment."

"You can't," I say desperately, grasping at straws. "It's not safe. You don't want to risk Angelica's li—"

"Please don't." She sounds like she's on the verge of tears and is holding them back with a sheer force of will. "Please don't use my love for my daughter against me."

I fall silent. She reaches behind her neck and unclasps the necklace I gave her. Carefully, she sets it on the coffee table. "I'm not going to stop you from seeing Angelica; you're her uncle, and she loves you. But you're not in my life any longer. Whatever we had—it's over."

VALENTINA

CHAPTER THIRTY

Dante doesn't want us to leave. I know him—I can read it in every frustrated line of his body. But he doesn't stop me. He might be perfectly okay forbidding me from going on field missions, but he isn't going to imprison me here against my will.

He's not Roberto. He's not going to take his happiness at the expense of mine.

I move on autopilot, my heart breaking with each step. I head upstairs to my bedroom and throw my clothes into a suitcase. I'm still doing that when Angelica returns home. "What are you doing?" she asks, a note of accusation in her voice. "Why are you packing your clothes, Mama?"

"We're leaving tonight," I say flatly. "I heard from the contractor, and our apartment is ready. It's time to go home."

Angelica sets her jaw mutinously. "But I don't want to leave. I like it here."

Have you ever felt the urge to lose it and scream at your kid? I haven't, not until now. Angelica is generally a very good child. "Our apartment is ready," I repeat through gritted teeth. "We had to stay here while it was getting painted. That's all. This is not our house, Angelica. This is Dante's house, and it's time for us to leave." I press my lips shut to keep from screaming and silently count to ten. "Pack your things. Please don't argue with me."

My kid is very emotionally intelligent. She never told me about the princess bed Dante bought her. And she hinted that she would like me and Dante to get together but never outright said the words. So she must hear the emotion I'm trying to suppress because she takes one look at my face and realizes I'm not okay. "Okay, Mama," she says, oh-so-quietly. "I'll pack my stuff."

I help her get her belongings into a suitcase. "Don't forget Diny," I say, reminding her about the tutu-clad velociraptor guarding the windowsill.

She looks at the toy. "Diny can stay here," she replies. "Uncle Dante will be lonely when we leave. Diny can keep him company."

I swallow the sob in my throat. "Good idea."

I don't know how I will survive the next couple of hours. Keeping busy helps. Angelica's stuff is, predictably, all over the house. I climb up and down the stairs, gathering everything. I dread running into Dante—my composure is a fragile shell that will shatter at the slightest pressure. But he stays out of sight, locked in his bedroom. It's only when I'm zipping up Angelica's suitcase that he appears, standing in the doorway. "I'm going to the office," he says, his gaze flickering to my daughter before resting on me. "Leo will be here shortly. He's going to help you transport your computers."

"I don't need them."

The words come out instinctively, but the more

I think about it, the more I know it's the right thing to do. My world has been tilted off its axis at this revelation. When everything slots into place for this new normal, I don't think I'll be able to work for Antonio's organization again. The padrino kept the true circumstances of Roberto's death a secret from me for ten years. I only went to work for him because I thought I owed him a debt of gratitude, and he knew it. He wanted my skills and let me believe a lie. Antonio Moretti has a reputation for being ruthless, but I've never seen it before.

I see it now.

But Antonio's betrayal doesn't cut as deep as Dante's. It's Dante I can't face every day at work. My crushed heart won't be able to stand it. Not now, not after what we shared. I need to walk away from this life, no matter how much I love it.

Dante stares at me for a long moment but doesn't say anything. He turns and climbs the stairs, heading back to his bedroom. I load a game on my iPad for Angelica, then go to my bedroom to continue packing.

The pendant Dante gave me for Christmas, the

one I left downstairs on the coffee table, is on my pillow.

Doing my best to ignore it, I stuff my clothes into a duffel bag. But try as I might, my gaze keeps returning to it.

It's a lovely piece of jewelry—delicate, understated, and beautiful. The man who commissioned it knew me. I named myself Sparrow because it was a small, unobtrusive bird, and that's how I saw myself.

But Dante's sparrow isn't unobtrusive. It gleams golden, perched on a ring of diamonds, cherished and infinitely precious.

My eyes prickle with unshed tears. My fingers trail over the pendant, and then I jerk them away. Nobody's ever seen me the way Dante Colonna saw me.

But it was all based on a lie.

The doorbell sounds, and I hear Leo's voice. He says something to Dante, and Dante replies. There's a murmur of conversation, and then the front door clicks shut with a finality that tears at my heart.

He's gone.

It's over.

I sink onto the mattress, fighting the urge to run after Dante, fighting the urge to forgive him. There haven't been many people I could lean on for support in my life. Not my parents, for sure. I looked after them more than they looked after me. Lucia's parents were comforting and stable influences for a while, but they died when I needed them the most. All through school, Lucia was my best friend, but after her parents died, she fled Venice and didn't talk to me for two years.

Dante was the only person there for me from the day I met him. He's been an annoyingly steadfast rock at my side. When I was sick, he brought me coffee and made me take my migraine meds. When I was nervous about my first field mission, he arrived to be my bodyguard, irritating me so much that I forgot to be afraid.

But it goes back much longer than the last few months. Every time I've needed him in the last ten years, he's been there with sarcasm and support. He could have gone back to Rome after Roberto's death, but he stayed in Venice. I can never forget the first time he watched Angelica for me. She was six months old, her first tooth was coming in, and she was miserable. I swear to God, she cried for thirty hours in a row. She would fall asleep for about ten minutes, then wake up with a scream, her tiny face scrunched up and red. She would cry and cry, and I couldn't seem to make it better. I held her in my arms, fed her, and changed her— nothing seemed to help.

Then, I had a migraine flare-up.

I never knew how Dante found out, but when I was at the point of passing out, he knocked on my door and said, "You need to rest. I'm going to take her out for a bit."

I was torn between gratitude and suspicion. "Do you even know how to handle a baby?"

"You figured it out," he said with a shrug, plucking Angelica out of her crib and cradling her in his large hands. "I will, too." He looked at me then, his expression serious. "I will keep her safe, Valentina. I promise."

I expected it to be a disaster. I fully expected him to be back in under an hour, worn out and at the end of his tether. But I hadn't slept more than an hour at a time in more than a week, and I was almost delirious with the lack of sleep. My head was pounding, my migraine so bad that I could barely keep my eyes open, and there was no one else I could ask for help.

"You have to text me every hour," I said. "I need to know she's okay."

"I will."

It hadn't been a disaster. The texts came like clockwork. Photos of Angelica at the park. Photos of her giggling at the flock of pigeons in Piazza San Marco. Photos of her swaddled in a blanket, asleep in Dante's arms.

I slept for twelve hours, then asked him to bring my daughter back. When he returned with Angelica, she was in a new dress, wearing a clean diaper, and she smelled like a mixture of clean baby and soap. "See you later, patatina," Dante said, blowing a bubble into her tiny palm and making her giggle.

"You're good with her," I remarked, surprised.

"She's family," he replied. "And you are, too. If you need help, Valentina, call me. I'm happy to watch her while you get some sleep."

We've always bickered. Dante can be overprotective, and I like my independence. But I never doubted he loved Angelica like his own daughter. And I never, *ever* doubted that he would be there if I needed him.

Which is why this is so hard and so tempting to keep leaning on him. To brush his lie away and pretend it didn't happen.

I love Dante, and he loves me back. But I can't be with someone who won't tell me the truth. I can't let this slide. A little lie here or a little lie there will build up, and before I know it, I won't be Dante's partner. I'll be his golden sparrow, cherished and protected, but in a cage.

Leo comes up the stairs. "So, you're leaving," he says, his expression troubled. "Create a lot of extra work for me, why don't you?"

His tone is light and teasing, but his words cause a dam to burst inside me. Tears turn into deep sobs that wrack my body. "Valentina," Leo says in alarm. The security chief is forty-one years old, so you think he would have dealt with crying women before, but his expression betrays that he has no idea what to do with me. "Come here."

He folds me into his arms. "You are amazing," he says. "Did Dante tell you that? Because you are.

I was here when we took Padua, and it was a bloody mess. But Bergamo?" His tone is admiring. "We took over Bergamo without bloodshed, without a single battle. All because of you."

He pats my back as tears roll unchecked down my cheeks. "It's going to be okay," he says.

I let myself cry for three minutes. No more. Then, I dry my eyes and pull myself together. I don't have the luxury of wallowing. I have a daughter to take care of. "Sorry about that," I mutter. "I got mascara on your shirt."

"That's okay." Leo flashes me a smile. "Maybe your pretty friend Rosa will make me a new one."

Antonio and Lucia are getting married. Leo wants to ask Rosa out. It's just a reminder that life goes on, steady and relentless.

Yet I feel broken.

It seems like I'm destined to be hurt by the Colonna Brothers.

Roberto broke my bones and put me in hospital. . .

But Dante just crushed my heart.

Somehow, this feels worse.

DANTE

I have to leave because I cannot watch Valentina and Angelica move their things from my home. I don't have it in me; I'm not strong enough. If I stay, if I linger, I don't trust myself not to stop them. I don't trust myself not to beg them to stay.

So I go to the office. Where else is there to go? A stack of folders is on my desk, waiting for me to review them, and when I turn on my computer, email after email comes flooding in, the near-constant stream inevitable when you manage an organization with over five hundred employees.

Leo comes back to the office two hours later. "I dropped them off at home," he says. "Valentina cried. A lot." His expression is reproachful. "What happened?"

A flash of grief rips through me. I made Valentina cry. In this, I'm no different from my brother. "She found out I killed Roberto."

Shock fills Leo's face. "You killed your own brother because of what he did to Valentina?"

"I didn't shoot him in cold blood, Leo," I bite out. "Don't get me wrong, I wanted to hurt him. I was going to beat him senseless. Break every bone in his body. I vowed that for every day Valentina spent in the hospital, Roberto would spend ten."

My mind burns with the memory. "Roberto was in hiding. He knew he'd gone too far. Knew he was in trouble. When I got to his location, I found him drunk on vodka, belligerent, just looking for a fight."

"And you gave him one."

"We started arguing. He pulled a gun, I lunged for it, and in the tussle, it went off. He was dead before I could even call an ambulance."

Leo whistles between his teeth. "And you've never told Valentina. All this time." He shakes his head. "Dumb move, my friend. She's going to think you don't trust her."

I feel my throat close up. "I know," I choke out. "But she's wrong."

I trust Valentina; I always have. What I didn't trust was *us*. I didn't trust that our relationship would withstand what I'd done.

And surprise, surprise. It hasn't. Talk about a self-fulfilling prophecy.

Leo stares at me for a long time. I know he's thinking that this situation is of my own making, but he's kind enough not to point it out. "I'm sorry, Dante," he says finally. "I know you love her. But honestly? I don't know how you come back from this."

I don't either. Despair floods through me, and I bury my head in my hands.

"How did she find out?" he asks.

"I don't know," I say tonelessly. "Antonio knew, but he was the only one. Maybe he told Lucia?" Just thinking about it sends a fresh wave of guilt through me. Lucia's one of Valentina's closest friends. If that's how she found out, no wonder it feels like a betrayal.

I've been such a fucking fool.

"You think Lucia told her?" Leo sounds skeptical.

"Who else could it be?"

"I don't know, you tell me. Who else knew? You called the paramedics? Was it them?"

"No. I covered it up. Two officers of the Carabinieri showed up to investigate, and I paid them off. Pietro Casali, who retired six years ago, and Bruno Trevisani."

Silvio passes by outside my office. When he hears me say Bruno Trevisani, his head jerks up. "Should I have stopped him?" he asks worriedly. "He said he needed to talk to you urgently, and he's on the known associates list, so I let him in."

"You let him into Dante's house?" Leo barks. "What did he need to talk about?"

"He said it was about a background check Signor Colonna asked him to run. It was for an English name. I can't remember—"

"Neil Smith."

Leo raises an eyebrow. "The guy Valentina went on one date with?"

"Yes. Fat use his report is going to do now." I clench my hands into fists. "Trevisani must have told her," I say grimly. "I'm going to kill that fucker."

Leo puts his body in front of me. "Stop," he says calmly. "I know you're furious, but you're not thinking clearly. As angry as you are with Trevisani, you cannot beat up a member of the Carabinieri. Leave it alone. He's not responsible for this situation. You are."

He's right. It might be momentarily satisfying to beat Trevisani senseless, but then what? I still have to go back to my silent, empty house. The lights will be off. There will be no cartoon dogs with Australian accents on my TV. No pieces of Lego waiting to be stepped on. No Valentina sneaking up to my bedroom after Angelica falls asleep.

There will just be emptiness.

"Fine."

I settle back at my desk and bring up the never-ending stream of emails. I had everything, and I lost it all. Work is the only thing I have left.

VALENTINA

CHAPTER THIRTY-TWO

Our apartment is freshly painted. The living room window, the one that lets in an icy draft every winter, has been fixed. The kitchen has new counters, the cabinets have been sanded and painted, and there's a brand-new dishwasher. New electric outlets have even been installed in my office so I don't have to run extension cords everywhere.

Renovating our apartment so we could sell it and move to a bigger place was the cover story we gave Angelica to explain the move, but I thought

Dante had forgotten all about it. I certainly had. I don't even know when he found the time to have it done. Not to mention how much it cost.

I stare wordlessly at my renovated apartment, and fresh tears spring from my eyes. I blink them away before Angelica can see and go help her unpack. I can't let myself be weighed down by the huge knot of sadness inside me. One foot in front of the other—that's what I need to do to survive.

The week goes on. The one good thing about being miserable when you have a child is that you can't fall to pieces. If I didn't have Angelica, I would lie in bed all day, eating my way through tub after tub of ice cream. I would keep my drapes drawn so I never saw the sun and refuse to shower. I would just wallow in my misery.

But I can't do that. I still have to take care of her. Angelica is off for Christmas break. She's pretty good at keeping herself entertained, but I still have to shop for food, cook meals, do dishes, and make sure she doesn't spend all her time on the computer.

I decide that I'm going to resign after Lucia and Antonio get back from their honeymoon. I don't want anything to get in the way of their happiness, and even if it means seeing Dante more often than I want, I can hold on. It's only a month away.

But seeing Dante at work *sucks*. We give each other a wide berth, but he is my boss, and I can't avoid him completely. Every time we meet, I snipe at him with increasing venom. But of course, the Broker never responds. So frustrating. As much as I want to be indifferent, I can't stop from lashing out. I'm still in love with him, and his betrayal *hurts*.

The atmosphere at work gets increasingly poisonous. The rest of the team—Leo, Joao, and Tomas—start giving me a wide berth, which only angers me further. I'm not the one who screwed up. They should be avoiding Dante, not me.

Antonio loses his temper the day after his wedding. "Enough," he says, glaring at Dante and me. "It's obvious there's some sexual tension between you two."

I see red. "Sexual tension?" I sneer. "With all due respect, Padrino, not even if he was the last man in Venice."

Dante usually doesn't respond to my provocation. This time, he does. "You wish," he bites out, and I feel perversely glad that I've goaded him into snapping at me.

Antonio leans forward. "I'm delighted to hear you say that. Because you work together. Dante, you're Valentina's superior. If we had an HR department, they'd be freaking out about workplace harassment."

Anger yields quickly to guilt. I can't let Dante take the fall for this. He didn't harass me— everything between us was enthusiastically consensual. "He's not—"

"I'm not done," Antonio interrupts. "Your personal issues are disrupting team morale. So, I forbid it. There are to be no dates. No cozy, intimate glasses of wine after Angelica has gone to bed. No sneaking around and no sex. Do I make myself clear?"

The days tick on, slow and miserable. Rosa calls me in the new year. "I just got back," she says. "I feel like I haven't seen you in ages."

"You saw me at Lucia's wedding," I point out.

"That doesn't count," she says. "Let's go out soon. Talk to Dante and figure out when he can watch Angelica, and we'll have a girls' night out, okay?"

The mention of Dante sends pain stabbing through me. I push it to the background. Time is supposed to be the great healer, but it's been two weeks, and I'm just as miserable as I was the day I left his house. "Are you free tonight? Angelica has a sleepover at Mabel's."

"Yes," Rosa responds enthusiastically. "Let's do it."

Angelica sets off with Silvio for her sleepover, backpack slung on her shoulders. I watch her leave with a pang. The last couple of weeks have been rough for her, too. I've done my best to keep a cheerful facade, but Angelica knows something is wrong and that it's connected to Dante. This sleepover with Mabel couldn't come at a better time. She'll have a puppy and a kitten to distract her, and if I know Zadie, she's arranged an evening's worth of fun activities for the kids.

As soon as Angelica is out of sight, I head to the neighborhood bácaro, where I'm meeting Rosa for wine and cicchetti. She's already there, tucked away into a corner table. The two of us fight our way to the bar, make our selections, and carry the platter of crostini back to our table.

"How was Lecce?" I ask her once we're seated. Rosa's parents moved to southern Italy three years ago. "And how are your parents?"

"It was all, 'Hugh graduated from college, isn't that great? Hugh has a girlfriend, Rosa. Why aren't you settling down and giving us grandchildren? Hugh got a job in a bank. When are you going to stop messing around with fabric and do some real work?'" She shrugs. "Same old. Hugh tried to deflect it, but my parents aren't easily distracted from their agenda of making me feel like shit."

"You have a boutique of your own in Dorsoduro. Do they have any idea how good you have to be to make rent every month?"

"No, and they don't care." She selects a piece of meat from the platter and pops it into her mouth. "Forget them. I want to talk about you." She gives me a concerned look. "Is everything okay with you, Valentina? You have dark circles under your eyes, you've lost weight, and at Lucia's wedding, you practically flinched every time you saw Dante." Her eyes narrow. "Did he hurt you?"

I haven't been able to talk to anyone about what happened. I can't talk to anyone at work—they're all guys who will undoubtedly take Dante's side. I don't want to trouble Lucia; she's deliriously happy, and I don't want to burden her with my problems.

But I'm tired of keeping things bottled up. Exhausted from having to maintain a happy face for Angelica's sake.

"He broke my heart." I tell her the whole story, all of it, starting with moving in with Dante and ending with finding out the truth about Roberto's death.

Rosa listens in silence, her eyes getting wider and wider with each revelation. "Wow," she says when I finish. "So, you're in love with Dante."

"Sure, but that's not what matters."

"Are you sure?" she asks gently. "Look, I'm not condoning what he did. It was a truly shitty thing to do. Secrets are bad. I'm just saying I understand Dante, that's all. Haven't you ever been so afraid of losing something that you make a mistake?"

I hesitate. I've made mistakes, bad ones. Staying with Roberto, for starters. I should have left the first time he hit me, but I didn't want to admit I was in over my head. As for secrets, I have plenty of my own. I've avoided talking about Roberto with Angelica. I've hidden the sordid details of the abusive relationship from her. I'll tell her about it when the time is right, but if she finds out before I can tell her the truth, would she hold a grudge against me the way I'm holding a grudge against Dante? Would she pull away from me like I pulled away from him?

"I don't know," I say helplessly. "He should

have trusted me with the truth."

"Sure. So scream at him. Make him grovel and beg for forgiveness. But don't walk away, Valentina. You're obviously miserable without him. Don't cut off your nose to spite your face."

Is she right? Should I have stayed and resolved our disagreement instead of running away? My head spins. I can't decide—I need time to think about it. "Forget me for an instant. I've been so involved in my mess that I haven't asked. Whatever happened to Franco? Are you still seeing him?"

"God, no." She rolls her eyes expressively. "If I want someone shitting over my career choices, I can always count on my parents. No, I broke things off well before Christmas. Not too long after our double date, in fact. Oh, funny story about that. You know Neil? Evidently, he disappeared. Just quit his job abruptly one day, with no notice or warning, nothing. And Franco says his phone's been disconnected. So weird."

The hair on the back of my neck stands on end. That's odd. Why quit without notice? It's the sort of thing that burns bridges, and there aren't that many accounting companies in Italy that Neil can afford to do that with.

Just then, my phone rings. It's Zadie, Mabel's mother. "Hey, Valentina," she greets me. "I just wanted to see if you're running late or if there's been a schedule mix-up?"

Ice slithers down my spine. "A schedule mix-up?"

"Angelica's not here yet. Mabel's quite disappointed, of course, but if you—"

Angelica's not there. I interrupt, my voice harsh with fear. "She should have been there half an hour ago." Panic grips my heart. "Zadie, I'll call you back."

My fingers shaking, I call Angelica's cell phone. A synthesized male voice answers. Someone's running their voice through a filter to prevent recognition. "Hello, Valentina," he says. "You have a hundred million euros of my money. If you want to see your daughter alive, I suggest you return it. I'll call you back in two hours."

Then the line goes dead.

Revenant's kidnapped Angelica.

I can't think.

I can't breathe.

I need Dante.

DANTE

CHAPTER THIRTY-THREE

I finish up work and start the short walk back to my house. On the way, I pass a bistro. Light spills out of it, warm and inviting, as does the appetizing smell of tomatoes and garlic.

Two weeks ago, Valentina was teaching me how to cook while teasing me about my lack of survival skills. Those days are in the past. There's no food at home; my refrigerator is bare.

Bare and cold and empty. Just like my life.

"Colonna," a familiar voice calls out. It's Bruno Trevisani.

I stare at him with barely concealed dislike. Leo's right. I was responsible for what happened. But that doesn't mean I have to like Trevisani. The man is a born troublemaker, the kind of person who likes to stir shit up and watch the resulting chaos with glee.

I keep my temper under control. "What?" I snap.

Trevisani raises an eyebrow at my tone. "I never heard back from you about the background check you had me run," he complains. "I thought it was urgent. And you never paid me either."

"It's not an issue any longer," I say, my voice clipped. The longer he stands here, the greater the odds are that I'm going to punch him. "You'll get your money."

He nods expansively. "You found out it's a cover, then? It was well done, I'll admit. I almost thought everything was okay, but—"

I go very still. "What do you mean, it's a cover?"

"It took me a while to spot it. The driver's license, identity card, and passport all looked legit. All came up in the databases, no issues. But then I looked at the photos. You know what I found?"

"Get to the fucking point, Trevisani."

He frowns at my tone but is too intent on telling me how clever he is to take offense. "He was wearing the same outfit in all the pictures," he says. "Three different photos, same clothes, as if all the photos were taken on the same day. So, I dug harder. The ID documents are real, but they belong to one Nicola Sardone, an eighty-seven-year-old man living in Milan. Neil Smith or someone close to him must have hacked into our databases and swapped out the details."

Someone hacked into the national identity database, which is not an easy task. Someone skilled. Someone who's successfully evaded our every attempt to find him.

Revenant knew Valentina's name.

It's all adding up to one inescapable conclusion.

My phone rings, loud and shrill. "Dante," Valentina says, her voice shaking. "He's got Angelica."

DANTE

CHAPTER THIRTY-FOUR

I've never moved so fast in my life. It usually takes twenty minutes to get to Dorsoduro from Giudecca; I get there in seven, taking a boat and speeding across the lagoon, breaking several traffic laws along the way.

Leo's with me. We race into the bácaro. Valentina is seated at a corner table, and her friend Rosa has her arms around her. Several people give the two women curious looks. "Empty the place," I order. I crouch next to Valentina. Her face is pale, her eyes wide and staring. She's in shock. "I'm here," I say, wrapping my hands around hers. "Tell me everything."

"Angelica had a sleepover at Mabel's. Silvio came to get her, but they never got there. Zadie called me." She takes a deep, shuddering breath. "I called her phone, and a man said that I had a hundred million euros of his money, and if I didn't return it, I wouldn't see Angelica alive again." Her grip on my hand tightens. "Dante, I think it's Neil. Neil Smith is Revenant."

"I know," I say grimly. Leo's on the phone, finding Mabel's address. "Bruno Trevisani came to tell me his ID was fake. You have a way to track Angelica's phone. Have you tried it?"

Her bleak expression is answer enough. "It's okay, we're going to find her. What time did Silvio leave with Angelica?"

She looks at her phone. "Thirty, no, thirty-five minutes ago. They set out, and I came here. They were going to walk along Campo Santa Margherita. Mabel lives on the other side of the bridge, on the east side of Campo San Pantalon."

Two of Leo's guys set off in a run.

Rosa is still here. She shouldn't be. I'm going to

do whatever it takes to find Angelica, no matter how bloody and violent, but she doesn't need to see it.

I gesture to Leo and draw Valentina away. "We're going to find her, Valentina. I promise you. He wants his money; he's not going to hurt Angelica. We have time." My jaw tightens. "He took a child. I'm going to make him pay."

"Yeah." Her voice is flat. "I know."

"But I need you." I grip her shoulders and stare into her eyes. "Don't fall to pieces now, sparrow. I can't do this without you."

"We found Silvio," Leo shouts, interrupting us. "Let's go."

Silvio is slumped in an alley, his stomach bleeding. Omar's kneeling next to him, putting pressure on the wound. "Someone stabbed him," he says tersely. "I've called an ambulance."

Silvio's eyes are closed, his breathing strained. He's in no condition to talk. "Did he say anything?

I bark at Omar. "Who hurt him? Who took Angelica?"

He shakes his head. "I'm sorry, Signor."

The paramedics arrive in record time and rush Silvio off to the hospital. I step up to Leo. "It's been fifty minutes since Angelica was taken," I say in a low voice. What is my niece going through right now? She must be terrified. She's probably crying, and the thought of her tears shreds my insides. "Do you have someone watching the bridge to Mestre?"

"The bridge, yes. But I can't monitor all the boat traffic. We need more information, Dante."

"I know." I look around and spot the camera at the corner of the building. "Maybe I can get it to you."

Valentina spots the camera at the same time I do. Her eyes sharpen, and her back straightens. That's my sparrow. "I can hack into that," she says. "But I'm going to need my laptop."

Valentina breaks into the camera feed in record time. Eight minutes after we get to her apartment, she pivots her screen to Leo and me. "I'm in," she says, clicking some keys. "Okay, this should be five minutes after Angelica left home." For a moment, her composure breaks, and she almost sobs out loud. Then she bows her head and collects herself.

I rest my hand on hers and watch the screen. It's dusk, but thanks to the ever-present streetlights, the video is surprisingly clear. Tourists walk by, their gazes glued to their phones. A teenager bounces a basketball on the cobbled street.

And then there's Angelica. She's chatting with Silvio, laughing at something he's saying.

Then a man in a trench coat approaches them. Silvio's head lifts, but before he can react, the other man stabs Silvio, sprays something in Angelica's face, and lifts her unconscious body up. Then he looks up. . .

We all recognize him at the same time.

"That's Andreas."

Fury envelops me. Andreas has worked for us for two years. He's one of ours. He was trusted enough that Leo assigned him to guard Valentina when she went on her first field mission. I thought he was loyal.

I was wrong.

"Fuck," Leo swears, smashing his fist into the wall. Plaster goes flying everywhere. I understand his frustration. First, Antonio gets shot, and now this?

He sprayed a gas in Angelica's face. Something to render her unconscious. There are a handful of aerosols that can knock someone out, but they're rarely safe to use. Angelica is nine. A child. What if he got the dosage wrong? My stomach churns with helpless rage and numbing fear.

My anger is useless now—it will only slow me down. If Valentina can put her fears on hold and do what's necessary to catch this bastard, so can I. "Hold it together," I snap. "This isn't the time to lose it. Let's assume Andreas has been working for either Verratti or Smith. It doesn't matter which one. He's got a child with him, and he's got to move fast. Where does he go?"

Valentina presses her hands to her cheeks. "Not to his apartment," she says, her voice trembling. "That'll be the first place we'll check."

Leo's knuckles are covered in blood. He holds up his phone to his ear. "We'll check there anyway," he says grimly.

I nod. "Where else? What about family?"

"He doesn't have any," Leo replies. "He's an only child, and his parents are dead. An aunt lives in Canada, and there's an uncle in England, I believe, but he's not close to either of them."

"Hang on, that's not true." A frown creases Valentina's forehead. "At that farmhouse in Bergamo, I was nervous. Andreas was making conversation, and he said his sister could take on the caretaker."

"You're right." Leo looks *pissed*. "He did say that, and I should have caught it."

"Not now," I say sharply. "Flagellate yourself later. Did he say anything else? Something that can help us find her?"

"Yes." Leo jerks his head up. "He said her name was Cecelia, and she lives ten minutes away from that farmhouse."

Valentina immediately turns to her computer. "Got it," she says after a minute. "Cecelia Girelli. I'm sending the address to your phone."

I'm already moving to the door. Valentina's voice stops me. "Dante," she says. "I want to come with you."

Fuck. "If I find Andreas and Angelica isn't with him, I'm going to have to make him talk." I don't want Valentina to see what I'm capable of when someone comes after the people I love. "It won't be pretty."

"I don't care," she replies, her eyes glittering with tears. When she was hacking into the camera feed and looking for Cecelia's address, she had something to do, something to keep her mind off her daughter. "I can't wait here not knowing what's happening. Silvio was stabbed in front of her eyes, Dante, then Andreas sprayed something in her face to make her unconscious. What if she never wakes up?" She makes a jerky, convulsive gesture in my direction. "Please, Dante. I'm begging you. She's my daughter. She's all I've got."

No, I want to say. *You've got me, sparrow. Now and forever.*

When Valentina watches me torture Andreas, it's going to change the way she sees me. There are some things you can't come back from, and this will be one of them. But I can't deny her now. If it's a choice between my needs and Valentina's, I will always pick hers.

Even if it means the end of us.

"Let's go."

VALENTINA

CHAPTER THIRTY-FIVE

The only thing keeping me from falling to pieces is Dante. I can see the rage in his eyes—the same rage I'm feeling—but he's not letting it get the better of him. The Broker is calm, controlled, and terrifyingly competent.

I load up my supplies. I shove my laptop into a backpack, add a code breaker, some drones, and finally, the most effective weapon in my arsenal, an EMP generator. One pulse from this baby and every electronic circuit in a hundred-meter radius will get shorted out. It's not exactly a hacker tool, but it's extremely effective.

While I'm doing this, Dante readies Antonio's helicopter so we can get to Bergamo. A stray thought strikes me. "Will Revenant be able to find our flight plan?" Neil Smith, not Revenant. He's not a faceless adversary any longer. He's real, he took my daughter, and we're going to make him pay. There is no safe place on Earth for him anymore. If even a hair on Angelica's head is harmed, I will make it my life's mission to hunt him down.

"Helicopters don't need to file one," Dante replies. "We fly using visual flight rules." He glances at the phone in my hands. "He touched your phone," he says, frowning. "When you were walking Angelica back from school, remember? Could he have planted a tracer on it?"

"No. I wipe it down to the factory settings every week." Leo gives me an astonished look, and I shrug. "What? It's just your average everyday paranoia. The two of you should probably take burner phones, though, just in case."

"You wipe your phone every week." A half smile touches Dante's lips. "That's my sparrow." When I hear him call me sparrow, my heart pangs. I push it deep down inside. I need to talk to Dante, but not now. Not when my daughter's life hangs in the balance.

We rush back to headquarters in Giudecca, where the helicopter is on a landing pad, its rotors already whirling. Leo, who's been with us the entire way, hangs back. "I fucked up," he says, not looking at me. "Andreas was one of my guys. I hired him; I vetted him. I'll understand if you don't want me to come along."

What? Leo thinks this is his fault? I'm the one to blame here. I hacked into the Verratti computer and stole their money.

Dante's gaze meets mine. Our thoughts must be running in the same direction because he turns to the other man and says, "For fuck's sake, Leo, we don't have time for this. Just get in the damn helicopter."

The next thirty minutes are a blur. The only thing anchoring me to reality is the reassuring warmth of Dante's hand over mine. We arrive in Bergamo, where an armored SUV is waiting. More of Dante's competence. We navigate to Cecelia Girelli's house, parking the vehicle a hundred meters away so Andreas doesn't get wind of our presence.

The house is small but cared for. The exterior is freshly painted, and the wooden window shutters gleam. Somebody— Cecelia, probably—loves this place.

Leo glances at me, his expression concerned. "Valentina, I don't think you want to come inside."

This man took my baby. Leo thinks Dante wants to hurt Andreas? He has no idea what I want to do to him. "You're wrong. I need to be here."

DANTE

CHAPTER THIRTY-SIX

There is not a damn thing I can do to stop Valentina. She wants to see Andreas hurt, *and I get it.* But the truth is, she's not bloodthirsty. The moment she sees me stab a knife into Andreas to get him to talk, she'll see me differently.

And there's not a damn thing I can do about it.

"It could be an ambush." I point to a spot to the right of the door, where she'll be protected from stray gunshots. "Stay here until we give you the all-clear."

"Okay."

I smash the door with my shoulder. It's solid oak and doesn't yield, not even a little. But the frame is another story. It gives way, and I kick my way inside, Leo at my heels.

Andreas, the fucking coward, is cowering in the basement. He puts up his hands the moment we burst in. "Don't shoot!" he yells. "I'm unarmed."

My temper snaps. I slam him against the wall, my forearm pressing into his neck and restricting his breathing. "You fucking traitor," I growl. He tries to kick free, and I hammer a punch into his gut. He goes down, his breath coming in short gasps. "You betrayed your oath of loyalty." I aim a vicious kick at his face. "And you took a child."

"Why'd you do it, Andreas?" Leo asks tightly. "Why did you turn traitor?"

Andreas gets to his feet slowly, wiping blood from his mouth with the back of his hand. "I was hurt," he spits out. "All summer, I couldn't work. I was worried about money."

"Worried about money?" Leo sounds apoplectic with rage. "The padrino paid you. All summer long."

"And how long would he have kept paying me? Forever? If I got hurt on a job, would the padrino take care of me for the rest of my life?" An ugly sneer covers his face. "I don't think so. I did what I had to do."

"Let me guess. You did something unsanctioned, and Revenant found out and used it as leverage." The fucking piece of shit. "Where's the girl, Andreas?"

A defiant look fills his face. "I don't know anything."

I pull a knife from the inside of my jacket. "This is a filleting knife," I tell him. "I like it for delicate work. I could torture you, Andreas. Take my time and fill every waking moment of your existence with pain. But I'm not going to. I don't have the time for that."

I drive the knife into his body, just under his right ribcage.

"I hit your liver," I tell him conversationally as shock blooms in his eyes. "Luckily for you, your odds of survival are pretty good." I hold my burner phone just out of reach. "If you get to a hospital, that is."

He gasps in pain, clutching at his side. "I wouldn't pull out the blade if I were you," I continue. "It's helping to slow the blood loss. Did you know the human body can lose between two and four liters of blood before it goes into shock? A wound like yours will take ten to fifteen minutes."

I toss the phone into the far corner of the basement. Valentina is standing behind me, her eyes wide and staring. She's looking at me like she's seeing me—truly seeing me—for the first time. I feel an acute sense of foreboding and focus on the task at hand. "You have two options, Andreas. If you persist in your defiance, I'll stand here for the next fifteen minutes and watch you bleed out on this cold, concrete floor. Then, when your sister returns from her overnight trip to Milan tomorrow morning, she'll discover your body in her basement."

"Option two is to answer my question, and I'll kick that phone toward you. If we find Angelica unhurt, I might even let you leave Europe alive." I can't allow myself to picture my niece being harmed because I will not be able to function. "I'm going to ask the question one more time. Where is the girl?"

He stares at me, exhaling hatred and pain. But he's not ready to die today. "He took her from me thirty minutes ago."

"This guy?" Valentina pushes forward and thrusts her phone to his face. She's got a photo of Neil Smith on it. "Is this the guy who took Angelica?"

"Yes."

"Where did he take her?"

Andreas coughs a mouthful of blood. "The farmhouse."

"The farmhouse," Valentina repeats. "The one where I got the computer?" Andreas nods, and she continues, her voice disbelieving, "But we know where it is. Why would he reuse the same farmhouse?"

"Because he's an arrogant fuck who thinks he is the smartest person in the room," I say grimly. "He's about to find out he isn't."

I pull out my gun and point it at Andreas. His eyes widen, and I see the precise moment when he realizes he's going to die. "You said I could walk out of here—" he starts to say.

"I lied." I shoot him at point-blank range between his eyes, ignoring Valentina's gasp of horror, and then turn around. "Let's go. Our work here is done."

DANTE

CHAPTER THIRTY-SEVEN

We drive to the farmhouse. It's a dark, starless night, the moon obstructed by thick clouds, the air heavy with the feeling of an oncoming storm.

Valentina's still sitting next to me, and she's still holding my hand. She saw me kill Andreas but hasn't said a word. She's either waiting for a better time or, more likely, just thinking of Angelica.

It's been two and a half hours since my niece was taken. Almost two hours since Revenant made his demand for money. He's going to call her again any minute now. Is he at the farmhouse? Is Angelica?

The building is dark and silent. I pull to a stop and cut the engine. "You want me to wait in the car?" Valentina asks, her fingers picking at the straps of her backpack.

Angelica might be in there, and Valentina looks like she's hanging on by a thread. But I don't want to leave her alone.

"No, come with us." We get out of the car. I squeeze her hand and kiss her forehead. "Stay behind me, though, please? It would wreck me if anything were to happen to you."

"Same," she says softly. "You be careful, okay?"

Leo clears his throat. "If the two of you are done—"

That's when a shot rings out. Leo clutches his side and dives to the ground. I drag Valentina down and fire my gun in the direction where the shot came from. A man screams and crashes to the ground, and then. . .

Nothing.

"Leo?" My heart is racing. That was too close. I need to be more careful. I can't let my worry for Angelica make me lose my focus.

"I'm okay. The bullet just grazed my side." He moves over to me, taking care to say low. "You think you got him?"

"There's only one way to find out." I get to my feet, gesturing for Valentina and Leo to stay where they are. I make my way as silently as possible to the thicket of trees where I heard our attacker cry out.

Sitting on the ground, holding his bleeding shoulder, is the last person I expected to see.

Romano Franzoni, Salvatore Verratti's missing second-in-command.

I keep my weapon pointed at him. "Franzoni, what the fuck are you doing here?"

"Colonna?" he asks, his voice threaded with pain. "Is that you?"

"Yeah. Put your gun on the ground and kick it away."

He does that. I pick up his weapon, tuck it behind my back, and move closer. "How badly are you hurt?" I ask, shining my flashlight at his wound. I only clipped him. His shoulder is a mess, but he'll live. "Are you working for Revenant now?"

"Not willingly," he replies through gritted teeth. "The bastard kidnapped my mother." He jerks his head toward the farmhouse. "He has her in the cellar. Says he'll kill her if I don't do as he asks. What are you doing here?"

"He kidnapped my niece," I say grimly, giving Leo and Valentina the all-clear. Romano inhales sharply in response. "Where is he now?"

"I don't know. Not here. He put the child in the cellar and left."

"And you didn't attack him while he was doing this because. . .?"

Leo and Valentina join us. I shine my flashlight at Leo's wound, which isn't as minor as he suggested. He needs to get to a hospital soon. But Leo blames himself for Angelica's kidnapping. Knowing him, he won't go anywhere until he sees this through.

"The cellar is booby-trapped," he replies. "That's what he told me. If Revenant doesn't check in every hour, it's rigged to explode."

That's why Franzoni hasn't just taken out Smith. Damn it all to hell.

"He keeps the door locked," Franzoni continues.

He needs to get to a hospital, too. And I need to get Angelica. We're running out of time. "Some kind of complicated digital lock."

I glance at Valentina, and she nods. "Let me at it."

"I can't do it." Valentina stares at her codebreaker in defeat. "He used a ten-character code, and I can't brute force it."

"Help me understand. You were able to get inside the last time we were here. Why is this different?"

"Last time, I didn't brute force it," she explains. "I had to guess a ten-digit passcode that Salvatore Verratti used. I tried his birthday and then his wedding date. That gave me eight of the ten digits I needed. I don't know any of Neil Smith's personal details, and even if I did, he wouldn't make the same mistake. His password would be random and include uppercase letters and special characters."

My heart sinks. "How long will it take to break in?"

Her face crumples. "Anywhere from one month to fifty years."

Angelica is on the other side of this cellar door. We can't lose hope now. "Let's work the problem. Can we break into the cellar?"

Franzoni answers. "You think I haven't thought about it? The bastard warned me against it when he forced me to do his bidding. If I try to break in, the place will blow."

Fuck. We're running out of time. We have to get Angelica out before Revenant realizes Andreas talked. If he finds out we're at the farmhouse, he could blow the entire place up. The longer we delay, the more likely that scenario becomes.

The nagging feeling that I'm missing something intensifies.

And then I remember my conversation with Massimo Rinaldi in Brescia, and it all clicks into place.

As if on cue, Valentina's phone rings.

VALENTINA

Chapter Thirty-Eight

It's Revenant again. Or Neil Smith, or whatever his real name is. "Hello, Valentina," he says mockingly. "Have you been waiting for my call with bated breath?"

"What do you want?"

"My money. Do you have it?"

"Yes." I work hard at keeping the fear out of my voice. "Is Angelica okay?"

"Of course. And she'll remain that way as long as you do exactly as I say. Send me the private keys to my bitcoins. You have thirty minutes."

Dante takes the phone from me. There's a hard light in his eyes. I look at him, and my heart leaps.

He has a plan.

"No," the Broker says, putting the call on speakerphone. "It's not going to work that way. We're doing nothing until we get proof of life."

"Colonna." Revenant's voice ices over. "I was wondering when you'd show up. Do I have to remind you you're in no position to negotiate?"

"Neither are you." There's quiet assurance in Dante's voice. "It took a while to figure it out, but I've got it now. You're Federico's bastard son. You killed your father because he ordered your mother's death, and you tried to ruin Verratti's organization as part of your revenge."

I stare at him in shock.

"But it's over now," Dante continues. "Salvatore's in jail, but his allies aren't. You killed his father, so now it's personal. He's going to make it his mission to hunt you down. And unlike you, Salvatore grew up drenched in blood. The odds aren't in your favor."

Dante makes a fist, his knuckles white. But when he speaks, his voice is steady. Unaffected.

"You need the hundred million euros you stole from Verratti to disappear. Without it, you're fucked. You'll spend the rest of your life looking over your shoulder for an assassin." His voice cracks like a whip. "I need proof of life. Get it for me. You have ten minutes."

He hangs up. I stare at him with desperate hope. "You think he's going to come here?"

"Yes. He's used to being in control, having all the answers. I've flustered him. I wasn't making up the threat; he's in real danger. He's going to rush over here to get the proof of life we need." His jaw tightens. "And we'll be ready."

Dante turns to Leo and Franzoni. "The two of you need to get out of here." Leo starts to protest, and he raises a hand. "No, Leo. We can't risk Revenant spotting our car. If he gets the slightest whiff that we're waiting for him, he'll get spooked. Take the car, get to a hospital. Go to Milan, just in case—Ciro Del Barba owes me a favor. That's an order. Oh, and can you do something about Andreas's body? His sister shouldn't find it."

I swallow the lump in my throat. "What about me?"

I can see Dante wants to send me away, too. He wants to keep me safe—it's etched into every line of his taut body.

But he doesn't.

"No, sparrow," he says. "I need you."

DANTE

CHAPTER THIRTY-NINE

After the tension of the last couple of hours, the next step is pretty anticlimactic. Revenant comes roaring down the farmhouse driveway, and Valentina and I hide in the kitchen and watch him march to the cellar door.

The instant he punches in the code and lifts the door open, Valentina activates her EMP generator. The device shorts out the electronics in the room, killing any potential booby traps. Revenant's still staring in confusion at his phone when I step out, my weapon pointed at his head.

"Drop the phone," I order icily. "And put your hands where I can see them. I really want to shoot you—don't give me an excuse."

I pat him clean and tie his hands behind his back. Valentina waits until he's immobilized, and then she rushes down the stairs. I'm at her heels.

Bianca Di Palma is sitting on a narrow cot, cradling a still-unconscious Angelica in her lap. A sob erupts from her throat when she realizes we aren't Revenant. "Romano?"

"He's alive." I'm more concerned about Angelica. "Is she. . .?"

"She never woke up."

Valentina's fingers are clamped around Angelica's wrist, her face white with fear. "Her breathing is labored," she says. "And her pulse feels very irregular. Dante, I think she needs a hospital."

VALENTINA

CHAPTER FORTY

We fly Angelica back to Venice and race her into the ER. The doctors whisk her away immediately to run a battery of tests. "What did she ingest?" one of them asks me urgently. "Do you know?"

I don't, but Leo does. It seems he found the aerosol can when he went back to deal with Andreas's body, and instead of heading to a hospital, he rushed it to a lab so they could analyze what was in it.

That decision saves Angelica's life. The doctors

give her a drug to counter the toxin's effects and place her under observation. I refuse to leave her hospital room, and so does Dante.

It's three in the morning when Angelica stirs and opens her eyes. "Mama?"

I swallow the sob in my throat. She's awake. She recognizes me. "Hey, kiddo. What's four plus five?"

"Nine." She gives me a puzzled look, and her gaze pivots to Dante. "Uncle Dante? Where am I? What's happening?"

Dante doesn't get a chance to answer. A nurse comes rushing into the room, followed by a doctor. After a long examination, they pronounce her okay. "We're going to keep her in the hospital for at least another night," the lead doctor tells us while the nurse gives Angelica something to drink. "And then she can go home."

I bury my head in my hands and let the tears fall freely. Dante places a comforting hand on my shoulder, and then he's gone.

At five in the morning, Leo comes to relieve me. "Go home and get some sleep," he says bluntly. "You look dead on your feet." He looks at Angelica's sleeping face and then at me. "I'm sorry. My failure led to this. I understand if you can never forgive me—"

I cut him off. "Thank you for getting that aerosol. If you hadn't..." I don't even want to think about what would have happened if Leo hadn't done that. "You saved her life."

"No, I didn't," he corrects. "That was Dante."

"I know," I whisper. For all his assurances, I have no faith that Revenant would have returned my daughter unharmed. If Dante hadn't taken charge, if he hadn't held it together, we would have never found Angelica in time. "Where is he now?"

He didn't stay with me. He waited until he knew Angelica would be okay and then made himself scarce.

Because he thought I wouldn't want him around.

But if there's one thing I've learned tonight, it's that Dante is as essential to me as air and water. As essential as Angelica is. I can't live without him.

Leo makes a face. "The office, where else? I tried suggesting he go to bed, and I got my head bitten off."

"And Revenant? Is he still alive?"

"For the moment. He's also at headquarters. I don't know if Dante's questioning him or—"

"I want to go there."

Leo starts to protest and then stops himself. "I'll give Tomas a call. He'll escort you there. He's handy with a weapon."

"Tomas?" I ask doubtfully. "Our mild-mannered accountant?"

"He has hidden depths."

Tomas escorts me to headquarters. "I hear they're going to discharge Angelica tomorrow," he says quietly as we take a speedboat across the lagoon. "I'm glad she's going to be okay. How are you doing?"

"I'll be okay." It all seems like a bad dream. "Dante killed Andreas."

He gives me a searching gaze. "Are you surprised?"

"Yes. No. I don't know. I've never seen anyone shot at point-blank range before." There was blood everywhere. Blood and brains. On the wall, on the floor, on Dante's clothes.

"You know why I like numbers?" Tomas asks. He doesn't wait for me to answer. "It's because there are clearly defined rules that govern them. Our world is violent and messy, but there are a few cardinal rules. Andreas broke the most important one of all: You don't target children. They're always off-limits. Save your empathy, Valentina. People like Andreas don't deserve it."

Dante looks up when I walk into his office. I've been too busy sniping at him to notice, but he's lost weight, and there are dark circles under his eyes.

The last few weeks haven't been easy for either of us.

"I was just going to interrogate Smith," he says. "Do you want to come?"

I've been so concerned about Angelica that I've almost forgotten about the man at the root of this all. But if I'm ever to turn the page from this episode, I need to hear from him. "Yes."

He leads the way to the attic. One of the rooms has been converted to a makeshift holding cell. The room is sparse—an air mattress on the floor and a bucket in the corner. Nothing else. No table, no chairs. Nothing the hacker can use as a weapon.

Neil Smith is sitting on the air mattress. He lifts his head when Dante and I enter the room but doesn't get up. "The heroes of the moment," he says. "Triumphant and eager to rub my failure in my face."

"Talk," Dante says tersely.

"That's it?" Neil gives him a mocking look. "No threats, no promises of torture? How civilized. Very well, I'll play along."

"You're Federico's son," Dante prompts.

"Yes," Neil confirms. "His bastard son. My mother tried to hide, but his assassin found her when I was a year old." His lips twist. "I don't remember it, but the records show she was killed in front of me. I don't know why I was spared. Maybe Federico's hired muscle couldn't kill a child."

Tomas's voice sounds in my ear. *You don't target children. They're always off-limits.*

"When I was twelve, I hacked into my records and discovered the details of my mother's death. It was only a matter of time before I found my mother's online diary and learned all the sordid details of the affair that led to my conception."

"You wanted revenge."

"I did. So, I became a hacker. I worked for a handful of criminal organizations, building my reputation and my resume. I called myself the Revenant. A fitting name, I thought. My father left me to die, but I came back from the dead."

Dante rolls his eyes. "Then you were hired by Verratti's organization."

"I did. Finally, my dream was within reach. I had it all planned out. Federico was alive while my mother was dead. Salvatore had grown up the favored prince and heir while I bounced from foster home to foster home. They would pay for it."

I take a deep breath. "You stole a hundred million euros from the organization."

"Yes." A smile plays about his lips. "I made it seem like all of Salvatore's investments had failed. I wanted him broke and desperate. I wanted him to suffer. For a while, my plan worked brilliantly." He fixes me with a poisonous glare. "Then the idiot went to the Russians, who approached Antonio Moretti."

"And that's when I got involved."

He nods. "At first, I wasn't paying attention. I even thought it would work in my favor. The rank and file of the organization hated that Salvatore got involved with the Russians. There was a lot of discontent among them. But then you took the files from the computer, and I realized I had a new adversary."

"I was arrogant," he continues. "I see that now. Andreas told me you were going to the farmhouse to get the computer, but I was confident you couldn't get past my encryption. I didn't realize I was dealing with the legendary Sparrow."

"Why kidnap Bianca Di Palma?"

"I'm a hacker," he replies. "Brains, I have. But I

needed muscle. Romano Franzoni was loyal to Salvatore and suspicious of me, but then I learned that Bianca Di Palma was his mother. He came around once I threatened to hurt her."

"Franzoni told you about Marco," Dante guesses. "Didn't he?"

"Yes. If I were to ever get my money, I needed to weaken your organization. But the idiot couldn't pull it off. He missed, and Antonio Moretti lived."

I glance at Dante's face. He's definitely not as calm as his voice suggests. If I were Neil Smith, I'd be very, very afraid. "Who shot Giorgio Acerbi?" he asks. "And why?"

The hacker's face darkens. "I did. Renzo Acerbi killed my mother. I thought it was fitting that I should kill his son."

"Giorgio Acerbi didn't do a damn thing to you," I say hotly.

He shrugs. "There's a certain sense of symmetry about it, you must admit. The sins of the father, and all that. But it started to unravel. I hoped to spook you when you decrypted my files, but you didn't stop. You stole my money. I met you to see who I was dealing with, but I couldn't get to you. You were too well-guarded at Colonna's house."

Guilt floods through me. Dante puts his hand on my arm. "Don't let him mess with your head," he says. "There's only one person here who stooped to kidnapping a child." He gives the other man a frigid glance. "Keep talking."

"What else is there to say? People were asking questions about my identity. Some cop in Venice was on the verge of unmasking me."

Dante winces. "Bruno Trevisani," he says. "I had him investigate Neil Smith because I thought you wanted to date him." His expression is bleak. "I'm sorry, Valentina. This was—"

"Not your fault," I say firmly. "Like you said, only one person here stooped to kidnapping a child."

"About that." Neil looks directly at Dante. "You want to kill me. But before you do, consider this. I know your secret." He gives me a meaningful look. "If you want to keep it that way, I suggest you let me go."

"His secret?" I ask. "That he killed Roberto? That was your ace in the hole? I already know."

I watch with satisfaction as the blood drains from his face. Neil isn't repentant. He isn't feeling any remorse. And people who kidnap innocent children don't deserve to live.

"I've heard enough," I tell Dante. "Kill him."

I leave the room. The moment I step out, a gunshot rings out. He's dead. Revenant will never hurt my family again.

"How's Angelica doing?" he asks. "I called the hospital a while back, and they said she was sleeping peacefully."

I nod. "Leo's there. Dante, I want to thank you for—"

"Don't," he says harshly. A shadow passes over his face. "I don't want your gratitude, Valentina." He runs his hand through his hair. "I should have told you everything right from the start. And I definitely should have told you when we started dating. But you are everything to me, Valentina, and I was terrified I'd lose you." His lips twist in a bitter smile. "I'm not a good person. You've seen the evidence plenty of times."

There's good, and there's *good*.

"You didn't want me there when you were going to question Andreas, did you?" I ask him. "I saw your face when I begged to come."

"No," he admits. "I knew I would do whatever it took to get him to talk. I saw your face when I stabbed him. When I shot him. It's changed the way you see me, hasn't it?"

"You did what needed to be done. If you didn't want me there, why did you let me come?"

"I didn't want you to be alone." He shrugs his shoulders. "But that's not the only reason. I'm a killer, Valentina. A monster. I will do whatever it takes to protect the people I love. It's not pretty. It's ugly as fuck. But this is who I am."

He hid the truth from me once, trying to spare me the ugliness. Not this time. This time, he showed me everything. He laid himself bare for me.

I thought Dante didn't see me. But I didn't really see him either.

"After what you saw," he continues tonelessly,

"I understand if you're concerned about me spending time with Angelica."

"What?" My mouth falls open.

"I murdered two men in cold blood today, and I don't regret doing it. Neither of their deaths will keep me up at night."

"I asked you to kill Neil," I point out. "I might not have the stomach for killing, but that doesn't mean I disagree with what you did. I could have stopped you from stabbing Andreas, but I didn't. And I could have stopped you from killing Revenant, but instead, I asked you to shoot him. If you're a monster, so am I."

He stares at me with so much yearning that it feels like someone has wrapped their fist around my heart and squeezed. "Where does this leave us?"

I've let the past cast a shadow over my life for ten years. That's long enough. I take a step toward him. "If you hadn't seen me in that hospital room," I whisper. "If we met for the first time at a party, what would you have said to me?"

"I would have said that you are the most beautiful woman in the room. That I could not take my eyes off you." His gaze is as soft as a caress. "I would say, 'Something in my heart tells me that you are going to be the most important person in my world.'"

I blink rapidly to keep the tears from welling up. "Good start," I murmur. "Keep going."

He laughs softly, his expression slowly filling with hope. "Then I would have said, 'Want to get out of here so we can get to know each other better?'"

He holds out his hand to me.

I take it.

And it feels like coming home.

Dante wraps his arms around me and hugs me tight. "I love you, sparrow," he breathes. "I never want to lose you again."

"I love you too, Dante," I whisper into his neck. "I love you so, so much."

We stay that way for a very long time. Finally, I tilt my head up at him. "What happens now?"

"In a fantasy world, I'd take you to my bedroom, where we would make love for hours." His lips brush against mine. "But we're not in a fantasy, and you need to sleep. You look exhausted. When you wake up, I thought we'd stop at the shelter and pick up the dogs Angelica wants so that they're waiting for her when she gets home from the hospital."

My heart melts. "I look exhausted? Have I told you you're terrible at compliments?"

His lips twitch. "At least once."

"And have I mentioned that when you tell me what to do, it drives me crazy?"

He laughs out loud. "Twice a day, minimum."

He kisses me again, his lips soft and perfect. A glow of happiness warms my heart, and a stray thought occurs. "Hey, Antonio forbade us from dating, remember?"

"He did," Dante says. "He didn't say anything about us getting married, though." He tilts his head and looks at me. "What do you think?"

"Yes," I reply, giddy and effervescent, a million bubbles of champagne working their way through my body. "Yes, yes, yes."

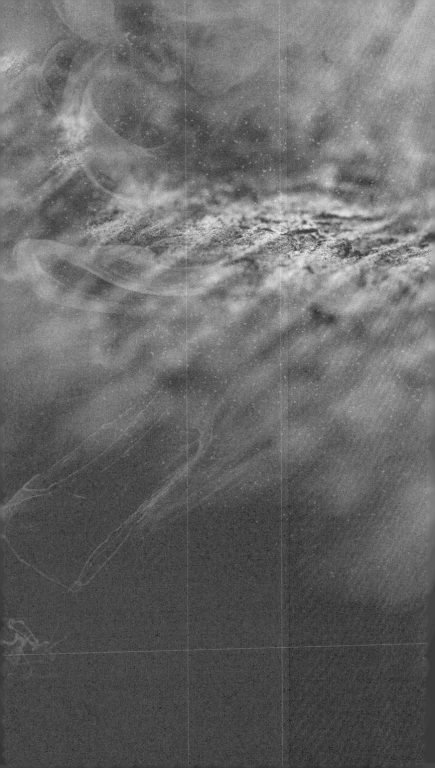

EPILOGUE

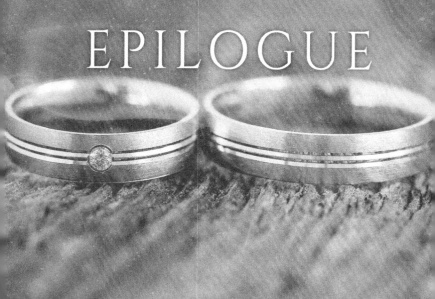

A week after Neil Smith's death, the Carabinieri find a capsized boat in the Adriatic Sea off the coast of Bari. Divers find three badly decomposed bodies. It takes the authorities a few weeks to identify the victims, but eventually, they issue a report that Neil Smith, Andreas Sbarra, and Marco Cartozzi drowned in a fishing accident. Without any other red flags raised, they close their file.

"Did you kill Marco?" I ask Dante.

"Not me. Antonio."

I'm not surprised. The padrino couldn't let Marco's death go unpunished—a message had to be sent. And I bear the man no fondness. Marco was Roberto's best friend. The first time Roberto hit me, Marco showed up at my door, warning me it would be a very bad idea to leave. "Roberto loves you," he said. "It would be a shame if you left him. His heartbreak might make him do something reckless, you understand? And it would be a *shame* if something were to happen to your parents."

"Did he. . ." I hesitate over the right words.

"Did he torture Marco?" I nod, and Dante shakes his head. "No, I offered Marco an easy death if he talked. It was quick."

"And Romano Franzoni? What happened to him?" Franzoni sent Marco after Antonio. Granted, the man was acting under extreme duress, but Marco aimed at Lucia, and the padrino's anger runs deep. "I'm somewhat surprised he wasn't among the victims."

"Romano sought Ciro Del Barba's protection," Dante replies. "It's for the best. Antonio didn't really want to kill Franzoni, and this way, he doesn't have to."

"Franzoni is talented and loyal. Sending him running to Ciro—"

Dante gives me a wolfish grin. "Turning into quite a strategist, are you, sparrow? I'm a little terrified."

"You should be. And so will everyone else once I share the results of last week's security audit."

Dante groans. "Let me guess. You were able to hack into everyone's account again."

"With laughable ease."

His eyes narrow. "Were you able to hack into mine?"

"Of course." It wasn't easy, but I'm not going to tell him that.

"How?"

"I'm not going to tell you." I wink at him. "A girl's gotta have a few secrets."

I debated quite seriously with the idea of quitting. Antonio and I had a long conversation after he returned from his honeymoon. "I'm not going to lie," he says. "I needed you at the time. But that's not why I didn't tell you about Roberto."

"What was the reason, then?"

"Dante is more than my second-in-command," he says. "He's one of my closest friends. I wouldn't be where I was if it wasn't for him." He gives me a small smile. "He wasn't ready to tell you. I didn't agree with him—it's not his smartest decision—but he was my friend, and I respected his wishes. What would you have done in my situation?"

Probably the same thing. And Antonio didn't kill Roberto, but I owed him a debt anyway. He cleaned up the Venetian Mafia, getting rid of people like Marco. He's always paid me well, always been a good boss. He even remembers Angelica's birthday every year and sends her a present without fail.

"You're my wife's best friend, Valentina," he continued. "I don't want animosity between us. What can I do to make amends?"

I thought about it, and then I had it. "I tracked down another '54 Spider," I said. "Well, it's the chassis of one. Evidently, it sustained extensive fire damage in a race. There's a lot of interest in this car. People are going to be bidding aggressively."

"Done," Antonio said promptly, a smile flickering on his face. "Consider it a wedding present."

Neil Smith had no known family, so he's buried in an unmarked grave in Bari. Marco's family in Lecce had a long, extravagant funeral, but there's a marked absence of real grief. Andreas's sister Cecelia didn't seem to mourn her brother much, either. I think she's simply relieved.

And so it ends, not with a bang, but a whimper. The fishing accident barely rates a mention in the local newspaper. Life moves on.

Angelica suffers no ill effects from her kidnapping. The actual abduction happened so quickly that she didn't even register it, and thankfully, she was unconscious after that.

Even so, Dante hires a child psychiatrist to talk to Angelica. But after a couple sessions, the psychiatrist tells us we might be wasting our time. "Angelica is very resilient," she says. "She's not burying the incident; she's quite happy to talk about it. She says that if she's in danger, her uncle Dante will protect her."

"He will. She's right about that. But are you sure—"

"I am. Angelica is thrilled about your upcoming marriage and very excited about her new dogs. She's a happy child, Signorina Linari. You have nothing to worry about."

We set a wedding date for the summer. Dante's not a fan of the delay, but I'm determined not to rush it. "I'm only going to get married once in my life," I tell him. "I'm not going to rush it. Besides, you waited for ten years. What's another six months?"

"I don't want to wait six months precisely *because* I waited ten years," he replies, exasperated. "But okay, fine. Where do you want to go on the honeymoon?"

I know the answer to this. When Angelica was three, the two of us went on our first vacation together. We boarded a plane and flew to Nice.

Lucia joined us there.

I have so many happy memories from that week. It was the first time Lucia met my daughter, and she brought a gigantic teddy bear bigger than Angelica with her as a present. Angelica took one look at it and promptly burst into tears, and Lucia was so horrified she made my daughter cry that I couldn't help laughing. The weather was gorgeous. We took Angelica to the Promenade du Paillon, where she scrambled over the giant climbing whale, and to Place Massena to run between the water jet fountains. Neither Lucia nor I had very much money, but we went on picnics and gorged ourselves on cheese and wine, and I felt more like myself than I had in a very long time.

On the flight back to Venice, I sat next to a woman in her thirties. She asked us about my vacation and showed me pictures of hers. "My boyfriend and I rented a boat for my birthday," she said, showing us pictures of them cruising the canals in the Canal du Midi region. "It was amazing." I looked at photos of her boyfriend and her lying on the deck, glasses of champagne in their hands, and felt a piercing sense of envy. I vowed one day that I would have enough money to do something like this.

When I tell Dante this story, he listens with a strange look. "You should have told me," he says quietly when I finish. "I would have made it happen. Hell, I would have bought you a damn boat."

I kiss his neck, just below his ear. "You can't magically arrange to buy me everything I want." It wasn't just the idea of cruising down French canals that was magical. Her boyfriend had cared enough to do something special for her birthday. The photo of them laughing on the deck as they drank champagne made my heart pang.

She was loved, and I couldn't imagine that future for myself.

And now I'm marrying a man who will do anything for me and Angelica. I never have to doubt that Dante loves me—he shows me every day in a thousand ways, large and small.

"I think you'll find that I can." He moves ever so slightly, and I bite back my smile. My fiancé might think he's only ticklish on the soles of his feet, but I know better. "And trust me, Valentina," he says, kissing me possessively, "I will be spoiling my wife and child rotten."

We get married in July in Antonio's vineyard north of Verona. A hundred guests gather on the banks of a gently rolling hill to watch our wedding.

The day is a blur, and I remember very little of it. Angelica walks in front of me, scattering rose petals down the aisle. Then Dante is there, his eyes on me, and a lump wells up in my throat.

It's been ten long years. But Dante Colonna was worth the wait.

We fly into Montpelier and pick up our boat at Toulouse. While Dante is getting a crash course on navigating the locks on the Canal du Midi, I go into the bedroom and call Angelica.

It's the first time I'm taking a vacation without her. She's staying with Lucia and Antonio in what is arguably the safest house in Italy, but I still worry. A mother's prerogative.

Angelica answers the video call on the first ring. "Hi, Mama," she says. "Guess what Aunt Lucia bought me?" She holds up a leather case.

I bring the phone closer to me, and my mouth falls open. "Is that a lock-picking set?" Lucia comes into view, and I glare at my friend. "Are you teaching my daughter how to pick locks?"

Lucia takes the phone from Angelica. "This is not my fault," she says defensively. "She was already watching YouTube tutorials on how to pick a lock. I had to show her how to do a good job. You don't want her to get caught, do you?"

Dante arrives in the bedroom, hears the end of that conversation, and starts to laugh. After an outraged second, I give in to my amusement. "I guess it's unavoidable," I admit. "I'm teaching her to hack, and you're showing her how to pick locks." I give my husband a pointed glare. "Do not teach her how to stab someone."

"No knives for a few more years," Dante agrees. "But a few self-defense lessons can't hurt."

No, they can't.

Angelica overhears Dante. "Yes," she says enthusiastically, taking the phone from Lucia. "I want to learn how to punch people."

"Hitting is bad, Angelica," I point out, torn between laughter and chagrin. We're bringing up a little criminal. At the rate she's going, my daughter will be the best thief in Venice by the time she's eighteen.

"Uncle Dante says I'm allowed to hit anyone who hits me."

Did he, now? I'm not saying I disagree with that, but I doubt other parents are going to see it the same way. "We'll discuss hitting when I get back home," I tell her. "Are you having fun?"

"I am. I'm practicing picking locks, and tomorrow, I'm going to bake an almond cake all by myself. Then Aunt Lucia is going to take me to her museum, and then I'm going to—"

"Do all the things. Okay, kiddo. We're going to go now, okay? Call me if you need anything. Otherwise, I'll call you tomorrow."

"Bye, Mama. Bye, Uncle Dante."

Dante kisses my neck as I hang up. "We can fly back home and get her if you want."

My heart swells with love for this man. "I'm fine. She's obviously having the time of her life. She's just growing up so fast, you know?" I smile at him. "Let's get underway. I'm on my honeymoon. I have a bikini to change into and some champagne to drink."

He gives me a wicked smile. "And I have a wife to ogle."

I have visions of us wrecking the boat before we even set out. "Who's steering the boat?"

"It's docked." He leans against the door and folds his arms across his chest. "Get changed," he says. "I'll watch."

Watch, he says. But, of course, he helps me undress, kissing each bit of exposed skin as it comes into view. Needless to say, it takes a very long time for me to get into my bikini and even longer for us to get moving. Not that I'm complaining. Eventually, the two of us settle on lounge chairs on the deck, tall flutes of champagne in hand.

"To my wife," he says, his expression uncharacteristically soft and full of love. "I don't deserve you, Valentina, but I'm going to make it my mission to make you the happiest woman in the world every day for the rest of my life."

"You already do, Dante," I reply. "You already do."

Once upon a time, I saw photos of a woman on vacation with her boyfriend in the south of France, and that dream felt impossible for me. Not any longer. I love Dante, and he loves me back, and we're going to live happily ever after.

Thank you for reading
The Broker

More Dante & Valentina?!

I've written some bonus content exclusively for my newsletter subscribers. Sign up to read it at http://taracrescent.com/bonus-the-broker or scan the QR code below.

Want more Venice mafia?

The next book in the series, **The Fixer**, features **Leo & Rosa**. Preorder this age gap, arranged marriage, mafia romance today.

ABOUT TARA CRESCENT

Tara Crescent writes steamy contemporary romances for readers who like hot, dominant heroes and strong, sassy heroines.

When she's not writing, she can be found curled up on a couch with a good book, often with a cat on her lap.

She lives in Toronto.

Tara also writes sci-fi romance as Lili Zander. Check her books out at http://www.lilizander.com

Find Tara on:
www.taracrescent.com
tara@taracrescent.com

Also by Tara Crescent

CONTEMPORARY ROMANCE

The Drake Family Series

Temporary Wife (A Billionaire Fake Marriage Romance)

Fake Fiance (A Billionaire Second Chance Romance)

Spicy Holiday Treats

Running Into You

Waiting For You

Hard Wood

Hard Wood

Not You Again

Standalone Books

MAX: A Friends to Lovers Romance

MÉNAGE ROMANCE

Club Ménage

Menage in Manhattan

The Dirty series

The Cocky series

Dirty X6